REVELATION

A NOVEL

James Faber

Salem-Danvers Village Press

James Faber

Salem-Danvers Village Press
Sprydom House

Published by Salem-Danvers Village Press, a division of Organ Group Corporation; and Sprydom House, an imprint of Salem-Danvers Village Press

First Edition; Hardcover

Publication note:
This work is a creation of fiction. Any events, places, and or people in this book are fictitious, even if they might seem real. This book might be based on and contain real people but any and all events that take place are fictitious and have been made up. Any person indicated in this work of fiction is clearly an idea of the author. Nothing represented in this work of fiction is real, even though actual things might seem real. The publisher nor the author, or anybody affiliated with them are responsible for anything that occurs. This means that you may not file any legal action against us for something that occurs or occurred in your life.

Cover Image by Alexandre Rotenberg © 2017

Unidentifiable woman in the distance looking at a church in the dense fog of the Lombardy region of Italy during the winter, frozen corn field

Cover Text and Design by James Faber © 2018

ISBN 10: 0-9984311-6-8
ISBN 13: 978-0-9984311-6-1

REVELATION

A NOVEL

James Faber

ACKNOWLEDGMENTS

People are often included in this section to portray why they should be acknowledged. Well, this isn't that type of section.

This section acknowledges the dangers of evil and why it must be stopped.

This section acknowledges the importance of doing good things to better society.

This section acknowledges the heroes of World War I and World War II.

Lastly, this section acknowledges that freedom, liberty, and the pursuit of happiness are important in a constitutional federal republic and that no right shall be trampled upon, as the rights of people are derived from God and not government.

Revelation: A Novel

James Faber

REVELATION

A NOVEL

James Faber

Nothing Belongs Here

Contents

Chapter One	5
Chapter Two	17
Chapter Three	37
Chapter Four	53
Chapter Five	67
Chapter Six	79
Chapter Seven	98
Chapter Eight	114
Chapter Nine	122
Chapter Ten	136
Chapter Eleven	154
Chapter Twelve	175
Chapter Thirteen	192
Chapter Fourteen	205
Chapter Fifteen	217
Chapter Sixteen	231
Chapter Seventeen	242
Chapter Eighteen	263
Chapter Nineteen	296
Chapter Twenty	307
Chapter Twenty One	315
Chapter Twenty Two	328
Chapter Twenty Three	343
Chapter Twenty Four	359
Chapter Twenty Five	370
Chapter Twenty Six	383

Chapter One

And then there was fire, glowing bright blue and violet, yet was bright yellow and red from a distance. An entire town was on fire and no one knew who or what was behind it. Could it be that it was intentional or was it an act of God? No one will ever know.

As a matter of fact, there could be an issue with everything, but no one wants to question their own beliefs. As much as it will pain people, there is no reason to hold such a belief.

It is only an understatement of what imagines people within a case of opportunity for the time being. So, it is very noteworthy for people to claim.

Before anything ever becomes clearer, there is a sense of a new wave of hope, which does not really exist, yet it is not a crime to have hope. So, for that, it is not that bad to hope for freedom and change, but there is always a reversal of hope.

Clearly, there is a sign of something wrong that is indeed going on. Are there even any people around? There seems to be no one around. But, what about the people screaming, or are those all fictitious as well? No one wants to be in this situation where an entire town is burning down. It is just a product of sin and torture, so it would be solely at the behest of every other person. How would you like it if someone controlled your fate? You would probably not like that because you want to control your own life. But, as people always say, no one is ever entitled to anything because you must earn that privilege doing hard work. Besides, the entire town is literally on fire, so don't worry about a thing, or so you believe.

It is not a matter of when but is a matter of why and how. It could be it is a sign of punishment for people to experience forever, but that is not the case of how everything ends. There is no one to find but there is something to gain. No one would want to ever experience this wild fire but it is just a sign from God that the end is near, or so people thought, as anything could happen soon. But, then there is the sign of who knows what is happening, and that does need to be answered, or else people will start demanding answers to which they can't and won't ever be able to understand, because they do not understand gibberish. So, it is the goal for all of the people to die in this fire, or so you thought, because really, are there even any people? You can have that opportunity to decide for yourself.

A girl with long but not too long brunette hair was seen afar, but no one was able to see her, because she was the only one left remaining, or so people thought. But, this girl was the only survivor because no one else could be found. Yet, it was a sign of nothingness, because it was just her, and it was in a place where people were usually happy. It was a place where people never lived in a poor or lower class society. It was the land of the rich, the wealthy, and upper class.

It was a cold December morning in the year 1939, and an eighteen year old brunette girl by the name of Carina Alexander was all alone in the town of Winslow, South Dakota. And that was about it, or so the rest of the town thought, but it was just about to get worse. At the least concern to the people was the possibility of a person playing with a set of matches because the adults knew it would be blown out by the cold wind. But, at the worst, the entire town would be engulfed in high flames.

Carina didn't see it coming, but she was lucky to escape the wrath of a burning fire before it ever begun. It was good that she avoided the fire but it was bad that everyone was caught by surprise in their homes. Carina would probably be the only survivor but no one knows if anyone survived. It is such a shame no one is to the rescue to do anything. There is nothing but cold and dry air. Carina does not know what to do so she just walks away from the rest of her town and moves on. It is just a sign that goes nowhere until it has begun, or else there could be another bad event.

For the time being, Carina is walking away from her family and her hometown, and as she just passes by each home and street, she sees it all the same, but does not know what to do.

There are no signs of police. There are no signs of firefighters. There are no signs of EMTs or paramedics. Everything is completely silent, except for the wind and the sound of people screaming in buildings and their homes. Everyone was dying in front of Carina and she just didn't want to get into the madness of what was happening. She couldn't do a thing to help save anyone. She just continued to walk, but no one even noticed her, because they were either burning alive or were trying to hide in some building that wasn't on fire. But the entire town was on fire, unless if somehow a building and or home was not in vicinity of the flames. It was just a lost cause.

On the other hand, Carina was disguised, so no one would even notice her. She was wearing long pants and a hooded jacket with gloves. She did not even feel cold but that was probably due to the fire burning down everything. But if there was even anyone else alive, people would suspect Carina as a person of interest, yet there is no proof she even did anything wrong.

The town of Winslow, South Dakota was a very thriving vibrant town and it once was at the attention of the California Gold Rush. People from all around the world would travel to Winslow just so they could get to California easier. It wasn't their intended destination but just a quicker route to bypass all other paperwork. Everything was just so very tiring and people did not want to wait, so they paid people in Winslow, South Dakota to put them in front of the line. And then it was part of the plan of why it was happening. Well, there was nothing but corruption and greed. It was never about being morally right because it was always about making sure the wealthiest people were given the right of way before anyone else.

But, keep in mind that everything is not as it seems, since those very wealthy people who came to Winslow, South Dakota were all liars, crooks, and thieves. They all stole their money from banks and trains without getting caught. It was a time when the innocent were bad and the guilty were good. Anyone could be blamed but they all left their old lives behind in order to profit off of the gold rush in California. No one would even know if their best friend was a thief. That is why it is important to not trust anyone, and as people think, it is a time to reflect of why it happened. To most people who already lived in Winslow, they did not care for gold, because they were already wealthy. It was this new wealthy class who were crooks, liars, and thieves who made their money illicitly. But, no one seemed to even care.

But where does all of this connect to what is currently happening in 1939? Well, no one even knows for sure, but there was said to be a person by the name of Corinth who promised destruction and chaos upon everyone and everything if his demands were not met in a timely manner.

This man or person by the name of Corinth was said to be a ringleader of a very notorious gang, *The American Justice*, who constantly tortured any person he wanted because he could during the mid to late 1840s until 1861. He was a very ruthless and evil-minded person who could not be reasoned with. It was like talking to a piece of wood or to the wall, since he never responded back, as he wanted to keep his victims or his critics in suspense. It was a very psychological in nature but he was the reason why anyone even lived during the California Gold Rush, as he owned many hotels and general stores in California and the surrounding areas. Sure, this Corinth guy was a ruthless person in charge of an American outlaw gang, but he was a very rich man who could get away with anything, yet he only liked to torture people at night when no one was around for him to be found. It was more of a hobby for him, as he also had a very excellent reputation of being the nicest person around town and all of the areas surrounding California.

And then his reputation went down the drain on the day of his death, after the Confederate Army captured him for desertion in 1861. He promised that one day he would make sure people will suffer because of what the Confederate Army did to him by capturing him. Corinth promised to offer the Confederate Army everything he knew about the Union Army, and he set demands as well, but that plan failed to persuade them.

So, Corinth said, "failure to meet my demands in a timely manner will cause chaos and destruction in the near future to all of your family members, friends, and descendants to everyone and everywhere." Sadly, the Confederate Army failed to heed Corinth's offer and advice, and he was hanged immediately after he spoke those last words about destruction and chaos. Everyone moved on from there, and soon it was all forgotten, except for that only certain people within Winslow, South Dakota even knew of the threat.

Except for one reason, no one in the town of Winslow, South Dakota knows of the people, since a fire is currently burning down all of the buildings with the people inside. As that December day in 1939 continues to draw to an end, there is just one thing, the fire is not going to end because there is just no stopping a very powerful wind that likes to burn down anything in its path. It was a never-ending fire and it continued to grow and burn until there would be nothing left, but there was another problem—the buildings were not melting or turning to ash and the people were just stuck screaming inside with nowhere to go. Not one even tried to exit any building because they feared that they would die.

The people were rightfully scared but they did not know that they could escape, yet they never even tried to open the doorknobs. Anyone in any of the buildings could escape and no harm would be done to them. The fires were real but they were kind of magical, since no person was getting burned from the flames. People were clueless and Carina did not even know what to do. She thought that all were going to die because everyone and everything seemed to be on fire, so she continued to walk away from the crime scene with no sympathy whatsoever. It was a bittersweet moment but there was nothing that she could do and she could not think of even a remote thing that she could do. Everything seemed like a lost cause.

And then, people dressed in black ski masks started to arrive, and they went into the burning buildings one-by-one, but no one even saw them again. It was like they entered the building and then disappeared. Carina didn't care, even though she saw those mysterious people in the black ski masks entering into those burning buildings, For all kinds of purposes, those people in black ski masks could be responsible for the fires, and that is what Carina thought, but she just continued on her way into the central business district.

Arriving at the central business district, Carina sees no one and nothing but tumbleweeds and dust. All of the general stores and other public and private businesses were completely empty. It was a sign of something sinister. No one was here and it seemed that no one would ever be back, if people were not lucky enough. So, why is all of this happening, well no one knows? All that Carina saw were people in black ski masks going into what she perceived as burning buildings. She thought they were all goners because of the flames and smoke, but she did not know everything. It was something like an alternate dimension. Carina heard all of the people screaming and yelling for help, but no one dare to go inside.

Everything was at the behest of Carina, as she is the only known witness to see the fires and flames trying to burn down buildings and do nothing about it. Something must end but it is not yet known of how to solve such a problem. It is just a case of not how to do something. That is just the opinion of how people decide to do everything in some country or another. It is just that Carina does not want to do anything because she does not want to get involved in any criminal situations. To Carina, it is just the reason to keep everything to her and pretend like it never happened. Nothing is off the hook for anything. Carina does not want to get into the specifics of what she just experienced but she could not care less and is looking forward to getting out of Winslow, South Dakota, but certain events will make it so she will experience the most terrible and horrible gruesome events that she has ever even experience. It will be a test for her judgment when the events start to appear or happen, and she must be able to walk away unharmed or alive with some form of injury.

Carina will not take it lightly but she must

face her fears when she is at her weakest, in order to feel accomplished and brave. Yet, the people in the black ski masks are nowhere to be found, but it is that reason why there must be a change. It must be so apparent to solve the case as to whether there is an existence to develop.

It was Corinth who promised destruction and chaos if his demands were not met in a timely manner. It was Corinth's promise of destruction and chaos that could have caused that fire to begin and engulf everything in sight. Corinth or his ghostly spirit is probably the person behind the burning buildings for some reason at all, and so it is his own spirit that should be held accountable. But that is such craziness and so psychotic that no one will ever believe anyone. It is for that reason why there must be another explanation. There just needs to be another possibility. Nothing could go wrong but it needs to be solved now. It needs to be answered, but there is a case-by-case basis of when such events will ever happen to Carina. For her, it is just a thing of the past.

But, that is not what is going to happen, as there is still the possibility that the people in the black ski masks could be behind everything that has occurred in the past several hours during the entire day. But, Carina is waiting for a bus, hoping for a change, and hoping that she will be able to escape this place once and for all. It is such a shame that she needs to act at once in a certain time to save her own life and the rest of humanity. It is something that must be solved and it needs to begin now, or so people believe.

Chapter Two

Then a bus appeared out of nowhere, from down the road. "Miss, are you getting in," asked the bus driver. "Oh, I'm not sure what I'm looking for, but sure, I will get in," said Carina. "Where would you like to go," asked the bus driver? "Anywhere but staying here, because I want to start a new life somewhere else," said Carina. "That is what I was expecting you to say," stated the bus driver. With that, the bus driver began to drive again until he ran out of gas or until he wanted to stop.

An hour has passed and Carina was just sitting down doing nothing. "Hello, my name is Sean Preston, and I am going to see my grandma in the Deep South," stated Sean Preston. "What is your name," asked Sean? "Why do you want to know my name," said Carina? "Feisty, I like that in a good woman," said Sean. "Fine then, my name is Carina Alexander, and I am getting as far away from here as possible," stated Carina. "Why," asked Sean? "Well, because everything that I knew burned down and I want to start a new life," said Carina. "That is such a fine name; Carina is indeed a very fine name, and it sounds delicious," stated Sean. "Where are you from," asked Carina? "Oh, me, I'm from the same place as you're from," said Sean. "And, where would that be," asked Carina? "Winslow, South Dakota," stated Sean. "How come I never seen you before," asked Carina? "Well, I was always doing other things, and I never had the time to do what I like until now," said Sean.

Carina just stared at him, and thought that he was a troublemaker. Then, all of a sudden, the most mysterious thing happened. The road just started to crack and it is only getting worse. A person appears in the middle of the road, and everyone on the bus except for the driver and Sean believe he is real, yet Carina does not care. "Slow down, there is some person in the middle of the road," said one of the passengers. "I'm not slowing down, because there is no one there," said the bus driver. But the bus driver did see someone and he knew who it was. The bus driver knew it was John of Patmos trying to reveal what would happen in the coming hours and days to the rest of the world, and it indeed was his ghost that looked as though John of Patmos was alive and well standing right there, but it was more likely his ghost, since it resembled a hologram. The bus driver told everyone that everything would be fine and that no damage was done.

Others, though, well they thought they were in for a murderous spree from an evil bus driver who did not care about anything, except for Carina, the bus driver, and Sean. Still, though, all of the other people felt unsafe and wanted to get off in a quick manner, but the driver indicated he would not stop for people to get off because there was nothing bad happening anywhere. In fact, the bus driver did know what was happening but he was on a mission from God or the Devil to deliver people to them for a specific purpose. But they didn't know it, except for Sean, while Carina could care less, as she will probably be long away from the bus when all of those other people are delivered to whoever they are delivered to.

People have a tendency to overreact but it is quite rare for them to see ghosts or people who have already died. Usually if people claimed they have seen dead people, they are usually in some house or other building that is haunted, and then they decide to hire paranormal investigators to get rid of those damn ghosts. But in this case, the passengers have made a claim that they believe the bus driver is an insane maniac because they believe they have just seen a live person who was in danger of being run over by their bus. While they might claim that it could be real, they themselves are probably in a very delusional state of mind, since they do not know where they are going, which caused them to experience hallucinations of non-existent people who have died many centuries ago. It is a price that shall be paid but no one will ever know what will happen to them. It is such a sad case of people being in a state of mind that they don't care about what they are doing for the better of society. They are just afraid but they need to be quiet, or else they will just get into trouble along the way. It is a time and place for none of that stuff, but that is never the case, as people always tend to hold a grudge that should never exist in their right mind. No, what these bus passengers are experiencing is a state of mind that causes danger and angst, as they do not know what is happening and also because they just got on the bus because it would take them to a place where they always wanted to do. But the bus driver never told the passengers where they were going. It is something sort of like they believed the bus driver knew everything about their planned or soon to be planned vacation. Yet, the bus driver only told them to just hop on so that he will see where the road will take the bus. That is not how to drive a bus.

Meanwhile, there is something that is very much needed. There is something about that bus that isn't right, and it is about to get increasingly worse, or so the passengers think. It is such a bad case that it has never been heard of, but no one even knows how to achieve anything. Most of the passengers on the bus do suspect a thing but that is just paranoia, or so they think. They should have something to worry about because it will only get worse from here and from now on.

That is to say, if they don't get to their place of interest. And if they did get to their intended place of interest or their dream vacation spot, then they will have nothing to worry about. However, all of the bus passengers are only worried because they believe they will be called as witnesses to a murder trial that will happen in the near future and they do not want any part of that. So, yes, the bus passengers are very worried about where they will go. But, it is a chance that might escape them, since the bus driver will not reveal where he is going.

Everything seems like a mystery because it is indeed a mystery to everything that does not belong in the current place. It is a time when hopes are high and when people are distracted for all the wrong and correct reasons.

Suddenly, there was a loud noise, but it

wasn't the bus or any person on the bus. It was the earth shaking and it continued to shake for unknown reasons. It could be due to the road cracked down the middle. It could be an earthquake, which is the likely reason for why most of the bus passengers are now in a mode of panic. They fear for their lives and they have the right to be scared, but they do not know if they are going to survive. It is the time when all hope fails because everywhere where it is going to happen will just cause a lapse in space and time due to a current crisis.

"Everything will be okay son," said one woman to her son on the bus. It is just another time when people have an adrenaline rush, "But I'm scared," said the son. Well now, there is something to worry about and it is indeed troubling. It is a sign that needs to be known or else something else will be not known to the rest of society. It is just that and it shall always be that, because that is that the cause of action that is currently happening.

But no one cares, since it is always about the never-ending crisis. It is such a bad thing that no one is even listening to each other on the bus. That is such a case of being doomed, or so the passengers seem to think of now.

And then, the situation has only gotten worse, because now the crack in the road is so wide that the bus will fall in. But, the bus is not going to fall into the very wide crack, as somehow the bus is using the crack in the road as some type of guiderail for some other specific purpose. But everyone else, except for Carina and Sean were not scared at all, while the bus driver didn't care because he knew what he was doing. There was crying and screaming, and it was like a wide amusement ride. The bus should have fallen in but it think it is a monorail or even some type of train on a railroad track. That is very silly and interesting for all crazy purposes and it should be into the blank void of society. Yet, everything seems to be a mystery, or else everything else is dead wrong. That is such a sad case but it shall begin and it has already begun. But the passengers on the bus won't see it that way because they are frightened.

And if all else fails, the people are currently in the midst of a mental health crisis because they fear they will die. It is nothing new but each of them still believe they are all going to a different place or a different destination, and it seems they are all wrong, due to the fact they are all going to the same place, and that is the Deep South, or so they don't know. It is an ugly situation that needs to be resolved now but it shall never be resolved because of the current and evolving situation that is currently happening on the bus.

It is such an evolving and changing crisis that

no one will know what will happen unless everyone has a clue about everything. It is a crazy situation and it should be known that no one should be trusted. It was a type of situation that needs to know about the rest of society and nothingness. For all other purposes and all known reasons, it is quite exciting to see all of those bus passengers getting nervous and anxious about something that isn't going to turn bad, but they need to be scared so the real plot is not revealed to them. That is a scenario where everyone needs to be out on the watch in order to protect each other so that no one will ever find out anything. If it doesn't make sense, then that is correct, because it is meant as a confusing tactic that will lead to the death as well as the destruction to everyone and everything. That is such a sad case of affairs and it needs to be fixed so that there is a case to the basic principles of nothing new and important.

On a positive note, the bus driver reaches the next town and decides to pull into town so that he can eat and take a short break of about an hour or so. Yet, he is going to tell the passengers to do the same, as they shall be relieved of stopping for rest.

On the intercom, the bus driver spoke, "We are stopping in a deserted town, where there are no people, but you are allowed to get off the bus in order to eat, drink, and use any facilities that you see, but please be back in your seats in two hours." With that, the bus driver pulled into a vacant parking lot with only a few vehicles. It was a surreal experience, but all of the passengers got off the bus, including Sean and Carina. The bus driver was the last to get off, as well as Sean and Carina, because it was protocol and because Sean, Carina, and the bus driver wanted to avoid the massive crowd that would be caused by the other passengers when people are trying to depart a bus.

As the people are leaving the bus, Sean and Carina waited for all of them to depart, and they felt as though something was wrong with them. To Sean and Carina, the passengers felt paranoid, but that is always a cause for concern, as it is that time that shall be known. That was something worth waiting for, but that was probably an exception to everything else or something like that. It was an experience that should not be dismissed but it will be dismissed due to what people believe in.

At last, it took some time, but all of the other passengers got off of the bus after fifteen minutes and they all headed toward the front entrance of what seems to be a mall. Carina, Sean, and the bus driver then departed the bus and it only took them a few short seconds to depart. The bus driver locked up the bus and all three of them headed to a separate and much smaller building that the other passengers did not see.

It was an experience that probably should not exist, but there could be a reason why Carina, Sean, and the bus driver where headed to a different place than the other passengers. Carina could be getting special treatment. But what about Sean; is he also getting special treatment? Probably, but there is a good chance that at least two people are up to no good, which could be the bus driver and Sean, both of whom Carina met on the bus. Everyone else might be wondering where they are, but they will probably be all happy since the bus driver is nowhere near them. There is a chance that something sinister is going to happen to all of the other passengers, and they probably don't know it yet. All of the other passengers will probably start to scream if they feel something bad is happening to them, such as a fire or another earthquake start to break out. It is always the worst thing that could happen but no one ever suspects a thing because they are always too pre-occupied with something else. But to Carina it is very different, as she could care less about anything, since she wants to go on an adventure for some reason due to probably seeing burning buildings but none of them actually burning down. That is such a bad case of not wanting to be here, or so people think. But it is for that reason why none of the other passengers should be upset with the bus driver. It is for the opposite reason why everything is happening to those passengers, because they are idiots because nothing bad is ever going to happen to them. They are either delusional or actually afraid, but they are probably delusional because the bus driver never told them where he is taking them.

As the bus driver, Sean, and Carina continue to walk toward the other building, there seems to be a sense of hope for them but not for the other people who feel differently. "Where are the other passengers going," asked Carina? "Oh, well, where they are going, you don't want to go there, because that is the place where no one can return, and it is a place where once you enter you can never escape," stated the bus driver. "It sounds fun," said Carina. "It is indeed fun, but they think they will be getting back on the bus when they are ready to get back on the bus," stated the bus driver. "Well, do they know that they are not getting back on the bus because it would not be possible for them to get back on the bus, since they will be stuck there forever," asked Carina? "Well, no, because all they care about is safety and they believe they are safe, but they also believe they can get back on the bus because they need to get somewhere, yet actually they don't need to be anywhere," stated the bus driver. "That sounds interesting yet intriguing, but I prefer to go with you and Sean into the smaller building," stated Carina. "It is interesting and very intriguing, but the building we are going to is much better than what they are going to experience, and we will be always protected, unlike them," stated the bus driver.

Everything seems interesting, as it is, and it is for that reason why Sean, Carina, and the bus driver must stay separate from the passengers, as those other passengers are going to experience something awful that no one wants to ever experience. There is no room for speculation but the reason for that is due to the fact that the other passengers might die because they saw something they liked, but it could actually be a trap that will doom them all. And that is why it is good to always to not be the first ones out of the bus, because by being so the bus passengers were not able to see the other building, as it was not there for them to see it, since they could only see what they perceived as a mall. It was impossible for the other passengers to see the smaller building because it was not even visible to them. And it wasn't because they were all pre-occupied looking for or doing something else, but it was due to the building not being there in the first place, as only certain people could see the much smaller building. And Carina did not care, since she liked the much smaller building, as it is more of her lifestyle and personality. It is simple and plain on the outside, which intrigues Carina much more than a mall.

On the other hand, Carina does not really care about those passengers who went into what looks like a mall, because she believed malls were overrated and dirty. While the other passengers took several minutes to get off the bus, they rushed into the much larger buildings in a matter of seconds. Yet, Sean, the bus driver, and Carina are just entering the smaller building. "Where is the key, did I misplace it," asked the bus driver. "Oh, here it is, it was deep within my pocket," said the bus driver. "Here we go, but just remember one thing, we can see everything that is going on, and we will know when it is time to use the bus again," said the bus driver. "Then, the two hours remark was something that was meant to be made up for specific and certain reasons," asked Carina. "Yes, that is right, and once everything is finished we can all leave together, but we might pick up passengers along the way," stated the bus driver. "That is so good to know, but what do we do now," asked Carina? "Well, we just wait, and we can order food and watch and do anything we choose," stated the bus driver.

Sean, Carina, and the bus driver enter the building finally, and it looks much larger inside than expected. It was surely a spectacle of amazement, as it seems that it looked and resembled a speakeasy, but it was more than just that. It was actually a full service bar, restaurant, and clubhouse with anything people could imagine. Everything about that place was such amazing that it awed Carina, but then she got over it and moved on. But Carina has yet to get to the most exciting part.

The level of the building where all of them entered is the only visible part of the building to any person who is able to see it. All other floors or levels of the much smaller building are below ground. It is for that reason why everything about this place is a secret, but the other passengers did not see the much smaller building, as they were unable to see it, since it was probably invisible to them. Then why did Sean, the bus driver, and Carina see the much smaller building and not the other passengers? Well, that is very interesting and intriguing, because it could be that Carina, the bus driver, and Sean are so special that they can see stuff that other people can't. It is such the case that they can see what the rest of the passengers saw but can also see stuff that is not even visible to anyone. The smaller building could just be hidden due to a cloaking device and if that is the case, then only certain people with specialized and very special equipment can see its existence. So, it would seem that Carina, Sean, and the bus driver could have specialized equipment or they could just be enchanted beings. Anything is possible but no one else would be able to know. It all provides a thing to worry about that people should not worry about when no one is worrying about anything. For most parts, it is the reason why Carina, Sean, and the bus driver do understand their surroundings, and for that purpose it is necessary for everyone else to know nothing. And that is exactly the case. Or if anyone else cares, then there is certainly something special, or there could be an institution being ravaged with harm. It is just for the sole reason of nothing.

And then there was nothing else but the sole divine purpose of happiness. Carina was very happy at what was happening to her and she did not care for anything else. She was enjoying herself by doing any and all things she could possibly do in such a small or what really turned out to be a large building. And it is that case that seemed to be the craziness of why the other passengers are idiots, because they think a very bad thing might happen to them. They could be right if anything does indeed happen to them, because they would have been right all along. But they still do not know what will happen to them because it is still too early to know. As of now all of the passengers who went into that building that resembled a mall are safe, because they feel safe and have nothing to worry about, but they also don't believe anything bad will happen to them anymore since they are not on the bus anymore.

Since the passengers are off the bus it is not surprising that all of them are happy, because they were extremely nervous when they believed they saw a person in the middle of the road and they thought he was going to be run over. The bus driver claimed they saw nothing but they did see something because they claimed they saw someone. It was not a person who was still alive but it indeed was a person who died many centuries ago. But it was some type of vision that they all had because of something that was probably meant to be.

Was this vision of a man in the middle of the road some sort of dream or was it foreshadowing an event that will happen to them in the future. They could be in a lot more trouble than being the prime and only witnesses to a possible hit and run, which could ultimately make them suspects to a crime due to what they believed the bus driver did. Instead, the more serious crime or trouble the passengers could face is that they might die in the building that looks like a mall. And then they might be all doomed, yet it is not yet known what will happen to them. It is all of a sudden that nothing of the sort will be prevented, due to the prospects of other events that are already in the crosshairs of turning into reality. That is the fate that is worse than a hit and run because then they would all die in an enclosed environment with no room or air to breathe.

No one would ever want to experience such a terrible death, but as a matter of fact, Sean, Carina, and the bus driver will not die today because they are all safe and immune from everything that will happen to the bus passengers. It is a good thing so far that everyone is safe for now, but something could happen in the next few hours or so. Yet, it is not known if people will actually die because they will die if they do something they are not supposed to. It is something that Carina, Sean, and the bus driver do not care about because they are having the times of their lives.

But now, it has only been one hour since the bus has parked, and there is only one hour left to get back on the bus. Yet, there is a chance that none of the passengers will get back on the bus, but Sean and Carina are not really considered passengers because they are not with the other passengers. It is just due to the fact that something is going to happen, and no one needs to know that.

Forever more, there is just something wrong with those people who think they are safe in what looks to be a mall. It is precisely their immaturity that is the real reason why they might get into trouble or into a mess they can never get out of. That is not how everything is supposed to be. Instead of those people who believe that a mall is safer a bus, they should really consider trying to make their escape, yet they are still very happy they can spend time having fun in a deserted or what seems to be a deserted building in the middle of nowhere.

As it all seems to sound, there is a crisis at hand and there is the possibility many people will be unable to escape, but that could be a good thing or whatever civilization means. People know no better than what they believe and this is exactly one of those situations, as they believe the mall is safer than a moving bus. Well, it could be safer, only if nothing bad happens inside of the mall, and that would lead to more chaos and havoc. It is such a slippery situation that no one can handle and it should be approached that way. If anything else that was learned by them in an immediate second right now, well, those people who got off the bus first should be worried and try to get out of that mall building as quickly as possible, due to the fact that they are in trouble but they don't know they are in trouble. For that reason, they will try and get out of the mall but they will end up in further trouble if they refuse to depart now, since a possibility might exist that the mall or whatever it is could actually be on lockdown as of right now. That shall always be a possibility because there is no one in the mall but those passengers. None of them even knows what will happen to them. It is such a sad case for today.

Of course, you have Sean, Carina, and the bus driver having the time of their lives and they could care less about some crazy passengers. But in the real world there is something more to worry about, and that is when how the people will escape from what seems to be a mall. No one knows what is going to happen to them and they aren't even aware about their current circumstances. Everything is not what it seems because everything is an illusion and mirage with an intended purpose of trapping them there for a specific purpose. It is for that reason why Sean, the bus driver, and Carina are safe and the passengers are in deep trouble for being idiots and walking into the first place they see, since they do not even know any better.

That is the tragedy that will always end up on the news but there is a possibility the news won't even exist because they might all be dead, and then you will have relatives looking for their loved ones in a very serious way. So, to put it lightly, there is a case of not being correct and that is the way it is always meant to be because of how the world works. That is always the solution of nothing. But it seems that there is another problem—which is that Carina, Sean, and the bus driver don't seem to care about them—and that is not even a problem. At any rate, it is almost dark, and there is a saying that goes like this, ‘if you don’t find your way out before dusk then you will be trapped there forever and eternity.’ Nobody wants that, but it is just that way, and the passengers barely have fifteen minutes to get out before they are doomed for eternity in the middle of nowhere.

Chapter Three

Three minutes to complete darkness, and there is already a problem for all of the passengers who decided to enter into that building of what looked like a mall. The passengers are trying to get out of the mall or whatever it is but they are having trouble, due to the matter that all of them are pushing and shoving each other. It resembles a brawl and it soon will be a melee, because everyone will either have injuries or they might die. Everyone will die some form of death because no one can live forever, but there could be an exception for Sean, Carina, and the bus driver due to them being in a different building.

It is surely coincidental that the three of them ended up going to a different building than the other passengers, or it could be the fact that they are just magical beings or have the power to see stuff that no one else can. The latter sounds more plausible to the rest of the world because of certain people being able to see stuff that isn't there. It could explain why some people are hallucinating and hearing things that do not exist. For the passengers in the building that looks like a mall, well it could be the end of the line for them, since they seem to be having a problem of escaping or exiting the building. That is certainly a bad and worrisome thing or event to happen when you are able to think about it. But it does happen, yet not in a way that screams murder mystery due to the fact everyone died from trampling upon everyone else. That would indeed be a tragic death that no one would be able to cope about because there could be constant nightmares.

Barely a second has passed and there is still madness going on in that building. It just won't stop because the passengers keep on trampling on each other. And for the rest of time, it is something like the end of the world. That will surely be the reason why no one will live to tell the tale of why they could not escape the wrath of a mall. It is just so sad that none of them will be able to survive and it will only be due to their own expense. That's right; they will suffer a painful death by stampede because they are not even paying attention to what they are doing. All of those passengers do not even know what is happening to them but they will soon learn they will not live to see another day. It is their own fault that they are going to die at what looks like to be a mall, and all of this could have been avoided if they just waited on the bus and or not push and shove each other when trying to depart the bus. It is what matters but that could be karma, and karma can be a bitch, so they were given a warning before yet refused to act appropriately like normal functioning adults.

Thirty seconds have passed and there is still this fighting going on between the passengers, since all of them want to exit the building at the same time. But by doing so, the passengers created a blockade of sorts, and this blockade will cause the exits of the said mall or building to be blocked, forcing people to trample upon each other and leading to the deaths of many innocent people. But the question to ask is if this was all planned from the beginning. It is the time and place for anything and it too shall be the reason why there is a revolution of the dead. It is for that one reason why people must die in order to make sure the rest of the world can live.

As there is something wrong with those people trying to escape from the mall, they seem to not comprehend what is going on around them. They have no clue and they will be sorry about what will turn into a disaster. And from that point on, there will be something that is not necessary for the rest of the world in their opinion because they shall not exist in the next few minutes. They shall die when they are trying to escape but they won't know it until they are finally happy. So, it would be at their behest to not do anything that could be described as too dangerous or else they might actually die. But, they will never listen to anything, as they believe they are under attack again. For them to learn will be incredibly hard, as it seems they lack the basic comprehension skills of being able to live a normal life, but only because they act like idiots and repeatedly ask for an explanation each time they don't understand. It is not that they are not smart because they are smart; it is due to the fact that they repeatedly ask idiotic and or stupid questions that make no sense to the rest of the society.

The passengers just need to get their heads together and think of something more productive but that will never happen. It will only be a matter of time until they die, but the only question to ask is how they will die. That is up to the building or the people it, because anything can actually happen to anyone. No one can escape death, not unless you are Sean, Carina, or the bus driver. Without anything, there will be no society, and that is the premise of what is going on with those passengers trying to get out alive. They are their own problems and they are the reasons why they shall die. If they never even panicked during the bus ride, then they could be safe, but that could actually be proven wrong if the bus driver already had planned on doing such a sinister act, like what is happening right now. It is for that very reason why it is good because it is always a part of life of not doing anything.

With less than three minutes to spare there is nothing that can be done. It is a complete and utter mess that is currently happening in that mall and no one will help them. They don't even need any help as they don't appreciate it. Everything will be just for a lost cause, but they actually never knew where they were going because they believed they were going to their dream vacations. So, they made up their very own destination, each and every one of them, which does not make a lick of sense. The passengers are such morons that they can't see their delusions and nonsense are going to kill them. It is too bad that they will end up nowhere, or that is what they don't want to believe.

For all other purposes they shall be ignored, since they will not live that longer. It is just the way it works, and if it was the exact opposite of that then all of them will become immortal or something like that. It would be the worst possible thing that could ever happen to society because there would be too many people. And then there is just the utter hope for some small change that could happen, and it seems there could be something wrong with that. It would seem that there is no hope for anyone because every one of those passengers in that building will die but they do not want to die, since they believe they actually have a purpose in life.

With one minute to spare, the passengers still have hope, but they shouldn't, as they will all die in a matter of seconds. It is just simple as that and they will not know what hit them. It will be sad but also a very happy day. It will be the beginning of something new for the rest of society. Nothing will ever be the same because it was always the same. That will be the day.

At last, the passengers were able to open the doors, but then something happened later. They were able to see the bus but then there was a loud noise that no one could describe. It was a rumbling noise and it sounded like it was the building. "Look up," said one of the passengers to the rest. "What is going to happen to us," stated another passenger? "Are we all going to die," asked a third passenger? "We are safe for now and we have nothing to worry about like on the bus," stated another passenger. But there was something wrong indeed.

Suddenly, the building came crumbling down upon the poor helpless passengers, even though all of them were 1000 feet away from any structures of that building. It was just something that didn't make any sense at all, and it seemed like the building had a mind of its own. Or, it was just vengeance for some other divine or demonic purpose. And then it was very clear because it wasn't.

The bus driver alerted Sean and Carina to the incident, seeing that all of them were too busy to even notice anything. It is for that reason why no one should trust anyone, since these types of distractions can always happen during the most important times of a person's life. But there is something good in all of this, which is that the passengers died in a freak accident that was supposed to happen, yet not in their own minds because they believed they were safe. All of those passengers thought wrong because they are dead now. They should have not complained on the bus but that is their own darn fault for being people who know nothing.

It's too bad only three people survived the collapse, but then those three people were located in a different building. So it doesn't really matter, since all of those passengers died, because they were supposed to die anyways. None of them ever made it back to the bus because they were never supposed to get back on that cursed bus. It all remains a mystery of why they got on the bus in the first place. It could be that they wanted to escape something or they also thought it would take them wherever they want, but the latter has a better chance of being true, only since they wanted the bus to take them wherever they wanted to go. The bus driver did not care for all of their problems, since he was only doing his job, by transporting people.

For all other purposes, there is really nothing wrong with what just happened because all of those passengers deserved what they got. They had nothing better to do then complain about seeing a dead person who was in the middle of the road, doing possibly a very sinister thing, or he could be just reciting some sort of verse about the future. And if that is the case, John of Patmos predicted the future of those crazy and whiny passengers accurately, but they would have never of known it because all of them are said to be bonkers or just plain mad about not getting to where they want to go. It figures those passengers became angry and annoyed at the bus driver, only because they believed they were lied to, but the bus driver never said he will actually take them to their dream vacation destination. All the bus driver stated to them is, “that what I was expecting you to say,” which was never really a promise of anything. It was only something that they believed in their own minds that the bus driver would take them anywhere they wanted to go.

Only idiots would believe a statement like that from the bus driver, and they just took his words out of context, because they already thought the bus driver knew where they wanted to go. So says the bird who is all wise, but that is something that is not meant as you thought it was, because the passengers were never the bird. But from another perspective, the passengers were just worried about their own lives or something too simplistic like wondering what they would eat the next morning. It isn't funny but it is at the same time, because everything is at the center of the universe to them, but that should never be the case.

If all else fails, they should have been alive, if they never boarded the bus, but each one of them saw it and thought it would transport it to their intended destination for some reason. They weren't even a little reluctant because they thought it was an actual bus for some reason or another. But the craziest part of it all was that none of them even purchased a ticket at all, which is a reason for doubt, as all buses usually require some form or payment, unless it is subsidized by a government or government agency. None of those passengers even thought about the reason that they didn't have a bus ticket. They all thought that it was a free bus ride, which they were right, but then they died trying to get back to the bus, and that was not a good decision on their part. So, for all of that old misery, it is up to nothing now, and it could be the sort of thing that should be ignored for all types of reasons.

And then, it was time to leave again. Sean, Carina, and the bus driver all went back to the bus in order to leave the middle of nowhere. No one in the world even knows what happened to their relatives, if they even had any relatives on the bus, and if they had none on the bus then they should feel fine and dandy due to the fact that their relatives are alive or have died from different causes.

Alas, there is nothing that can be done to save those dead passengers, but that is no problem, since everything is without anything for the most part during these situations. But hey, why is there a rush to get to the problem? Nothing is perfect and that is and shall always be the case, or it shouldn't bother Sean, Carina, and the bus driver, and it won't. So, to put it into something easier for people to understand, the people died because they were idiots. It is sad but true, so no one should be outraged. It will be the end before anyone even knows it and that shall be the day when people become more idiotic. That is the time when there will be more severe problems, and it will happen during the lifespan of Sean, Carina, and the bus driver, so the rest of the world needs to be very careful about what happens, or else something bad might actually happen to them. That is just crazy to think about.

Besides that, there is simply nothing to worry about, because no one even asked. But it only took Sean, Carina, and the bus driver about a few minutes to get back to the bus. Now, back at the bus, Sean, Carina, and the bus driver think for few seconds, in order to decide what they will do with the luggage left behind by the passengers. But the bus driver ultimately decided to throw it all overboard, just like he had done many times once before. It was probably something out of a science fiction novel but it does occasionally happen to certain people. There is just a time and place for anything. And it is at the peril of the people behind the mystery.

"What are we going to do with their luggage they left behind," asked Carina. "We are probably just going to leave it behind," said Sean. "Really, or because it will weigh down the bus," asked Carina to the bus driver? "Well, we will just leave it behind because it will weigh down the bus and we might also need more room if other passengers have any luggage of their own," stated the bus driver. "That is fine by me," stated Carina. "Good, so now we can open the doors to the storage compartments. It won't take long, because those people didn't bring much with them, except for a few passengers who chose to pack heavy.

It is a cold afternoon and all three of them are trying to see where they will put the passengers' left behind luggage, if they had any at all. Sean, Carina, and the bus driver are probably going to place all and any luggage on the side of the bus and leave it there for anyone to pick up, which isn't unusual at all when the landlord has already evicted a person from any type of apartment, if those tenants didn't take some or any of their property with them. And then all of the relatives will wonder where all of the belongings have gone, if said relatives ever found out. But that won't probably happen, since no one knows who the deceased bus passengers are related to. In the end, all or any of the bus passengers probably do not have any relatives alive or well. And to put that into some sort of conundrum, all of those relatives probably do not care about their deceased relatives because all of the deceased relatives who tried to exit the building are probably the black sheep of the family and also deserved to die.

Everything was finally all said and done but it took a while. Sean, Carina, and the bus driver all did not estimate enough time at all. Underestimating the time it would take, they finished the task anyways, with some time to spare for a surprising reason. And that is something that seems crazy because it doesn't even make sense to underestimate time when there was time left to spare to do other things. It was for that reason why everything does not need to make sense because they set a set amount of time to complete the luggage removal but didn't believe it would take that long. Out of that set amount of time they set, Sean, Carina, and the bus driver thought it would only take about fifteen minutes, but instead it took around an hour with about thirty minutes time left.

So, what did Sean, Carina, and the bus driver do after unloading the luggage of the passengers who died? Well, they went back on the bus after they closed the storage compartment doors. It was like a sense of relief because of what has happened, but it was still a cold December day, but now it was a cold December afternoon. Everything always happened for a reason; but Sean, Carina, and the bus driver are just going to wait for a few minutes or when they are ready to depart this place located in the middle of nowhere. It is something that was just meant to happen—a delay in finishing the task due to some people packing heavy stuff in their luggage. It was a normal error that could probably be made again, but there is just something wrong with anything if they did not make an error.

After ten minutes or so of resting on the bus,

the bus driver started the bus in order to warm up the engine for about five minutes. It was a precaution of sorts in order to prevent engine damage or failure and to protect the asset of the bus. It was just something normal routinely done, and that is the case for how the rest of everything was supposed to be done in the correct amount of time.

Five minutes after the bus driver turned on the ignition, it left with Sean, Carina, and the bus driver to depart for some other place. Besides, the bus left early in order to get a head start. It is just something that has always been at the center of attention, due to the fact that no one can escape it, for the reason of having any sanity. But there was never a lost cause for some reason because there was a lost cause when the passengers reacted when they felt something was wrong. It was just a waste of time for all of those passengers, but maybe a new set of passengers will get on board.

It has been an hour since the bus left that place in the middle of nowhere and maybe it is too almost time to pick up more passengers. But there is no knowing of where the bus will end up next. It could be heading to California or it could also end up in Florida or some other southern state in the eastern part of the United States. Anything is possible and that should always be left up to the person in charge of the bus.

There is a sudden urge to do anything bus stay behind, but the only people who stayed behind were all of the dead passengers because they died. And that should surprise no one at all, since they have been constant complainers ever since they saw a man in the middle of the road, who was allegedly not really there, according to the bus driver. That is just what you expect that mysterious bus driver to say, but he too shall be unharmed for all the wrong and right reasons.

It seems to be that there is this curse with this bus and how it could lead to the demise of the people who board it. But there is a problem with this, since Sean, Carina, and the bus driver all seem to be immune to the said curse. No one else knows why but it could be that they are protected or they just know certain people. All three of them could just be a bunch of supernatural or magical creatures but no one will ever believe that, unless the believers claimed they have been abducted by other lifeforms, as it could actually be possible. There is just a vague and unknown certainty that seems suspicious to those who want to know more and it is bothering the rest of society who actually cares about no one, or so they always say. That is always usual until someone grows angry and starts a brawl. But in this case, that never even happened, as all of those dead passengers just pushed and shoved each other because they didn't know what they were doing. So, they were a dead cause to begin with.

After all, it is funny at times when you had those people trying to get off of a parked bus, due to the fact that none of them knew how to take turns or even get off a bus. They were just amateurs to begin with because they confused themselves by not doing the proper thing of practicing courtesy to each other, and by not doing that they made a big mistake of dying when trying to make it back to the bus. They should have thought and behaved better but all of them are dead now. So, who even cares about all of those low lives?

There is no one, not even one person, who can save humanity now, unless of course you count Sean, Carina, and the bus driver as heroes of some sort. It is all a mirage because no one shall ever get to know the whole truth and nothing but the truth. It will all just be a waste of time.

Chapter Four

Cruising along the highway, the bus just continued to pick up speed. It was something from a police chase but it was normal for this bus driver who has driven this route several times before. It was just natural for him to pick up speed once there was no one to pick up but once he was able to sense additional passengers waiting to go somewhere, the bus would stop at his behest, as it always has. It would take some time but it would be necessary. Besides, there are more people to pick up and this is not the end of a bus ride for some sort of reason. Everything has a purpose, even a boring bus ride.

At about the same time as people can think about anything, there is this sudden stop of the rest of the world. Nothing is happening to Sean, Carina, or to the bus driver, but everyone and everything could be stuck in time or they could be trapped by some sort of evil criminal enterprise who wants to get rid of the good people of society. Anything is possible but no one will even know if that ever happens, or so people thought. It is just what a doctor ordered, for the purpose of nothingness. That being the case, there is nothing that can be done, but that should never be the reason why the bus always stops. Besides, no one knows who even owns the bus. The bus could be owned by the same evil criminal enterprise who just wants to destroy the world. Sure, that is entirely and always possible, if the evil criminal enterprise is an actual organization. Or else, this criminal enterprise could just be made up for public relations, so that no one will complain.

Suddenly, the bus comes to a complete halt, indicating that at least one person is waiting to go to some unknown place. The doors of the bus open up and it seems to be there are people waiting to board this mysterious bus for some apparent reason. They do not know where they will go but when they saw the bus they were not going to leave.

Everything seems to be falling right into place where it belongs but the new passengers probably don't even know that. To the new passengers, it is just a normal bus that will transport them to the place where they want to go. But this isn't that type of bus to begin with. It is a different bus that seeks to do the opposite, by transporting the passengers to wherever the bus driver takes it. Sure, the bus could be sort of possessed, but no one would have ever thought of that being the case, because no one would believe that for a minute. People just want to go to some place that they always wanted to go to, but those passengers who are going to the bus just want to go to the next town or state over, but they do not know what will happen in the end.

"Where you all headed," asked the bus driver? "Well, we are all one group, but we heard about a convention in California close to the border between the United States and Mexico," said one of the passengers. "Then hop on, I will take you to the place you desire the most," said the bus driver. "How about our luggage," asked another passenger? "Don't you worry about that, because it will be packed in the storage compartments after you board the bus," said the bus driver. "So, all you have to do is to board the bus and take a seat, and everything else will be taken care of, just like magic," stated the bus driver to the passengers. "Don't we all need tickets," said the passengers to the bus driver? "Tickets are not ever required for this bus because it is free," said the bus driver to the passengers.

Without any further hesitation, all of the new

passengers got on the bus. There were about fifteen of them altogether going to a convention. But they did not mention what convention, only some type of convention near the US-Mexico border. That could be anything and no one will even know it. There could be something wrong with these passengers who just got on but they all seem and look nice, so no one will probably care. It would probably just be a waste of time to find out, but something needs to know who these new people are. No one can be safe because it is assumed people are being hunted by some sort of supernatural force that seeks the destruction of the human race and the rest of the universe. But no one will ever believe that because people tend to act and behave badly.

There goes the cause for good luck about finding out the rest of the truth. Everything will just be stuck in the past and no one will know who to blame. But anyone could blame the bus driver for some apparent reason or another because it is the bus driver who is always blamed for everything. And there is no problem with that, but people should only blame the actual parties responsible for death and destruction.

All of the passengers have boarded the bus and it is almost time to depart. They find a seat to sit down and once everyone has found a place on the bus to sit, the driver will close the doors. But if anyone looks out the window, they would see that the luggage of the passengers is not there anymore, since it is all under the bus in the storage compartments. And the bus driver never got out of the bus, because he was right about the luggage being placed in the storage compartments by the use of magic or some other unknown explanations. Or, it could be there is some unknown porter who is responsible for handling the luggage. But no one else is here. So who else could it be? There are no other people on this crazy bus besides Sean, Carina, and the bus driver. So, could it be any of them? It is possible but no one should care. Nothing is important right now, as the new mission is to get to this hidden or unknown convention, or what the bus driver or bus decides.

The bus driver shuts the doors to the bus and is ready to go. There is no knowing of where the bus driver will stop next. It could be near the border or it could be somewhere else. It will all be a mystery in the end, but no one knows if those passengers really want to go to a convention near the US-Mexico border. It could all be a ruse that would lead to more people dying. No one should feel safe because there are certain forces out there that want to destroy the rest of the world. Nothing can be considered safe anymore and it is apparent people are out to get other people. That will be the day when people actually kill other people by the masses. It will all lead to the end of the world and no one might even notice it. That is certainly something sinister, and as people might have thought it is.

And of course you have those people who will blackmail their friends and family for other types of reasons, just because they feel like it. No one is safe, not even family or friends; and it should always frighten anyone. That is what other people might call the end of the world, but that will probably be the only thing that will be considered safe. It is just for that reason why no one should be trusted for what they say to other people, because they could deceive the rest of society. And no one wants that but society will always believe anything people tell them for some unknown reason. It is just something that needs to be taken into consideration or there will be the force of nothing.

At each cost, there is just nothing to do, since it will be the end of reality, or what it is perceived as the end of the truth. But no one will find out because it will be in the middle of a vacant field in the middle of nowhere. That is the worst case scenario because no one will know who is in charge of anything, and people want to know who is in charge. And by that, there is something in the middle of nowhere, because there is nothing left.

After a few minutes of doing some

paperwork for some reason or another, the bus driver drove off from the bus stop where the people were waiting at and just zoomed away. He could be going to the convention or maybe somewhere else. It all remains a mystery. Everything that occurs is always a mystery to some other person. It never gets old but there is a time and place for everything. But, as people might believe, there could be something wrong with all of the new passengers who want to attend a convention near the US-Mexico border. It sounds like they really don't want to attend a convention but actually want to harm certain people.

That is the same thing that should happen to other people but it never does because of some other thing that constantly interferes with the process of the idiotic paper machine that continues to drive a wedge between society and humanity. No one likes that but these new passengers might. It could be something worse than a nightmare but stuff happens, so it is always necessary to end the day with a bang by doing the opposite. It never fails. Everything is constantly a disaster. But people always like it that way, as it is a promotion of chaos and destruction. That is the time when everyone decides to flee and cower. And then they will be scared. Because they are afraid of some dangerous event that could kill them, but that is understandable, at least from their point of view, if it is even viable. However, that is not what the most important situation is, due to the matter that there are strange people on the bus who are saying that they want to attend a convention near the border that separates the United States from Mexico. And if no one thinks that is strange, then they are probably part of the problem.

An hour has passed and the bus has still not entered the state of California. It is just somewhere in the middle of Montana. Probably it is near the capital, Helena, or somewhere close to there. The bus driver is surely driving a crazy route, but he is the expert who always drives the bus. So, he must know what he is doing, and if he doesn't, well, that is just his loss. But the new passengers are not scared of the bus drivers like the passengers who died when they were trying to go back to the bus. Who knows? Maybe some person will trigger an event that will lead to the destruction of the bus. That is certainly possible but it probably won't happen now. People can act crazy at times, and the bus driver is no different. So, that is that and it should begin at nothing other than the rest of society forgetting anything. By that way, people can have their own opinions whenever they want to escape a threat.

This bus ride is probably going to be very long, so everyone should be ready for the ride of their life, if they want to live. If the bus driver was smart enough, he would drive straight down from Helena, drive through Idaho and then Nevada, and quietly drive into the southern portion of California. But the bus driver would still have to go all the way to the US-Mexico border to get to a convention of some sorts. And besides, it will be a shorter route for the bus to take. But there is no knowing of which way the bus driver will go once the bus enters into the state of California.

It could be in Imperial County or it could be in San Diego County. But the passengers never gave a definitive answer about which border crossing that they needed to get off of. But, since it is near the US-Mexico border, it should be near it but not at the exact border crossing. The bus driver could know the precise location of where to drop off the passengers but he doesn't want to give away any secrets. That is why he is in charge and the bus driver. It is just the fountain of evidence for what needs to come in the near future. It would be at the center of attention for everyone to cross the border without any guard or federal agent watching, but there is still that same exact question about if anyone is actually guarding the US-Mexico border. That will be the day when the people in charge of the border crossings actually do their job of stopping the drug cartels. Nothing could stop the drug cartels because they are just too big and too powerful, but no one even knows if those people who boarded the bus are actually members of any Mexican drug cartel.

It is still 1939 and there is already a drug problem in Mexico because of drug kingpins who want to smuggle dangerous and mind-altering drugs back to the United States of America. And by that problem, it actually means that these passengers who just boarded the bus could actually be members of local drug cartels. In fact, that could actually be the case why they seek to go near the US-Mexico border to attend a so-called convention. People will never know what other people do and it will cause the rest of society to become weaker. But, the passengers did not even say a thing on the bus. They were all quiet and it seemed strange to no one. Sean and Carina just looked at each one of them and thought the same, as it was strange.

The passengers had a blank stare on their faces and it looked all too serious, like they meant it for some reason. But that did not deter Sean, Carina, or the bus driver. The bus driver was just doing his job of driving a bus and no one knew if he was going to stop for a rest or to get some food to eat. It is just the type of situation that needs to be known, because people need to know what they are going to do. That is not something new.

That is the place that needs to happen. It is the poor man's game and it is here to stay. There is just no knowing of who will survive this bus trip, if it does indeed come to that. The bus driver has yet to say anything to those passengers since he asked them if they wanted to get on the bus. Nothing is for the fact that is truth.

There is nothing further to know and it is in the place of something else, to the extent that the US-Mexico border actually exists. There will be doubt put into place by the passengers' existence and then there will be the center of progress that will lead to the end of the universe. It is the epitome of the whole world to know who these people on the bus are, since they look and act suspicious. It is part of the situation in the manner of how to dissolve a situation in the new context of anything. That is no new situation of how to encounter the institution of justice, due to the fact that everything is crazy. That is the same exact place for something, and it is the reason why all of these passengers must be screened, just to make sure they are safe and not actually dangerous criminals or members of the resistance.

That is the very extent of immigration but that is not what actually matters. What actually matters is the people on the bus who boarded the bus a while back in the middle of nowhere. That is the kind of thing that is crazy, but there is no sudden change of heart. Everything will remain the same and it too shall be resisted.

The passengers will resist.

The people will resist.

The rest of the world will resist.

Sean, Carina, and the bus driver might not exist because someone needs to keep order in order to preserve and maintain peace. That will be the day and it too shall remain in chaos. But nothing shall be the real truth of knowing nothing. That will be the price to pay to resolve nothing. But the passengers are the ones who need to be worried because they represent what is wrong with the rest of society. It is how the means of time represents the bus and the rest of the world represents the rest of the world. That too shall be a waste of time.

That will be the day of resistance.

And time too shall pass to determine what is needed. No one will care and it will just lead to the chaos of the rest of society. That is not how anyone should live.

As the bus approached Idaho, it was almost certain that it wasn't going fast enough, but no one knows how fast this bus can go, with exceptions being Sean, Carina, and the bus driver. It is all too familiar because it has happened before, and that is what going on during the bus ride. That is how it must be accepted, and any other way is the wrong reasoning for fear of sanity and insanity. That is what not needs to happens. What needs to happen is that the bus driver needs to drive faster, and by drive faster, it means he needs to get to the destination at a quicker amount of time.

And so it was decided, the bus driver decided to speed up, just for no reason at all. It could be just for fun or it could be that he wanted to go somewhere else for deadline reasons. Instead of going the typical speed of about forty-five miles per hour, he increased his speed to over twice what he was doing, which was about ninety-seven miles per hour. That is very unheard of for a bus to go that fast, but no witnesses were in sight. There was no presence of police in the near vicinity.

There would only be a reason to go faster and it might be due to the bus driver knowing that all of these passengers are going to cause trouble for some reason or another. That is the only potential reason just to speed up, but it could be for some other reason that has yet to be known. It was that case for which the whole conspiracy is a waste of time. That will be the whole truth, but there is this thing called a bus that transport people.

At least five hours will be shaved from the speed and that is a good thing, but it will still drive into the night. It might arrive the next day but it will not slow down. That is how it is supposed to be and it has always been that way. It is about time and it is all about speed. Everyone else can go into the middle of a deserted location and they will get lost but not this bus driver. He shall always prevail. It is a precaution for the rest of time. But it will always be about how the people get there.

As the bus drives down the road it just picks up speed. In about three hours, the bus has already crossed into the state of Nevada, and there is just no stopping the speed. The bus just continues the very fast pace of ninety-seven miles per hour, and no one is even complaining. And then it was about five and a half hours later, and the bus just entered the lower or southern portion of the state of California. It was just a relief that time was flying by, with not one single complaint. There was less than three hours to go and the bus driver was making an all-time record by just going very fast. He knew where he was going and he knew that all of those passengers would be trouble for him. He sensed the trouble after they boarded the bus and took their seats.

At last, three hours later, the bus came to an abrupt halt. It was only a matter of time until all of the passengers got off.

Chapter Five

Nightfall has passed and it was almost the morning. It was actually in the middle of the night but no one cared, since everyone was asleep. That is something to think about. But the bus driver was not tired or he did not look like it. So, what would the bus driver when it was still dark? He would do what any normal person would. He just parked the bus in a deserted area in the city of Calexico, California. It was just a normal type of situation.

It was the next morning and the sun already rose. The time was six o'clock ante meridiem. Sean and Carina were already awake and so was the bus driver. The passengers are about to wake up and they don't know what to expect. It could be a dream but it could be something else. There is just something more powerful.

Sean and Carina could not care less, but then they must decide what they are going to do, or they could be doomed. It could be possible but it is at the time of day again. That is the time that it shall be known as. It is just how it is meant to be but this is something different.

What would Sean and Carina do?

What would the bus driver do?

No one knows but they must think of a plan quickly. They must know what is happening and they must know now. It is how it has already been. There must be certainty to help the rest of humanity before there is an apocalyptic event. Or that could be the end of the world more quickly and no one would want that to happen. As a matter of fact, there is a good plan to think about. There could be a problem with it but it can actually work.

The plan would consist of Sean, Carina, and the bus driver ditching the bus and going into town to see what it has to offer. There is no knowing of what will happen. There could be traps set but that can be very fun. It could be easy or it could be hard but then there is trouble for the meaning of being stranded in the middle of nowhere. That will just be the whole truth because it is just the beginning. Nothing will be into the oblivion. Everything shall be the same and it shall be right and good.

Sean, Carina, and the bus driver finally had a plan, and by a plan, they decided they will desert the bus and go into town. That shall be the time and place when everything is near the path or whatever the path towards the city path is. It won't be easy but it won't be hard. It will just be a matter of walking to the city center itself.

As Sean, Carina, and the bus driver start to leave the bus, they start to think for a few brief moments of what could happen to the bus, if they left it alone with the passengers inside. It could be fine and all, but no one will know what happened. These passengers could be part of the problem or they could be the wrong people to suspect of doing something bad and evil. But there is no way to know what could potentially happen to the rest of the people. On the one hand, there will be chaos, but on the other there could be destruction. Or, it could be that all of these passengers wanted Sean, Carina, and or the bus driver to leave. That way, the passengers could hatch up a plan in order to do something so sinister that not even the rest of society will think of. Sadly, no one knows if anything is true, and by that, it is the actual meaning of life.

Walking pass the middle of nowhere or what seems to be dry and barren with nothing but dirt and tumbleweeds, well that is great. But Sean, Carina, and the bus driver don't care about that, since all they want to do is go into town and see what will happen next. That is all society has to offer, but not if there is something to cheat for, such as this crazy appetite to destroy the rest of the world. That is just nothing, and as it comes to an abrupt halt, there is nothing to do but think about what is going to happen to Carina, Sean, and the bus driver. It is quite something, but do people really walk around in a shimmering place that looks as similar to an object to no allure. That is just the point of time people would have to deal with, as nothing is evident.

So, Sean, Carina, and the bus driver have only been walking for five minutes, and they still are not even in town. Five minutes of nothingness, five minutes of doom, that is that has happened so far, but so far they just see a glorified landscape of sand and cacti in the vicinity of their view, and the sun is on their shoulders trying to tell them to give up. But it is something other than that. It is a sign of new peace and a cause for change. As there seems to be a crazy reaction to something, this desert or wherever Sean, Carina, and the bus driver are at is a complete and utter shithole, because they can't do anything but walk to a better place.

As it turns out, they are closer than they might find themselves to be, but the confusion of the hot lush sand and cacti seeks to do harm to everything else in their dominion. Everything is a lost cause and it seems it will all be for a waste. Wait until all of the passengers start to wake up, because that will be the time of the century, and that too shall be nothing but why there is a problem with this trip to get to some sort of crazy convention. The writing is on the wall and it seeks the demise of everything in the path of Sean, Carina, and the bus driver. Everything is in the same exact place, but no one even knows that. It has been something of a game to everyone on the bus, but the passengers are probably behind everything. And so, there is something drastic to think about, and by that case, something is indeed different, or so they even know it.

An hour has already passed since all of the passengers started waking up, but they already knew what had happened. The passengers knew that Sean, Carina, and the bus driver stranded them in the middle of nowhere. But these passengers expected that to happen, since they knew what was going to take place. And by that, their evil plan can be put into place. Sometimes the plan needs to be implemented in a time of pity but this is not that, since this is a time of acknowledgement to get away with as much chaos and destruction as possible. That time is now, when people runaway, but the passengers do not know what is going to happen to them in a few short hours. They could die or could even start a war of the most sinister plots people have ever thought of. It is just the time of the matter that is important to how it is implemented. That is what needs to be said, and that is now, or so people believe, because that is the time when people die.

Meanwhile, it is still the same time where Sean, Carina, and the bus driver are, but they don't know that they have been walking for an hour. It has always been an hour since they left the bus in the middle of nowhere, but to them it only feels like five minutes have passed. That is all the time can be, due to there being something wrong, and it seems like it is all fine. But really, nothing is fine, yet it seems as though no one is sad.

At last, Sean, Carina, and the bus driver have entered the city limits, and they find it fascinating from something that looks as though it was part of the Wild West. Everything is grand and it seems all like a ploy. There are people in the streets but there is nothing but happiness. It seems like something is going to happen. But, there is still a long wait in order to determine what will happen next or what will happen yesterday.

Anyways, the passengers leave the bus and go somewhere that is secret in nature. And they all enter into the city limits in a fraction of the time. That is just peculiar for people who want to go to a so-called convention in California near the US-Mexico border. It is so peculiar, but nothing should surprise anyone anymore. At some point in time, the passengers will catch up to Sean, Carina, and the bus driver, but no one cares about that, since they don't give a damn about anything. It is all a hoax. It is the meaning of why people should not underestimate each other, and if they do then the passengers will be doomed as well as Sean, Carina, and the bus driver. Everything is a trap, as people are idiots. It should be noted that no one knows what is happening. But, at this time, Sean, Carina, and the bus driver are currently in the city limits of a gorgeous and vibrant city center that looks to offer an abundance of hope and change for the rest of society. It is hope that should be encouraged but it is hope that is inadequate for the rest of the world. It is the rest of humanity that must not do anything just so they can do stuff. But, Sean, Carina, and the bus driver need to get the anything of anyone here just to see if there is a convention. It looks as though no one is paying attention.

"Is there any report of a convention here," shouted the bus driver? "Hello, does anyone here know about a convention near the US-Mexico border," shouted Sean? Then Carina shouted to the people as well. “Does anyone even care to speak with us; we just want to know if there is a convention near here or someplace close to here,” shouted Carina. It is just a waste of time, as no one is answering any of them for unknown reasons. The town folks are just minding their business and keep on walking without giving a care in the world. It is so surprising but it seems that they are actually real people. But then there is a possibility those town folks could be evil robots in disguise. Or, they could just all be innocent but actually be mind-controlled for an evil and sinister purpose of unknown proportions. It is just so crazy about what will happen if no one finds out what is happening. It all seems too surreal here that no one is responding to Sean, Carina, or the bus driver, but they are not surprised at anything that is happening right now due to something they all suspect to be weird. It could just be a coincidence but this has déjà vu written all over it. Nothing seems to be good at all in this city called Calexico, California. It will just be a matter of time until other people find out the whole purpose of what is happening everywhere. It is all the same and it continues to be the same, without the whole purpose of truth. That is what is going to be at the center of attention for always and eternity, unless there is something wrong.

It is all a trap and it won’t be easy getting out

of this place. Since no one is helping Sean, Carina, or the bus driver, they must think of somewhere else to go, or they must leave this place once and for all. It is something difficult but a decision must be made to determine the consequences of what will happen next or people might not die. It is always for a purpose and it must be known. And that is still the problem with eternity, so says the rest of the world but not hell on earth.

Meanwhile, the passengers are nowhere to be found, or they could be going to their convention of some sorts. It is just so crazy that this is happening as of this moment. Nothing is going to be off the table, and that is the current problem with the rest of this society in Calexico. Everything here is the problem because no one cares.

Sean, Carina, and the bus driver decide that since no one will help them, they should go to the nearest place to figure out what is happening, for some reason or another. That is the very stressful situation that is currently happening, because all three of them are at odds with what to do. There is just no escaping this wild and strange situation. It is all just a waste of time and a mystery that is growing stranger by the second. That is such a terrifying experience because of what is happening to the rest of society in the midst of a national crisis of unity. That is not the price to pay but it is to demonstrate what must get done in order to protect the rest of the world. It is a crazy situation for everyone. It is just not viable for the purpose of unity.

The group of three finally enters into a local business or what seems to be a local business. It looks as though it is a saloon because there are round tables everywhere with a bar near the end. There seems to be stools instead of chairs. It is such a dark and quiet environment but no one is even inside the building. Everything seems like a mystery but there is just peace and quiet everywhere. The entire place is likely abandoned, but there is no explanation why it is empty when people were walking down the streets of the city.

Then it hit them, the entire city of Calexico, California has been abandoned or all people have died or moved somewhere else. Carina, Sean, and the bus driver must think of a plan in order to see what they will do next. It must be a plan of courage and it must be good, or else something bad could happen in the near end. They must think of something now and it must be quick. It seems they will be here for a while or so, as they could be stuck here for the rest of their lives if they don't figure out something sooner or later. But then, Sean, Carina, and the bus driver also experienced a revelation that all of those people they saw were probably not even people. It dawned on them that those could actually be robots of some kind or another.

There is just no peace of mind because it is the sign of the times. People should know better and it is at that point in time when Sean, Carina, and the bus driver decide to drink up before they figure out what they will do. That is such something that will not be part of the situation because it has already been a part of the plan.

But, it is that peace of mind that must be careful, so that the plan is flawless as possible, in order to do nothing but wait. One hour has passed and Sean, Carina, and the bus driver finally have a plan that they can implement. It consists of going back to the now empty bus and taking it closer to the border and they will then get off when they arrive at a specific location. It is an excellent plan but it makes no sense at all. It is crazy but it just might work for all the wrong reasons. The plan will take a while to fully implement but it should work within a certain timeframe if done correctly.

There is no time to waste. Sean, Carina, and the bus driver must be quick but precise in all of their determinations and decisions. It is a must and there must be something put into place. There is just some sort of crazy reaction, and as they decide to do the best as they can, they shall face many obstacles when they finally meet their match. And then the rest of the world shall watch.

Besides the truth, there is nothing more, and then there is something else. It is precisely what must happen. It is now and it always must be now, or else there will be something sinister.

Chapter Six

Departing the saloon, the trio finally decides that they will implement the plan. It is such something crazy but they must act right now. That is why they are all leaving this saloon. It all relates to something sinister that is happening in the midst of a crisis. It will take many minutes but it is eventually necessary to make sure it must be in the works.

Sean, Carina, and the bus driver arrive back at the empty bus in just a matter of minutes. It was very quick that they arrived, but they all got back on in order to get closer to the border, just so they can find out what is happening. But how did they arrive in a quicker manner than they left? Well, they don't know for sure, but they are not surprised about what is even happening. It could all be a trap for some reason or another. Nothing should frighten any of them, but as it seems, they believe everything is fine, due to the fact that none of them sees any of those passengers still on the bus. It is safe to say the bus is all clear of any possible threat, without the evidence of there being any threat. That is how the music flows, or so people thought. There is just confusion on some of the part from Carina, because she doesn't know why those passengers got on the bus. There is another thing that is complexing about why those passengers never told the bus driver where they were going. It is such a crazy situation, but Carina should get over it soon right away or at least in a matter of minutes by the end of the day. That is certainly hopeful but it all remains to an all distant future of what will actually occur in the wake of the disappearance of passengers who had their own plan to begin with. That is some sort of craziness right there. And if no one even gains a full grasp of what just happened, well it can be the reason why most people never understood any or even the whole situation to begin with. That is never a good sign.

Sean and Carina take a seat next to each other while the bus driver sits in the driver seat in order to warm the bus for five minutes or so, just so there will be no problems with the engine. It is such a warm day in California, but that is normal, that Carina, the bus driver, and Sean have to make sure the air is on full blast so that nothing actually happens to the bus while the bus driver is driving it. Sure, that might seem very far-fetched, but it has happen before, since the sun's rays just eats the vehicles by melting the plastic, rubber, and metal, making it rather useless and unmovable. Not one of them wants that to ever happen and it still remains to be a mystery why that is ever a case to begin with. It would be a true disaster of the worst possible outcomes, and then everyone would be stranded in the middle of nowhere. So, it must be for certain that no one dies in the middle of this journey, or else everything will go haywire. Be it the case, everything is normal, in the sense that normal means nothing, or so that is how people are meaningless.

After about seven minutes, the bus driver puts the shift into drive, and the bus drives off into the city to see what is happening. But there is just uncertainty to the fullest extent, because they do not know what is going to happen, and they do not expect to find any evidence of the sort. It will all be something that the rest of society has to live with for eternity and for the rest of their deaths. There is just doom and gloom for the rest of society. Everything seems like a shithole, especially the desert, because there is nothing that can be done. There is nothing there, but it will take a while for the bus to get into town. It will just be a matter of time.

For some reason or another, this city does not

like to show itself to outsiders. It is just some weird shit that seeks to undermine the reason of no hope for the rest of society. That is the way people die, so they will just be stuck in the middle of a hot desert for the rest of their lives. It is worth noting that there is something there in the city of Calexico, California, but it just doesn't want to show itself immediately in some fashion. It must be a well-kept secret or it could be a mistake. Whatever is happening, something is not quite right. It is just so surprising that nothing is there when really everything is hiding. That is what is as perplexing about the situation as it continues to unfold.

Everything continues to be a nightmare and it seems no one is going to help. That will be the end of times, or so it seems. It is not a good day for society and it seems to be the exact opposite of what is not supposed to happen in a utopian society, but there is just nothing here in this barren wasteland. It is still all sand but no buildings. Everything is wrong with this place but it will only be a matter of time until there is a sense of reality that hits them. Nothing is really going to happen to them but they just want to know what is really happening. That story might never be told but it is worthy.

At last, Sean, Carina, and the bus driver are in town. It took them twice as long since last time to get into town. But they should have arrived faster due to having a vehicle. It is just crazy, but if that's how it is, then they should all brace themselves for any and all future or return trips to become substantially longer because of some crazy thing about this city that doesn't want outsiders to find about. That is the cause of evil. Or it could be something wrong with the rest of time, and it probably is that, but no one wants to know that, for fear of being erased from the existence of the world. That is something that indeed is scary.

After arriving into town, there is no one to be found. All of those people Sean, Carina, and the bus driver have seen some while ago have mysteriously vanished into thin air. But they see a sign and they want to go to that place. So, the bus driver reads the sign and follows the road straight down a narrow path of an unpaved dirt road. It seems that everything here has a reason. But, arriving at the dirt road, there is only one way to go. So, the bus driver takes the left turn, and it takes them nearer to the border, exactly where they wanted to go to in the first place. It is just so surprising but the bus is no longer on the dirt road, but is actually close to the US-Mexico border. It is a sigh of relief.

All is so familiar, as Sean, Carina, and the bus driver seem to have thought they have saw this place in a dream before. They don't recognize it as the same place that they walked to earlier in the day, but it does seem quite the same. There is just an empty city of no one to be found. It is vacant and has no sign of life. There are sidewalks and buildings, which is a good thing. And the best part about it is there is no sand and desert anywhere to be found. It is much cooler here closer to the US-Mexico border, and it is sure a quaint little place. But there is just no one to be found. It is something that is in the near of the other waste of society, but at least it is nice and quiet, not like something that has been seen before. It is not a shithole for sure but other people could care less if they visited. That is not something to take likely but at least it is better than where they were before. At least this place is quite better. There are no fake people here, not like that other place they visited in Calexico. But they are still in town, yet they are in a better location that seems to look and feel better due to the vibrant landscape.

There is something about this place, with its lush landscape, historic landmarks, and small town atmosphere. But there must be something else to do in this city of nothing but emptiness. Seeing that no one is here, Sean, Carina, and the bus driver decide to look around a while. And then they shall spend the night here until they figure out what they will do next in this deserted or abandoned town near the US-Mexico border. It will sure be a strange occurrence if something does happen but no one ever cares about that situation. It will only be at the expense of no one but ghosts. That is the day when everyone is out of town and tries to do nothing. But at the behest of the rest of the world, there is nothing to do but pray and hope for the best.

After a while of looking around the place in the bus, the bus driver parks somewhere and turns off the engine so that all three of them can get out and about and explore the town by foot. It is such a great experience for everyone to have, even though if the rest of society is unresponsive. The architecture is just amazing, with detailed abstracts and its old style Hispanic-Latino heritage. There is just an amazing sensation everywhere. It is especially helpful that no one is in town, but that is not the best part of it. The best part of this place is that Calexico has such an old style feeling to Sean, Carina, and the bus driver, and to them that is amazing for some reason or another. It is just the surroundings that make everything come to life.

Such architecture and its vibrant feeling all around the city are amazing and it feels welcoming to the whole community. Everything that anyone can see is just like it's supposed to be. Nothing is off of balance. Everything is fine in its own way. That is how everything is supposed to be. While walking, Carina can see the small city atmosphere, the close buildings, and the smell of mom-n-pop stores and shops in the background. Everything is close together that it is easy to walk to each street corner. No cars are needed unless if you live in the suburbs. It is such a great experience to feel with the close-knit markets, stores, and shops that the entire area can be explored in less than a day.

Street-by-street, Sean, Carina, and the bus driver experience something orgasmic that no one has ever experienced before. It is such an amazing and down to earth experience that none of them can even remember when they experienced something like this ever before. No one would want to ever leave this place but even if they wanted to, it would be a very tough situation. There will be heart break and then crying, but what's most apparent is that no one will have the feeling to ever have the guts to leave a small-town community where everything is so small and independent. Everything is family-oriented and that's the way it should be. Without it, the entire town would lose its appeal and no one would ever feel at home. The only people who would leave such a small family-oriented business community are those who dare to seek adventure and travel, but those who want to experience might be limited in nature.

The whole situation about the town might seem creepy but that is only because no people are here. It is for the same exact reason why no one should ever be trusted. It is for that reason why there must always be a pleasant but invigorating sensation of smelling fresh coffee and fresh fruits and veggies in the morning and every time people shop in an open market atmosphere. Of course, it would be better if more than three people were actually present, such as the entire city. But no one seems to know where the people are.

Everything is still amazing though. It can be described as a dream of organic sensations that can cause anyone to hallucinate. Everything is such an amazing experience that anyone can feel that it is actually happening in real time. Nothing is ever off limits because everything is a sensational feeling that thrives on adrenaline and imagination. It is just about life and society but it is about how the person feels in the ways ahead of time, to the extent of how the whole world is recognized. That is such an amazing feeling that Sean, Carina, and the bus driver can't get enough of because it is a very addictive feeling that seems to never go away. Nothing can stop that good but crazy sensation of knowing when everything has been set into motion.

Several hours have passed and Sean, Carina, and the bus driver are growing tired, so they must decide if they are going to the nearest hotel or sleep on the bus. They have to decide quickly before the sun goes down, or else they could get lost in the middle of a deserted community. There could be monsters out there and no one wants to see that to happen. It is just a part of life and dangerous things might happen in a nick of time. So, a decision must be made, and it must be made soon. That is the question to ask, as that is considered proper in the whole context of a deserted village and possibly a deserted world.

A decision had been made and Sean, Carina, and the bus driver have all decided to find the nearest hotel. It will take some time, but it is worth the wait, if there is a long wait. They all walk down the streets to see what they can find and so far see nothing but stores, shops, and open markets. There are fresh fruits and vegetables everywhere but no one is in sight of anything. Everything seems like where it has been since it was placed there. It seems everything is fine, even if the entire town has vanished into thin air. It is quite the situation but that probably is normal. No one knows why that is. Sean, Carina, and the bus driver continue to walk, and as they walk down all of the side streets and main roads, they can continue to smell the fresh ingredients of something tasty yet probably delicious. It is only a matter of time but there are no signs of life here, so it could be a false sign of hope or even a trap. That is certainly the point of order.

Sean, Carina, and the bus driver finally found

a place to stay in the nick of time, because the sun has almost set. It seems quite close to the border but it looks amazing. It is a big long white building with red tiles for a roof. It seems quite nice and looks as though it is quite expensive. The hotel seems to resemble architecture of the Spanish colonial revival style. There are big words on top of the building, saying 'Hotel De Anza.' The name sounds like it was built for luxury. It seems like a very fine hotel for anyone who is interested. And so, Sean, Carina, and the bus driver walk inside the hotel, hoping to find someone that will help them. But they find no one and just grab random keys and go find their rooms in which they will stay.

Sean and Carina decide to share a room while the bus driver decided he wanted his own room. It is just something for the good of the group, so that the proper paperwork can be filed by the bus driver if it is necessary. And by that, it should probably be about those passengers who decided to leave for some sort of reason for evil purposes. That is something that no one wants to ever encounter. Yet, for the rest of that time, no one should think of anything but the hotel and nothing else. It would just be a waste of time to think of something other than luxury and that is the new normal.

Sean and Carina arrive at their room, were they will probably share a bed and sleep together for some peculiar reason or another. Meanwhile, the bus driver arrived at his room. All three look around their rooms and find that it is fascinating and amazing but all too spectacular. There are bright curtains as well as very gorgeous balconies in both rooms. It seems like something from heaven and no one should ever leave. It is quite a spectacle that some people can be addicted to the vibrant atmosphere. That is the very reason why people might stay in such a luxurious building for so long.

The light can be seen penetrating the room with its deep toned colors meant for something that can be described as gorgeous. The curtains are long and are a great look and match for a very quaint but rather large room that is enough to be a presidential mini suite. The bedding was opulent with clean white sheets that looked like they have never been slept on. It was surely a spectacle and it will always be a part of a vibrant clean atmosphere. Everything about the bed is so extravagant, with its plush and soft pillows and its decorated ornamental bed frame. There are just no words that could better describe anything. It is entirely amazing that the room will take your breath away. There is just no comparison because this place seems to be the grandest of them all. Nothing should ever defeat luxury but in a vibrant atmosphere, there is just no competition.

Extravagant and lavish furniture filled the

room and gave it a first class atmosphere, along with detailed carvings of its heritage. There were no signs of electrical-functioning gadgets such as televisions, microwaves, or mini fridges in the room. It was such an opulent room and all of its class was reserved for the rich and famous. "No wonder the rich and famous like to visit here, it is such an amazing but grandiose asset for anyone to do business," said Carina. That too shall be an amazing feeling for anyone to ever see such a place that gorgeous.

Looking around such a vibrant but sensual room, Carina notices something that interests her in a very fascinating look. It is the bathroom door but she does not know where it leads. So, Carina walks to the door and opens it, and finds such another thing that she likes. She opens the door and notices everything is just so grand inside, just like the room itself. It is a very opulent and vibrant bathroom that tends to have a sensual feeling in many cases. There is a shower as well as a tub, with such an ornate pattern. The shower resembles something from Victorian England while the bath tub is free standing and looks as though it is from the same era. There are fine brass faucets everywhere from the shower, the bathtub, and the sink. It is such a pleasant experience that no one should want to ever leave this place. Everything about the room just looks so well maintained and seems as it is brand new out of the box. There is just luxury all around everything. Even the toilet looks grand as its purpose, with a wide shape, and a very ornate wooden cover and design. Everything about the bathroom was so magnificent, from its tiling to its ceiling. Even its window was grand, in the sense that it invited a breeze sometimes. The tiling seemed very clean and vibrant, with a typical small-shaped pattern that matches well with everything else so vibrant and opulent in the room.

Tiles were made from clean white porcelain and looked very shiny, as though they were brand new. The sink, bathtub, and shower were also made from clean white porcelain, also making them look so vibrant and accommodating. But hiding in a small corner, there was a dated yet grand bidet. It looked so inviting that no one would ever want to escape. The whole bathroom was grand and vibrant. It seemed fit for the rich and wealthy, but Carina could not just get enough of it. Everything seemed like a slice of heaven. It was just all so clean and shiny for Carina and she valued every part of it. That way, it would be a reason to enjoy.

After exploring the room, Carina decided to lie down in the plush bed. She took off her boots and her clothes and only kept on her beautiful yet very expensive laced lingerie. There, she lay down in the bed, and Sean soon joined her in nothing but his boxers. It seems like a new-kindled romance or it could just be the water from the sewer that is causing all this. But, they lie down in the plush bed and look up at the ceiling.

Her eyes were locked into his. It seemed like a new romance will begin. Carina inched closer to Sean and both started to passionate kiss each other in a sensual manner. Carina's cheeks, rosy and white, were plump and sensualized. All was happy. Sean started to kiss her cheeks with such passion and it felt wonderful. It was a delight to everything that was in the room. Such passion, with their bodies moving with each other, they are one and another. Each move they make is just better and better. It is such a patient game and it continues to be until there is an end of time.

They kiss passionately on the lips over and over again. It is a never-ending experience that can be described as increasingly sensual. And it is about to get better and better. There is just no ending to this situation. Sean slowly slides his hands down Carina's panties making Carina feel happy and glad, while she starts to slide her hand down into Sean's boxers. It is a match made for heaven, or hell, but hey, that doesn't really matter a whole lot. As Sean and Carina start to caress each other, they feel something that they have never experienced before, and it is a very happy yet pleasant feeling. It is something not to worry about and it is a time when there is a thing to understand better. It is something that needs to be in the place of time and always never in an awkward position of loyalty. That is entirely the question that needs to be asked.

Sean and Carina are just having fun with each other now and they continue to caress each other in just a sense of happiness and other happy feelings. It is a sense of pride, a sense of happiness, and a sense of being in the clear. And then they start to kiss each other passionately again, like they don't have a care in the world. Kissing passionately, Sean and Carina start to make love to each other were Carina seems to be in control. Carina can feel a pleasant sensation from the feeling and it feels so pleasurable that she does not want to stop. Her thighs are working as hard as they can, and there is a never-ending sensation of such a wonderful experience. Carina is enjoying every second of it, but Sean decides he wants the same thing as well. Sean uses his body to gain the upper hand, and he is in control now. Carina likes the experience much more, and she just can't get enough of it. She is enjoying every minute of it, and it feels as though it just plain happy and too pleasurable for anyone to experience.

Carina starts to reach a sensation between her legs and it feels just pleasant to her. It is something sort of like fun, but she is enjoying it. And then it hit her, she has reached her climax, as she feels as though she is experiencing something pleasurable but relieving. It is indeed very pleasurable and there is always a time for everything. Carina starts to feel the tingly sensation again, and this time Sean and Carina are starting to climax together. It reaches an ending point of no return and then both feel an increased sensation between their legs. And the rest is history, for the reason that them making love has come to an end, as they both were completely satisfied. It is just the beginning but time is only on their side. That is just a matter of opinion, but time is indeed getting shorter, so everyone must act quickly. But no one will know when.

Sean and Carina clean up and go to what they see is a very opulent yet grand bathroom. They start the water in the Victorian Era bathtub by turning the shiny brass nozzles. It will take a few minutes for the tub to fill up but Sean and Carina wait to feel the water so they can get in together. It is something that needs to happen. It is about how it all began. And then it too shall commence, by understanding how hot the water is.

It has been about two minutes and both feel the temperature of the water. It is a fine lukewarm feeling. The temperature is perfect for them to get in and so they do. It is such a pleasurable but sensual feeling that they are noticing yet it feels quite fine and dandy. Sean and Carina start to wash and clean each other off and everything seems just so nice. Everything is fine and it is just a normal experience for them to feel. Nothing is wrong with that and it is just life. As they are cleaning each other, Carina starts to feel a sensation, and it feels quite satisfying for all the right reasons. It is a tingling sensation but Carina just wants more. That is just part of the way to understand what is happening. But time is not a friend of anyone, so they rinse each other off so they can get back to what they will do tomorrow or the next day.

Carina gets out first followed by Sean. Both are dripping wet with leftover water. They grab some towels and dry themselves off and then they leave the towels in the bathroom and walk naked back to their bedroom. Not knowing if they brought any clothes with them, Sean and Carina start to open an ornate but mahogany wardrobe. To their surprise, Sean and Carina find fresh new clothes, such as fresh shirts, blouses, shorts, pants, suits, and dresses. It is such a large wardrobe that it has its own corner, but soon they want to see about if there are other additions that exist as well, such as dressers. And to their findings, they see dressers and start opening the drawers to see what they can find.

One dresser drawer has additional clothing

while another drawer has undergarments. It seems that each dresser has ten drawers or five on each side. On the left side of each dresser there are regular clothes such as shirts, pants, skirts, socks, and shorts. On the right side of each dresser are undergarments such as brassieres, panties, stockings, underwear, and other undergarments. It was just a symphony of joy because everything was just so beautiful. And that is the way it was always meant to be. That is the real moment of truth.

Seeing that it is getting late, Sean and Carina decide to call it a night and go to bed. They don't put on any pajamas because they don't have any, but that just makes it more fun. So, they close the curtains and dim the lights in their room. It is not quite that dark yet in the room but Sean and Carina lie in their bed while comforting each other like they were meant for each other. It is just a fantastical time but it is what is meant to be. That is just a normal situation that should happen but it is quite fine. So, there is this and now there is that.

As Sean and Carina continue to lie in bed, they start to fall asleep in each other's' arms. It seems very romantic but that is not why it is important. And as they fall asleep, the already dimmed lights decide to turn off like magic.

Chapter Seven

Waking up by each other's side with nothing on, Sean and Carina decide to start kissing each other passionately and begin to make love. After a while, they grow board and go to the bathroom in order to take a shower with each other. The day is just getting started. They get out of the shower and put some clothes on. Carina puts on a dark black lacy dress while Sean puts on a suit and tie. Meanwhile, the bus driver has been up for about two hours and is already dressed in some expensive-looking suit.

Sean and Carina are ready to go and they go to the dining room area to see if there is anything to eat, while the bus driver is busy reading some sort of old newspaper. Sean and Carina arrive at the dining area and they hear and see no one, so they go to the kitchen to see if any ingredients exist. To their liking, there are fresh ingredients in the refrigerators and the freezers, and even in the pantry.

Since it is morning, breakfast is probably the best meal for the choice, but it is only eight o'clock in the morning. And the decision is made to make an excellent morning dish that will satisfy anyone—eggs benedict with an extravagant yet delectable golden yellow hollandaise sauce, fresh imported Scottish cold-smoked salmon with Black Beluga Caviar on some crostini slices, prosciutto-wrapped melon, fine imported cheese with red and white wines, freshly squeezed orange juice, and dark black coffee. It is a meal fit for the elite.

But anyways, Carina starts getting out the pots and pans so that she can begin making the eggs benedict. Carina turns on the gas stove after putting water in a specialized eggs benedict pan. She then covers it, since the steam from the bottom of the pan will cook it perfectly. While the eggs benedict are cooking, she separates the egg yolks and discards the albumen in order to make the Hollandaise sauce. She mixes and slides the sauce pan from an off burner to an on burner many times to keep a good and healthy consistency. It takes about seven minutes and then

Carina gets some fresh sliced round ham and English muffins to sauté in a separate pan. That takes about two minutes, and Carina turns off the burner for the eggs benedict pan. Carina places the sautéed English muffins on fancy white plates and puts one slice of ham on each side, then places an egg on top on each slice of ham. Slowly, Carina places some hollandaise sauce on top of each egg to perfect the extravagant but exciting recipe.

While Carina was making the eggs benedict, Sean was making the crostini by toasting the sliced French baguettes on a pan in the gas oven, as well as making the prosciutto wrapped melon. The bus driver, for some reason or another, showed up and made freshly squeezed orange juice and brewed dark black coffee. When Carina was done, she cut some fine imported soft and hard cheeses and paired them with red and white wines. The crostini were done and Sean took them out of the oven and placed caviar and imported Scottish cold-smoked lox on top. It was already complete.

That is such a perfect meal for anyone who can't resist. Sean, Carina, and the bus driver dig in to enjoy the entire meal. A total of about six eggs, six pieces of ham, and six slices of English muffins were made. Everything was delicious yet succulent but also satisfying to their delectable palate. The cheese went well with each paired wine, while the saltiness of the caviar and lox matched well with the toasted crostini. To finish it off the freshly squeezed orange juice made it the day, while the dark black brewed coffee helped energized them in order to explore what has yet to come. They wanted to enjoy every part of the meal so they took their time. One hour later, they are finished with such a fine breakfast that no one can ever imagine. Each of them place their dishes in a dish washer and turns it on in order to clean any mess.

The time is now, so now they decide to leave and depart the hotel to see what is happening around town. But instead of taking the bus, they decide to walk all over town, just because it will be faster for some particular reason. It is indeed something very strange, but they leave the dining area and exit the hotel in a matter of minutes. They did not know what to expect but they had no idea what they were doing in the first place.

It would be something unfortunate, but Sean, Carina, and the bus driver where still inside the hotel, and that is something strange. But, soon they realized something was strange. They have been mistaken and where actually in the hotel lobby. So, they saw some type of revolving door and decided to leave the hotel, as they seek to explore what is happening.

Outside, everything seems to be fine at first,

but as they look up, Sean, Carina, and the bus driver can all see bright flashes of light from above. It looks as though they are shooting stars, but they lack the necessary qualities and other features. But what are they anyway? There is the presence of the sun but that does not seem to be the problem, and there are the rest of the other issues to deal with. It should be normal but it doesn't seem that way. Sean, Carina, and the bus driver feel like something is ominous or at least is going to happen today. But nothing is even known yet, so there should just be patience and a way to know everything. It feels like there is something to hide but then there is something else. Suddenly, a very cold breeze starts to take over everything, and it is followed by the sun disappearing and dark clouds forming. It seems like it is going to rain but then Carina feels it is odd, due to the fact that none of those clouds look like thunderstorm clouds. It could just be her but then there is the possibility it could be the air. Yet, it is not the air, and something is indeed going to happen or is happening right now, but it is still unknown to the rest of society. There seems to be an odd smell coming from the other side of the street that seems to be of rotten eggs but if anyone got closer it would disappear or would smell like some person smoking barbeque with hickory and mesquite woods.

That is certainly surprising, but as Sean,

Carina, and the bus driver are looking around, they can sense the smell of rotten eggs. But they don't even think something is wrong with that, because they think something has gone bad because the city is abandoned. Everything is abandoned and it does not just end there. There are dark-stormy clouds from above but there is not even the slightest drop of any rain, snow, sheet, or hail. Everything is just dark and there is nothing to hope for. The sky is just making everything worse, yet Sean, Carina, and the bus driver feel fine. There seems to be no end in sight as there is this ridiculous darkness that makes no sense whatsoever. That is something to worry about but it could be more common as bread. It is just how nature probably works, but nothing will be able to reverse the course of time, unless someone says that they know Mother Nature or are Mother Nature. That will be the day when everybody laughs off the funny man who thinks he knows everything. It will be the test of time.

While the dark clouds are standing still, there is now something new to worry about. It is a deep and very bright light in the south. It seems like there is another sun but it is not what it seems. There is just something ominous about this as well. It is still only the beginning and time will tell from there. That is the craziness of it all.

Nothing is happening yet but it is just too

early to understand such a situation. That is how it shall always work if people even want to know about the constant reminders. That is surely not the way to live but people do it every day. So, now there is the possibility of what to do and how it can be achieved in order to escape this reality. The weather hasn't even changed but Sean, Carina, and the bus driver are still looking around. They haven't left that spot they're standing in since they got out of the hotel. It is just a surprise but they are probably looking for a clue to determine what is happening. Something to think about is relevant but no one cares about that for the sole purpose of sanctuary.

Before long, the weather has changed in a very dramatic fashion. The clouds grow even darker and darker, turning to pitch black, but there is still a lack of precipitation, which seems very strange and perplexing. It is all about timing, as something else could be next. There are just a handful of answers that can be acknowledged. Something is going on and it needs to be found out. That is the only answer that remains suspicious. It will be about substance and not about the actual stuff that needs to be answered. That will be extremely bad for the rest of society because no one but for a few people will actually know what is happening. That is the day when the rest of the world will finally learn about what truly is going to happen in a matter of seconds, just before anything drastic and dangerous occurs. It will be for the best but people shall put their faith in government and its leaders. But then it will just be a matter of seconds when the people actually find out that everything will be subjected to a gag order. It shall be revealed that no one in the government will be telling the truth, and people will be rightfully angry yet not surprised at what has occurred.

The clouds continue to grow darker and darker, even though they are already pitch black to the extent that it is impossible for that color to exist in reality. Everything begins to turn more ominous, as it seems something evil and dangerous is about to approach the way of Sean, Carina, and the bus driver for some reason or another. It looks dangerous but Sean, Carina, and the bus driver are unfazed of what they see. It is not surprising but they are waiting for something else to happen. They could know what might actually happen next but it is to the extent that no one else does. It is almost impossible for this to even happen. Nothing seems correct as all seems a bit too strange. But there is something else that is now on the horizon. It is a new formation but does not even look threatening at all. But nothing can be seen from a mile away.

Suddenly, there is a change in weather again, but the clouds still remain dark pitch black. There is now a heavy wind that can be felt by Sean, Carina, and the bus driver. But they do not fall over, even if it continues to pick up speed. They remain standing still on the sidewalk looking around. They still haven't move from their spots in front of the hotel. But it is something that is strange. There is just something that seems very irrelevant but not even one soul cares about the problem, should one exist at all. That is not how a storm is supposed to feel like. Instead, it is a new storm that brings doom and despair to anyone in its path, but Sean, Carina, and the bus driver don't seem to get it. They must be immune to everything they see that is dangerous. That is extremely strange and interesting.

For the most part, Sean, Carina, and the bus driver all seem to be fine. They are unfazed and have nothing to worry about. There is no sign of any threat to Sean, Carina, or the bus driver. There are no signs of any tornadoes, twisters, cyclones, typhoons, funnel clouds, whirlwinds, hurricanes, monsoons, or anything else of the sorts. There is just pitch dark black clouds as well as a very heavy wind that continues to develop. That is just something that might be normal but is actually really strange yet scary, since there is no type of precipitation. It is just plainly strange weather.

Then, after fifteen minutes, there was some new type of weather that appeared. It was a cloud of dust, and Sean, Carina, and the bus driver realized what they saw and quickly raced across the street to another building to possibly seek shelter. They must have known something was going to happen and it would happen soon. It was a bit of craziness and a bit of sensationalized propaganda. That is something that is needed to see this weather. But they had to find and seek shelter across the street in another building because they did not want to get caught in this sort of dust storm. Yet, they could have gone back to their hotel rooms but chose not to do so. It was just the reaction from Sean, Carina, and the bus driver. The first thing they saw that offered protection they went there because it was what they saw the closest to them.

Sean, Carina, and the bus driver did not know what to expect, but they tried their best to seek some shelter. It took them a few minutes to find out how to enter the building but they soon realized they were opening the door the wrong way. They were pushing the door inwards instead of pulling it in an outward manner. It got awkward for a brief moment amongst them but it was just a normal situation where no one knew how to open the door. Besides, there could be a trap that could trigger anything if they opened it correctly the first time, and no one wants that to ever happen. It would just become more awkward if that should ever happen.

Besides, no one knows what is happening to

them in the first place, except for maybe Sean, Carina, and the bus driver. No one seems to lock their doors around here as it seems. That seems quite not so good and dangerous because the business owners could be robbed blind. But there is no presence of any person here, with the exception of Sean, Carina, and the bus driver. Yet, Sean, Carina, and the bus driver do not know the location of those passengers, since they disappeared on their own. There is only a sense of safety but that is something different to the case of many people disappearing. The whole town practically disappeared from life on earth or they could be hiding somewhere. But anyway, there is just a sense of pride.

Sean, Carina, and the bus driver finally enter the building after standing outside and looking to see what's inside. They believe it is safe and they enter what seems to be a dark and dreary place with no signs of life. It is quite dark for the inside of any type of building in the daylight, but that could be due to the dark pitch black clouds outside. There seems to be nothing else but a heavy wind and the dust storm besides the dark pitch dark clouds, but Sean, Carina, and the bus driver are finally inside of a safe and very secure building. The door shuts behind them, and to make sure it doesn't open, they try to look for some type of heavy object to keep it secure. But Carina sees something that might be better. It is a high security door locking system consisting of four levels of locking devices. There is the main deadbolt lock, and then there is the sliding security lock, followed by the security padlock attached to another sliding security door lock, and lastly an electronic digital number lock to lock the bottom and upper portions of the door.

Carina locks the deadbolt first and then she locks the upper sliding security lock, and then the lower sliding security lock with the attached padlock device. Carina wants to lock the upper and lower portions of the door so the door does not get blown away or damaged, but she has no clue of what the correct code is. She looks around the wall to see if there is anything that will help her, so she decides just to push a bunch of random numbers. To Carina's surprise, the random numbers she pushed were actually correct. The upper portion of the door locks first, which is then followed by the lower portions of the door in just a matter of seconds. Since all of the automated locks lock vertically, it should work, but something could still go wrong. But, Carina thinks that the door is secure enough and so do Sean and the bus driver. Looking up, Sean, Carina, and the bus driver see some other object or thing that could help secure the door better. It looks like some sort of metal rolling door that tries to prevent the door from going into the rest of the building by blocking the impact from any outside damage. Sean saw a chain that could possibly lower down the metal rolling door, and so did Carina and the bus driver. It seems it was meant for that door, but there could be a problem if it could be for something else.

And then, Carina looked right next to the chain and saw a control panel, but then she looked to the opposite side of the chain and saw another sort of control panel. It seemed liked the control panels were both locked but they weren't, since they did not have a lock at all. The control panels were only closed since the doors were not opened. It should be easy for Carina, Sean, or the bus driver to open it, but then there is the situation of which control panel controls what. Nothing seems to be labeled on the exterior of the control panels' door. Any instructions could be located on the interior of the door. There is just some sort of strange happening. But it does at least solve one problem—hiding to get away from a rapid and growing dust storm.

Carina opens the panel on the left while Sean opens the panel to the right. They are actually very simplistic in nature. One of the panels has a label of 'outside' while the other panel has a label of 'inside.' It seems the left panel is for the outside while the right panel is for the inside. But there is still only one chain that can be pulled, but it looks as though it is a double chain that controls everything. However, after examining the chain further it is actually two chains, but it only seemed like one because both of them where close to each other. But, that could be less than appealing, so Carina, Sean, and the bus driver continue to all look at the two control panels. Each one has two buttons and a switch. The switch is dark black while the two buttons are red and green. Sean, Carina, and the bus driver believe the green button must be used to open it while the red button is the one to close the doors. The black switch confuses them at first but it is then reveled to be labeled as the main power switch for the motors after wiping away some dust.

The wiping away of the dust from each panel also reveals that they were indeed right about the red and green buttons. But right now it seems that the main power switches are switched to the off position, so even if a button is press, then nothing would be able to work. But then, Carina, Sean, and the bus driver see another control panel, yet it only has a small light indicator of three separate lighting diodes, a place to insert a key, and three metal toggle switches. Nothing is legible but then Carina wipes away dust and sees that it is labeled as a control panel for security bars.

They can all see that the conditions outside are worsening and not getting any better, but they cannot seem to find the key until they feel some metal object on their floor thanks to a scratching noise that can be heard. They found the key and Sean picks it up and inserts it to the control panel that says security bars. Sean turns it to the right and can hear some type of noise that sounds like mechanical parts turning. One-by-one, the indicator lights start to turn green, and since it seems they are off, Sean turns them in the on position by pushing the three toggle switches in an upward position. All of indicator lights start to turn orange, but something is wrong, since there are no signs of security bars. So, Sean looks for a button but finds none. Instead, Sean turns the key again after seeing if it will turn any further and it does, and now high-grade titanium security bars rise down from above on the exterior portion of the door, but not on the interior.

There is a locking noise and it is from the security bars, and after a second the indicator lights all turn red. But seeing that the dust storm is nearing the building and hearing the wind picking up speed, Carina and Sean both power on the black main power control switches in the upward position so that the rolling doors or whatever they are can be closed to prevent any damage. Some more noise can be heard and that is the sound of the motors. First is the exterior of the building and Sean pushes the red button. Something is rolling down and it takes a few short seconds. It makes it a little darker but it seems like automated shutters. Then, Carina pushes the red button for the interior portion of the building, and something decides to roll down in front of them. It is good that they are not too close or else something bad might have happened. The door locks in front of them, and then the motors turn off. Now there is just complete darkness, so they need to find a light switch or something.

Still looking at the control panels, they see some dust so they wipe it off. After clearing off all the dust there is something that reads, 'automated disaster shutter control system.' It seems as though Sean, Carina, and the bus driver were lucky enough to find this building because even the hotel isn't that secure like this. At last, someone is able to find what resembles a light switch. The bus driver flips it on in the upward position and now there is a better sense of what can be seen inside.

Chapter Eight

Wind can be heard howling, as the storm continues to intensify. The shutters are fine and nothing can be heard, so the wind must not be blowing that way. It must be blowing in a different direction because the shutters are not making any noises. There are no signs of any movement. Nothing is shaking and everything feels fine. The building is not even moving. All that can be heard is the wind and a dust storm. There could be rain but no one can hear it, since it might not be loud enough to hear.

Swirls of wind continue but nothing bad is happening to the building. It looks quite small from the outside when Sean, Carina, and the bus driver saw it, but once they turned on the lights it was quite large. Nothing seems to be happening right of now but no one will ever know. The heavy wind could easily destroy such a building this small while the dust from the dust storm will be able to scrape any glass and structures made from brick or concrete. It is surely a disaster waiting to happen. But that will just have to wait.

Heavy wind can be still heard howling but it has no impact on the building. It will be a very long time, so they must all be prepared to wait out the storm or whatever it is. Loud noises can be heard from inside the small building but it is not from the building itself. Instead, it is a vibration from the rest of the buildings nearby and deflects the sound onto this much smaller building where Sean, Carina, and the bus driver are currently inside of. It sounds like it is very close but that is the wind playing dirty tricks on the mind. It won't work but it certainly has fooled many other people who faced the same exact scenario before. This type of storm has in fact happened before but no one even knows why. It all remains a mystery. There is nothing that can be done but it is just part of nature so Sean, Carina, and the bus driver will just get used to it.

Before long, there will be some other problem that shall cause catastrophe, but that might already be happening, yet no one can be certain of when it will be, not even Sean, Carina, or the bus driver. They might not make it out alive but no one is supposed to be outside in the first place, and if they are then they must be crazy or really stupid. The intricate layers of the building could soon be gone and no one might be alive to live to tell the truth of what really happened. This will just be another day written in history books that led to a giant panic attack, if there are even any survivors left. Otherwise, no one will know what ever happened because civilization will be extinct for the rest of eternity.

Then, out of nowhere, something extremely unpleasant occurred. There was something that made a loud crash sound. It sounded as if something had actually crashed or fallen nearby. Sean, Carina, and the bus driver did not know how to react. They did not know what to do. But they remained calm and knew they had to wait out the storm or whatever it was that was happening outside. They are not afraid so that's a plus. There is just something that needs to be said but no one knows what. There is a sudden sound of thunder that is deep and ominous. Maybe that is what it is. The building is starting to shake but no one is moving. The trio just stays still, as if they never felt a thing. Not even one of them feels any type of sudden movement. It is like only the building is taking the damage from the outside. Nothing can be felt inside, which would explain the reason why Sean, Carina, and the bus driver have yet to feel any signs of sudden movement. That is highly strange and unusual, but it does occasionally happen, so there is that possibility.

Suddenly, there is a drastic change in the safety of the building. The lights start to flicker and flicker. It seems like the lights are burning out or something else is happening. Lights continue to just flicker and flicker. It is just nonstop and nothing can seem to stop it. All of them are just standing there and can't think to do anything but wonder what will happen next. And then there is the possibility of total darkness, a sign that could mean something bad has happened. But it's just too unsafe to go outside, so there must be another way out. There seems to be a pattern to this flickering madness. One side starts to flicker while the other side remains normal. And then when the other side starts to flicker the first side starts to flicker. It is a constant pattern of madness and it just continues to take place. That is the whole point of nothing.

There is no despair. There is no worrying. There is nothing that will make the world safer. It is just something that no one can speak about. That is the real mystery about what is happening. It is for that reason why Sean, Carina, and the bus driver must decide on how to get out of this place in some other way. There is a way out but it has yet to appear. It shall appear when the time is right. The time is not right. But the lights are still flickering on and off for too many times. The lights continue to flicker and flicker without any notice or meaning. There is just no reason for any of this. It is just a sign that there is some bad event might happen, besides the dust storm and the heavy wind. But those two weather outcomes don't explain why something bad will happen. It just explains something has led to another. It is always about one causing another. That is how it always has been.

The clouds turned darker and darker, which eventually turned the color to dark pitch black.

Then a heavy wind developed as part of the clouds turning into dark pitch dark.

And now, there is a dust storm, which was probably caused by the heavy wind.

All of these things have one thing in common.

They were caused by each other.

They are all connected in some form or manner.

It would be strange if they weren't

It would be impossible for some other event to cause them.

Everything else seems improbable and it does not explain why.

There is no other way to explain these crazy weather events, as nothing even makes sense about them to begin with.

It is a pattern of the climate having a change of heart and decency.

It is a pattern of change in science.

It is a pattern of how people view climate and science.

It is a sign that greenhouse gases are losing the war.

It is a sign that the climate has never changed to begin with.

Nothing even makes sense anymore.

It is just only an illusion.

Everything is an illusion as nothing makes sense to the rest of the world.

There is just a sense of nothingness to the rest of society.

Forget about everything that was ever said because it does apply to the current situation in which Sean, Carina, and the bus driver are currently facing in the midst of a crisis. They all seem to be doomed one way or another but that is why they are not all doomed. It is meant as a trap not to move and to find a way out. That is what the storm expects. That is what the wind expects. That is what the cloud expects. And that is what all weather expects so that it can scare anyone in its path. Nothing seemed so sinister before. But no one expects anyone to ever escape the path of this current storm or whatever it seems to be.

This is not a normal storm if it is one. Sean, Carina, and the bus driver did not expect to go back inside. They wanted to explore the context of this unknown convention in regards to the passengers who wanted to go to it near the US-Mexico border. It is a sense of craziness because there is no sense when it's going to end. That is why they must think of a plan as soon as possible.

Everything must come to an end though, but it is not time for that. No one is going to die and it should stay that way. But there are consequences for anything positive that continues to gain strength. It is just part of the problem.

The heavy wind picked up the dust and created a storm of dust. That is what probably did occur but everything is caused by each other. It is part of something else sinister. Nothing shall be at the forefront if this storm succeeds. Or it could have already succeeded but in another form or manner by just taking place.

Ten minutes after the lights started to flicker and flicker in a pattern of madness, nothing new has happened to Sean, Carina, or the bus driver. The lights are still flickering but now they are flickering all at once. There is no pattern of madness anymore, just a sign that the lights decide to flicker in unison instead of flickering at different times. It is not that much of a significant event. It was expected to happen and it means darkness could begin as soon as a matter of seconds or minutes. It could be a matter of hours as well but that won't be accurate, since the storm is affecting the electricity. It is not a surprise for this to happen. It is always about science and it is always about a natural change. There is nothing but the truth to exist.

Chapter Nine

Lightning has struck the building. It will only be a matter of time until the lights go dark. One minute later there is complete and sudden darkness everywhere. Chaos might ensue if anyone is outside and it will cause something sinister. There will be riots and then there will be disaster. Sean, Carina, and the bus driver are all safe in the building. But seeing as the building they are in has just lost electricity, it will only be a matter of time until the food starts to rot, the water starts to grow bacteria, and everything else starts to grow mold. Water could try and get in but that could possibly be the least damaging thing that could happen, as it might only be small leaks from the ceiling or from the walls.

But seeing as this building is still secure there is no indication of how a leak will get pass anywhere in the building. There should be back up power at least or not having back up power was always part of the plan. It could have been always part of the plan because maybe there is a secret passageway that Sean, Carina, and the bus driver can access to either escape or hide and seek shelter. That is quite the surprise if a secret passageway is ever found. It should be able to lead to the success of the rest of society.

Five minutes have passed since complete darkness has occurred. Sean, Carina, and the bus driver are still in the same place they have been since they secured the building or at least the door in which they entered. The building is still safe but it is just too dark because there are no windows or glass doors that they can see out of. All might look and feel safe but there is always a way for any building to be flooded. It could be from above or from below. There is just a sense of hopefulness, as there is no air and no power. It is a sign of bad events continuing the destruction and violence of everything else. That will be the day when everything turns to chaos. No one will know what to do and then people will start to kill each other by simply running them over. That is called the wrath of death because no one will know when they get trampled on by such a stampede of people. That will be the day of a revelation.

As seconds go by, there is a sense of hope for Sean, Carina, and the bus driver that the lights will turn on again. But that probably won't happen until everything is fixed.

Then, from out of nowhere, there is some sort of light that attracts the attention of Sean, Carina, and the bus driver. It is a bright white light that looks kind of yellowish from a distance, but is white when anyone gets closer. They see the bright white light in front of them to see where it will take them. It could lead them to a secret passageway or to some other place unknown.

A door suddenly appears but there is not even a handle or knob on it. Carina feels the door and it feels warm. The bus driver feels the door and he too feels it is warm. Sean feels the door last and he has the same reaction—it is warm. Since there is no sign of a handle or knob on the door, Sean, Carina, and the bus driver push it forwardly, and it opens for all of them to see. They see some sort of passage but don't know how long or far it goes. It could lead to the bottom of the world. It could lead to another universe or world. It could lead to nowhere. But they don't know where it will take them. They must find out and it must be sooner rather than later. That is the price that must be paid.

It is just a common and well-known reaction anyone will make. That is simply the truth and how people live. Everything should be like that.

So, Sean, Carina, and the bus driver all decide to take a vote on what to do. It is unanimous and they all agree to see where it will lead them. They want to know because it could lead them to a better place or at least to safety. There is a sense of craziness and restlessness. It is something that people always have to deal with, as a rush of adrenaline is paramount to know what will happen to them in the near future or at least on the same day. That is why it must be of the utmost importance.

By that sense of a plan, Sean, Carina, and the bus driver see torches on the walls already lit with a very visible and tall orange-red flame. It seems the passageway is very long, as Sean, Carina, and the bus driver all look down the path of stairs. There is just no knowing how deep it goes below ground. It could be feet or miles. That is something that needs to be known. At least all of them have access to bright orange-red lit torches that will help fend off the darkness. That is better than not having light at all because it will lead to a brighter future. It shall lead to something new for them to explore. It shall lead to the world being unknown unless there is some other price for the reaction. For that reason, it is a must that must be continued. Unless otherwise, they too shall perish in a building, so that is why it must be for certain that Sean, Carina, and the bus driver go see where it will lead them. That is just to know the truth and it is fruitful.

It is time. Sean, Carina, and the bus driver all decide to take a decision of hope. They decide to each take a lighted torch and go see where it will take them. One-by-one, Sean, Carina, and the bus driver all enter into the secret passageway, each making sure to grab a lighted torch. Carina is first, followed by Sean, and last is the bus driver. As the bus driver enters into the secret passageway, the door closes behind him. There is no way out now. They all look back and see no door. It has disappeared, and that is too surprising.

Now it is their time to find out what is going to happen. Something must have happened because the door just disappeared. It is without a doubt one of the strangest yet predictable things that has happened so far because all of the other events. What could be possibly down there? It will surely be a surprise that is waiting to happen. It is what matters the most and it shall be kind of crazy if it doesn't happen. That is why it is weird.

Not knowing what would happen Carina led Sean and the bus driver down a path of stairs to the deepest parts of the world. Bright-lit torches were just about everywhere on the walls of the passageway and it was sort of dark and creepy. It was just like a train tunnel that led to the next destination. It seemed like it was just a regular old tunnel where darkness always thrived. That is a tunnel for you, but this tunnel looks and sounds different. It does not look like a normal tunnel. It looks as though it is ancient with its long but narrow paths and its dark and deep ambience that surrounds everything in its path. That is just the price that must be paid. As Carina continues with Sean and the bus driver down the secret passageway, there is no knowing of where it will take them. They are just going deeper and deeper underground. It is a passage that might not lead to any place worth living. It is just so dark and nothing is well-lit even though there are bright-lit torches on the walls. But those bright-lit torches do not cover every area of the passageway. It only covers once every quarter mile or so and there will be at times very dark places that Carina, Sean, and the bus driver will find. They don't know what to expect but they are still going strong. The passage seems endless and endless like it will always lead anyone to an infinite destination determined by the tunnel itself.

It has been an hour since Sean, Carina, and the bus driver entered the secret passageway but it feels like forever. The torches are still brightly lit with no appearance of change or temperature. It is just that not one of them even knows where it will lead them. That surely sounds like a crisis because people might become scared. And if they don't, then there will be an awakening, for the truth shall be told to the rest of society.

Carina spots something ahead, and she thinks it is a way out. But Sean and the bus driver don't see anything, as Carina is blocking the way or she is just seeing stuff. Yet, there is nothing that can be known to all. Everything is seen as a way out, but it might just be an illusion. The trio does not know where this secret passageway goes. It is possible that it goes deep down into the Earth's mantle, but not one of them is close enough to know. It is just too early to tell.

Then, it looks as something is about to change for the better. Carina stops for a moment, as she sees a change in directions of the path. Instead of going straight down, the stairs level off to form a straight path. There seems to be no more flights of stairs after walking downwards for over five hours without any rest at all. None of them feel tired even though they have fatigue.

Meanwhile, after Carina stopped, so did Sean and the bus driver. It seems that there is only one more flight of stairs separating them from the leveled path and it shouldn't take that long. So, with that being said, they all must decide who will go first down the last flight of stairs. It won't be hard but it won't be easy as well, since the anticipation is just too exciting to escape. If Carina decides to go second or last, she will move aside to either the far left or to the far right, but the flights of stairs are wide enough that they can handle at least fifteen people standing from end to end all the way from the left to the right sides. But, it is still a wise choice to move aside in order to avoid the trap of getting pushed and shoved by two other people.

There must be a choice.

A decision needs to be made.

Before any harm occurs, it is wise to know who will lead who.

That should leave people rest assured that they are safe and have nothing to fear.

It would otherwise by the opposite for the wrong and right reasons. That is just the stranglehold of life that prevents change.

It has been revealed.

A decision has been made.

The bus driver decided to go first, followed by Sean, and lastly by Carina. It was Carina's idea to volunteer to go last because she wanted to make sure she was safe, since the bus driver seems to be wiser about everything, especially about those two different groups of passengers. Carina and Sean step aside to the left and right respectively in order to let the bus driver go first. No one knows if he will make it and no one will know who the last one out will be. It is surely an excitement of adrenaline. That is just the basis of everything.

Step-by-step, the bus driver goes down each step for the last time in this never-ending madness of infinite flights of stairs. He counts it but he is precise and slow, just so no mistake is made. There could be a trap door, especially in a place dark like this. No one can ever make a mistake in situations like these, so it is always wise to be careful. The bus driver is finally on the leveled-off path and he tells Sean and Carina that there are only fifty stairs to descend, but that can be quite far.

Sean is next, but he is quicker than the bus driver. It only takes Sean half the time of the bus driver to descend the stairs. It is now Carina's turn and she takes her time, but she is quicker than the bus driver yet slower than Sean. They are all united and are ready to follow the new path. With no stairs in sight to descend, the bus driver leads the pact to see where the path ends.

Ten minutes have passed and the trio has been making progress. It seems to be brighter down here in this path but that could mean they are nearing the end. Sean looks up and sees lights embedded within the ceiling but they are quite yellow and look as though they need to be changed. But that means they could be nearing a mine or something. It seems to be getting stranger and stranger. Soon there could be a fork in the road, making the decision much harder to choose. It will just cause confusion. Certainly that is not wise but it is part of it.

There just seems to be a pattern to this entire underground path. Everything looks exactly the same as before. The walls remain dark and there is nothing but embedded lights in the ceiling with an occasional torch every quarter mile or so. But that is all the light there is. Even with an occasional torch doesn't really improve anything. It is probably meant that way because of the design. Maybe it was meant for people to camp out? But it could be for the homeless. No one actually knows what this secret passageway is meant for. It could also be a mining camp and that is highly likely, but there are no visible signs of any markings on the wall. It is all blank and quite dark somewhere underground. That is not how people should die, especially if they are trying to see what is happening.

Two hours have passed since Sean, Carina, and the bus driver have been walking this new and straight path. The bus driver is leading and is not slowing down one bit of an inch. He does not seem any tired than last time or whatever last time was in this circumstance. But, there should be at least some form of fatigue. It just doesn't make sense. It seems abnormal if you ask anyone else. Time is surely on the side of no one and in this case there is nothing but patience.

There should be a way out of this dark and creepy passageway, but Sean, Carina, and the bus driver can't seem to find one. There is no sign of an exit and there is no sign of an entrance. The door just magically decided to close by itself and then to also disappear after the bus driver entered into the secret passageway. It seems like that door had a mind of its own but no one really cares about that. That is just part of the problem here. It sure is taking a while for the most part. But that is about right because they do not even know the depth of their descent to begin with. There are no markings indicating how far they have gone on the walls. There is nothing but what looks like solid brick made from mud, water, and sand because of its deep brown color. There is just nothing down there. It is just all too familiar to begin with and it is just strange.

Sooner or later something will happen and they will know where they are. It should only take a matter of time. Of course, there could also be some sort of ambush.

Carina decides to touch the surface of the wall to see if she can use that indication to find out the exact location. But she is certainly surprised at what she felt. "Ouch, that almost burned my hand,"

Carina said. “The surface of the tunnel felt hot or warm,” asked the bus driver? “It felt hot, like something was burning beneath us,” said Carina. “Like how hot,” asked the bus driver? “When you accidentally touch the surface of a hot pan by mistake because you don’t think for some reason,” said Carina. “Oh, that is hot but not that hot, because the way you screamed it seemed to be a higher temperature,” said the bus driver.

Sean decided to take a turn at the surface of the wall and his reaction was different. “Come here, I believe this part of the wall is cold,” said Sean. So, Carina and the bus driver went down to Sean and decided to feel the temperature of the wall. Carina and the bus driver put their hands on the wall at the same time and they both had the same reaction as Sean did. “It’s cold, but not that cold like when your hand sticks to the surface,” said Carina. “To me, I feel it’s cold to the touch, but there seems to be some other issue but just can’t put my hand on it,” said the bus driver. “We should be get going before we all get off track,” said the bus driver.

Sean, Carina, and the bus driver left to get back on course. And then there was something that seemed different. It was a sound that did not exist before. It sounded like they were getting closer or it was getting closer to them. There is just no other explanation that could be had. It would be a matter of life or death but death would probably win. There was just something about it that didn't make sense at all. To them it sounded like a roaring wave ready to attack people. It could have been that but then there is something else.

"Wait, stop, I hear something," said the bus driver. "What does it sound like," asked Carina? "It sounds like some tidal wave or the ocean is above us or something," said the bus driver. "Well, that makes sense because we descended too many stairs, but then it doesn't make sense for other reasons because I felt something too hot," said Carina. "We must be below the surface of the ocean or somewhat because it sounds like we are near a shipping channel or in the midst of a storm," said Sean. They all continued to move forward but stopped a minute later after a loud bang.

"What's that, it sounded like something hit this tunnel," asked Carina. "Guys, turn to the left, it seems like something is covered up or something," said Sean. Carina decided to volunteer and go to the left side of the wall. "It seems like there is dirt here or something because I can feel some type of grainy but abrasive element," said Carina. "Your hands are dark black," said Sean. "It seems you have touched black sand or at least something similar to it in nature," said the bus driver. "Look, there is something on the wall here," said Carina. "This might tell us where we are," said Sean. The sign reads, "*You have reached 10,000 feet below the surface of Mexico. You can turn back now but once you go forward you won't have that opportunity again. Good luck, should you wish to continue!*" Sean, Carina, and the bus driver read it and decided to just move forward. They ignored the warning from the sign, as they wish to find out where they are.

It has been five hours since they last saw that sign and they just continue to move forward, not knowing where they will end up.

Chapter Ten

Gases filled the secret passageway slowly in a matter of minutes after Sean, Carina, and the bus driver read the ominous warning or threat. They started to smell something and thought it smelled strange. It wasn't noticeable at first, but they started smelling what seemed like a mixture of Nitric Oxide, Tear Gas, Chlorine Gas, Mustard Gas, and Sarin Gas. It would be certainly dangerous but a decision must be made soon. A brief short few seconds after smelling the gas, Sean, Carina, and the bus driver all knew that they had to escape. It would be an escape like no other.

They must manage to get out quickly or resort to some other plan, or else they could collapse or even worse, die while escaping. It was a rush against time to determine what to do but any second more would lead to a possible tragic event. The time is now and there is just a rush of adrenaline. It is about time to make a decision before anything else happens that could start. No one wants that to happen, and in a time of panic there might be mistakes, which could lead to a disaster upon disaster. Anything worse would be catastrophic. It was a changing situation of the utmost importance.

A decision was reached in a matter of seconds and it was expected to be daring but dangerous. It would involve Sean, Carina, and the bus driver going as fast as they can while carrying torches. It was the only plan that could work and it was brave yet idiotic in nature. That would be a plan never to follow but if they wanted to get out alive they would have to follow it or risk dying of gas inhalation. There is just no other way to resolve it.

They were running as fast as they can in order to escape possible death. It was just a rush of a reflex and adrenaline in order to survive. It felt like they were getting nowhere because they were seeing the same stuff over and over again. Everything looked exactly the same and it was looking to be a waste of time. Could it be that Sean, Carina, and the bus driver would all die today in an underground passageway or tunnel? No one will know if they survive or die, because there is a lack of people. Everyone else has seemed to have vanished into thin air. There is not even a shred of evidence to indicate the location of the rest of society. Some mysterious people do appear but that is just a rare occurrence. It seemed like there are not many people left in the world after all. It seems that Sean, Carina, the bus driver, and those missing passengers might be the only remaining people on the surface of the planet of Earth. No one even knows if anyone is real. It will just resolve itself in a matter of days or years end.

As Sean, Carina, and the bus driver run as quickly as possible, they are getting tired but they just can't stop. They must continue or die. It is a must for survival of the fittest. If they just give up no one will win and the rest of society will not be better off. It will just be a matter of time. That is just the truth and it is about progress. But progress isn't getting anywhere. It will just be the whole truth and nothing but the truth.

Suddenly, Carina almost trips over something on the path, but her right hand accidentally rises up to the wall and pushes a brick. Carina sees what she has done or what has happened and so do Sean and the bus driver. A new secret passage has opened up and it was by accident. But, it could be a gift from above as well, since they got away from something deadly. It was indeed a gift from above yet Sean, Carina, and the bus driver all enter the new secret passageway in order to not die.

It takes a few seconds to think but they run for it. The bus driver is the last to enter the new secret passageway and after him the secret door disappears like it never existed. They don't look back but they continue to move forward one step at a time. It is just a new beginning. After a few minutes of just walking on the new path they come across a set of three different paths that could be taken. It all leads to the same place eventually but they don't know that until they take a route. But each of these paths could have something sinister waiting for anyone who chooses to take them. There could be traps and there could be dead ends. And then there could be several alternate paths within of the main path that was taken in the beginning.

A decision must be made again and this time it will be who will take each path. There are three: one in the middle, one to the left, and one to the right. It is all a race against time. Sean decided to take the left tunnel and the bus driver decided to take the right tunnel while Carina decided to take the middle tunnel. They each go their separate ways to see what is waiting for them. It could be the last time that they see each other. But knowing what the tunnels have in store for them, well it will be a very interesting day to see what actually happens.

As they enter they don't know what to expect. It could all be a trap or it could be something more sinister that never has been heard about. There is just the state of a crisis to begin with and it too shall be in the midst of something else. That is no reason to get into those sorts of situation. It would all be a mistake for anyone to help each other in a tunnel, as there is just no escape.

As Sean and the bus driver enter their own respective tunnels, it seems like there is chaos and havoc. There are loud yelps and screams coming from their tunnels. Carina, on the other hand, is still safe, and no screaming or yelps is coming from her tunnel. Carina is still walking but never even heard the yelps and screams coming from the other tunnels, so she just continued on walking her way to see what was out there inside to escape.

But why did Sean and the bus driver scream? It could be due to the fact that they were attacked by someone or something. It could be that they were up to something sinister in order to fool Carina, but if that was the case she didn't hear anything. Or, it could be that Sean and the bus driver actually fell down trap doors for some sinister purpose due to prior events. There is just no knowing what actually happened to Sean and the bus driver. Or is there? But there is just something sinister about everything. It is nothing about that but it is at the helm of the whole damn controversy. And Carina doesn't even seem to know what happened. Meanwhile, it has been one hour since the disappearance of Sean and the bus driver, and Carina is still walking through her tunnel. It seems nothing bad had happened to her or she is just too smart by knowing where all of the traps are set that she knows when to avoid them. That is just about the craziest and most logical things that could have occurred.

It seems that there is no end in sight for the tunnel to show light. There is just darkness with a slight sign of occasional light by embedded lights within the stone bedrock of this wall surrounding and protecting anyone who enters its domain. All Carina is able to see is the same thing over and over again—a bunch of brown bedrock. She can't seem to hear any noises in this place and it seems everything is just too quiet. There seems to be no signs of life and no signs of anything else. It makes it out to be a very creepy experience for anyone who can be easily frightened by just one out of line movement. It is just the type of thing that should be avoided if possible, but there is illogical to say the least. Sooner or later, Carina will find out something. But that is not even worth the expense.

However, Sean and the bus driver do need all the help they can get. But, they are safer than it was ever realized. Both of them where walking and made a mistake of not paying attention. At the same time, they walked over a false piece of bedrock that also activated a trap door. After accidentally triggering this false piece of bedrock in both of their tunnels, they fell down a trap door within a minute after stepping on the presumed switch. They did not know it at first but their lives would be spared, due to the reason that this is just a place of living and not death. There is nothing but hope. But, after a minute, the trap door suddenly appeared, even though it was not there before. It was kind of crazy at first but they did not know what to expect.

Sean and the bus driver thought it was the end of their lives but they never thought that. They fell down the trap door but then slid down what seemed to be a ramp slide. They are safe at the bottom of what seems to be a basement but that is not what is actually important. What's important is that they are safe but have to find a way to get out of this new found place.

Likewise, Carina sees some light at the end of the tunnel. After a few hours of moving forward in this new tunnel, Carina is able to see a future outside of this tunnel. It is getting brighter by the second and Carina wants to know where it will lead her. It is at a time of adrenaline that means luck does exist, but it is worth it. Carina is getting closer and closer but she doesn't know if it is a mirage or real. It is just a rush against time. This is just the kind of madness that will get everyone killed. It isn't worth it in any other mad and ominous situation but there is hope for the rest of society that they will understand everything, yet they seem to be missing at the minute. It is about time that the truth gets told.

On the other hand, Carina is now closer to the end of the tunnel, as she can see the light at the end of the secret passageway. At last, she can see some sign of land or life. She exits the tunnel and it brings her to the outside world. She is near the water but is safe and can see something better. Carina notices that she is now on a crisp warm beach in Mexico because there is a sign saying she is at a Mexican Beach Resort in the Yucatan Peninsula.

It was quite a surprise to her, but she exited the secret tunnel from underneath the resort via some sort of mysterious and luxurious grotto nonetheless. That's right, her exit point led her to a grotto and she ended up in a luxurious beach resort in the fine and quaint Yucatan. But she does not see Sean or the bus driver, yet her wish to begin a new life has now come true. But something is going to make her to give up her new found plans.

Carina feels quite satisfied that she has found dry land again. But she needs to get to the bottom of this place. Why is it that she is here but no one else is? That is the question to be answered. Well, it will just have to suffice for now. There is just no other thing that can be done to help anyone else. Nothing is able to help anything. It is all a bunch of nothingness and lack of an ability to care. That is actually what is happening.

Nothing is going to help Carina now and she will be stuck here until she can find a way out or until someone or something rescues her for some crazy and strange apparent reason. So, Carina decides to check what the beach resort has to offer. She does not know where to begin so she decides to see what the grotto has to offer, even though she exited from there but didn't actually see where she exited from since she only saw she exited from what looks as a cave that led her outside. Carina tries to find where the grotto is but can't seem to locate it. She is either looking in the wrong place or it has disappeared from the face of the earth. Most likely, Carina is looking in the wrong place, because she has wandered off into the beach instead and forgot everything since she was just so amazed by the beauty of its sand and world class atmosphere. She decides to go somewhere else instead.

Carina walks across the shoreline instead and wants to see what the deal is. It isn't really interesting but she wants to see something or believes it has it has to do with the disappearance of everything of why she is here in the first place. Sunset is nearly approaching and it is almost dark. Carina sees the beauty of the shoreline and she quickly runs across the other side of the beach in order to see what it has to offer. She finds thatched tree cabanas with ornate and very elaborate curtains and chairs. She sees what looks like a Tiki bar and a swimming pool. It all seems too nice but Carina approaches everything with caution just so she does not get hurt or fear for her safety. It is something sort of just being in the heat of the passion.

Alas, she is finally at the beginning of a large resort-style swimming pool that seems and looks very luxurious that she seems addicted to it. All of the scenery makes everything look so much better, with palm trees surrounding the pool and lush green grass decorating the ground. The actual resort hotel can be seen from behind and it casts a shadow upon the ground of the pool. But there is more than just one pool. There are five and each of them is all grouped together in the same area. The pools are right before the beginning of the beach and are in walking distance of each other. Hundreds and even thousands of eyes have access to the pool and the beach area and they can always be watching when they are visiting on vacation. It provides for a very special getaway for very special occasions but it is worth it.

Carina finds the view amazing from where she is currently standing but she wants to experience more than just that. She wants to look from above and see what everyone else can see from the back of a luxurious Yucatan all-inclusive resort. It is just worth the cause. Carina enters a gate into the pool area from what seems to be the back area of the resort so she can find a way in. She sees an ornate glass door close to the resort building and believes it must be an exit or an entrance.

Carina turns the knob on the door and to her amazement it opens up. Inside, she finds everything she has dreamed about or so it seems. She sees a very elaborate lobby that is all decorated with luxurious paintings and designs. The walls are painted with such atmosphere that it can take anyone's breath away. The lobby is just so nice that it too will make sure anyone is in luxury. Everything about the inside of this hotel just seems to be very luxurious. It is all about the atmosphere and that is what this place is about. But inside, Carina needs to find a room to stay in, for she wants to live here for the rest of her life and doesn't plan on leaving. It is all about getting what she wants from her life and she needs to find a way in. Carina is looking for someone, such as a bellboy or front desk person. She rings the bell at the front desk lobby and wants to know if anyone can help her find a room. She just wants a room key so that she can make a home or at least stay here until she figures out what is going on. That is all Carina is asking for. It's shouldn't be that big of a burden to ask for a room key. It's only a suggestion in order to celebrate the happiness of life. That isn't too hard for a person to ask. That is just life and people should give a care about safety. It isn't like it's taking some stuff without asking. It is about charity and offering help, but that crap does not apply in this case. In this case, everything is about finding out what is going to happen or what has already happened. That is the case of reality.

After a minute, Carina rings the bell at the front desk again. She just wants somebody to help her get a room. "Is anyone there or do I have to get the room key and check in myself," she asked? It is just so quiet but too quiet. There is no one here it seems and Carina is finding that out as well. So, she rings the bell one last time. The third time could be the charm but Carina is about to grab a random if nothing happens soon enough.

After waiting a few more minutes, Carina has had enough of waiting. She goes to a door that leads her to enter the employees' only area. Now behind the front desk counter in the lobby, Carina sees a bunch of keys hanging from a very large and long key hook board rack on the wall opposite to her. She grabs a random key from one of the upper sections in the middle and reads the room number. Carina reads the number on the key and it said '*RM 852*.' Carina decides to find a way to get to the eight floor of this grand resort. She exits the employee only area and sees if she can find a stairway or an elevator. It takes about five minutes to find the stairway and another minute to find the elevator. Carina decides to take the elevator instead since it won't take as long as climbing the stairs.

Carina opens a heavy duty steel door after peeking inside the window. She sees the elevator is present on the lobby floor. She turns the knob and opens the door to the elevator and then pushes the collapsible folding black ornate gate to the side in order to get inside. Now inside, the steel door slowly closes and after it closes completely Carina slowly pushes back the gate to close it. She pushes the button for the eight floor on a control panel to see if the elevator actually works.

The elevator starts to move.

It takes five minutes to arrive on her floor.

Carina pushes the gate to the side and then opens the steel door. She closes the gates and closes the steel door behind her.

There are signs indicating which rooms are where. She reads the sign and her room is located to the right. Carina sees more signs and it directs her to the left this time. After going to the left, Carina sees additional signs and this time it tells her to go the left again. She finally sees more signs but this time it directs her to her correct room number by going to the right and then stopping at the center near the proximity of a corridor. Carina can see her room from a distance away. She arrives at the door after a few minutes of walking and sees no other doors to the side of her room.

Carina takes out her room key and puts it into the door knob. She turns it to the left and it opens to her belief. The room is so large that she seems very happy she chose the key in the first place. She closes the door but as she enters her room she sees a golden plaque on the wall to the right that reads '*presidential suite*.' Carina is very happy as she chose the correct and largest room that meets her needs. It is such a large and lavish room that it has its own parlour, its own living room, and its own sauna. The map of the room also indicates there are two other bedrooms, a walk in closet, a large kitchen, and two extremely large bathrooms. There is an indication of square footage for each room on the map. The suite is so large that Carina can't believe what she is seeing with her eyes.

Carina decides to look at the balcony first to see if she can see the beach and pool from her room, and she sees such beautiful curtains. She takes a look at the beautiful white velvet curtains hanging from above the beautiful and gorgeous glass windows inside her room. It proves to be just wonderful to her and she just wants to experience all the beauty of the outside world. It is such a spectacular place that she doesn't want to live. She has fallen in love with all of the scenery, the ambience, and the atmosphere. It is such an incredible situation that she will never leave to go somewhere else. Carina can see what the room can offer her. It is nothing but beauty and she looks outside the window. She sees a wonderful set of five gorgeous and luxurious pools filled to the edge with clear blue water. And she spots cabanas surrounding the entire area of the pools. There are just trees and more trees in the proximity of everything in sight of the big glass window. It is just a sight to relax and do whatever there is to do.

Carina notices two embedded door handles nearby and sees that it is a door to open up to the outside world. She puts her hand on the embedded white door handles and slowly opens them outward towards her. It reveals a beautiful but spacious balcony with an exclusive view of the pool and the beach that no one else seems to have because it is on the highest floor of the resort. She is so amazed at what she sees that she wants to take everything off now and start swimming. It is just a wish but it is a wish that she believes needs to come true. But, there is just something more to do.

There is nothing more beautiful than the sight of palm trees surrounding a luxurious Yucatan beach resort. It is all amazing and the atmosphere just makes it more stunning and beautiful. It is simply the place to be if anyone ever asks. It is why Carina does not want to remove herself from the exact spot that she is currently at.

Carina removes herself from the balcony to see the rest of the room. She shuts the doors behind her and goes to the parlour to see nothing but very old décor and furnishings that resembles the era of the roaring 20s. She finds it interesting but moves on to the second bedroom and sees it is quite large but does not offer anything to her that she doesn't already like. She goes to the third bedroom and sees that there is something to offer but decides to go back to the main bedroom which is where the balcony was located. She takes off her shoes and tosses them aside and lies down in the bed to see how it feels. Carina finds it to be wonderful and luxurious. It is just a beauty of a bed that she is addicted and wants to lie on it forever. The texture is just so soft that it feels like sleeping on a marshmallow. Everything about the bed is just so fancy that it will be considered a crime not to sleep on this bed. Even the pillows are extremely soft and fluffy while also keeping their forms intact.

But she decides she needs to get up and see what else her suite has to offer. She goes to the first bathroom she sees and notices it has gorgeous tiles made from imported marble. The counters are made from fine granite and soapstone while everything else seems to be plated in gold. Even the walls are just so spectacular. The shower is so intricate and beautiful that it is a masterpiece by itself. Everything just takes her breath away, from the imported tile to the fine and excellent quality of solid gold. It seems all is good and done but Carina goes to the other bathroom to see what it has to offer. It is such a beauty that she leaves it before getting too addicted so she walks to the left and sees an indoor sauna. From the outside it seems small but on the inside it is just so gorgeous and breathtaking of an experience. She has to use this sauna before she leaves.

Black stone line the walls as a way to make the sauna experience more personal and as a way to better remove any sweat and other toxins within the body itself. Its sole purpose is to help anyone to just feel more relaxed and comfortable at the same time and to increase pleasure. Carina decides to end her tour here. She drops her clothes and lingerie in order to see how her experience will feel like. Looking for towels she can't find anything so she just walks in there completely naked. But Carina was looking in the wrong place to begin with. She turns the knob to turn on the heat and then pulls a lever from above to allow steam to be released. Carina is in her happy place now and does not want to leave for whatever reason. She can feel the heat penetrating her skin and the steam trying to rid her body of toxins. She feels just so patient and relaxed that she feels at home for once in a while. She feels so relaxed that she does not want to leave.

An hour later, Carina is still in the sauna and she decides it is time to leave. But she can stay for a few more minutes. There is just no time to waste and it is just too soon. Carina exits the sauna and her slim but sexy and gorgeous body is just so good to be in the midst of something sinister. But that is not to be known. Carina tries to see if she can find any clothes to wear and goes to the walk in closet and finds that it is so large that it can be considered another bedroom to find comfort and relaxation in. It is just about peace and quiet.

Carina puts on a bra, panties, and some type of dress. She decides to go back to the master bedroom in order to take a nap and rest for the next few hours. But there is something else to think about. It could be the weather or just her.

Chapter Eleven

Sounds of the earth can be heard rumbling as Carina is about to lie down in bed. There is nothing but noise and shakes coming from the outside. Carina decides it is not safe appear so she must take cover or leave but does not know where to go. Suddenly, some mysterious bright flash of light starts to appear and Carina wants to know what it is and how it got here. Carina takes a leap of faith and steps into the bright flash of light. She does not know where she will end up but it is worth a shot of finding out what's wrong. As she enters the light, there is nothing but silence but it soon disappears after she has stepped inside.

Carina finds herself in a place of uncertainty and does not know for sure what will happen. About five minutes later, the bright flash of light spits her out and then it disappears forever. It seems to be that it took her to a barren wasteland. There are no signs of people and no presence of life. It seems all has been abandoned. Everything just seems so riddled with crime and lack of opportunities that the place is unhospitable and uninhabitable. But there is just nothing to do here. It looks like a rundown mess with chaos and disaster. It seems terror has struck as well, seeing the mess that everything is currently in, and that's putting it nicely. Carina does not know what to do so she thinks.

It is just the sort of thing that didn't need to happen in the first place. But where is Carina at in this new reality. It seems she has entered some type of alternate universe because of what she can see and that is not necessarily a good thing. It is just a matter of what happens next because there can be dangerous things leading to more dangerous things. It would be the most significant waste of time to stand here in the middle of an abandoned wasteland or what seems to be what is represented. Nothing looks good here due to the fact the buildings are rundown, the streets are filled with garbage, the sidewalks are vandalized with graffiti, and the grass is flooding from too much water from broken fire hydrants. Yeah, sure, that sounds like a great place to live, but it isn't because that just makes everything bad. It is just a cesspool of what used to be once a great city. Or that could be how the city always was. Nothing even makes sense but there is surely one thing wrong: there seems to be a lack of people as well as the streets and sidewalks being rundown while buildings seem to look just like tenements. Everything is just a wreck and no one seems to notice because people suddenly disappeared with no trace.

There is just disasters waiting to happen but there is no proof of any disasters taking place before Carina got to her current situation. There is just a wide area of disarray that seems to have taken over at least one major portion of a city. There are no words for what can be said about what happened. It just looks like a mess that someone caused but it isn't for certain if a disaster ever took place. That is the thing that is actually frustrating. No people can be spotted in the nearest distance. The environment is absolutely destitute. Even if there is something to do it is very limited. There is just something wrong with this new place where Carina is currently at. It all just seems too ominous and too perfect. There is only silence along with water pouring out of broken fire hydrants onto the grass.

The buildings look in horrible condition and that is just being nice. Houses look like they have been broken into. Glass windows are broken and it seems like many houses have been burglarized or at least robbed in a potential attempt. Homes still see all fine with only the broken windows present. If thieves actually broke into homes then why is everything look as if nothing was stolen? It all looks like a bad nightmare that doesn't seem to go away. It is a way for a diversion of something more sinister. That is the theory.

Carina looks around and walks the streets to see what the city has to offer. She notices the broken windows, the graffiti, the fire hydrants pouring tons of water, as well as what seems a disaster rolled into town. But it didn't seem like a complete disaster to Carina. It seemed like everything was planned in order to institute a totalitarian dystopian society to maintain order and to implement a harsh reality of overbearing and illegal laws. It just seems like it was this that happened and it was this that would lead to finding out what really happened. Carina wants to take a closer look at everything but does not know where to begin. Something has to be wrong but Carina doesn't know what to think. It is just some type of distraction that seems to be taking place in order to hide something sinister that has already happened or is in the process of happening. It is a disaster waiting to happen, if it happens, and when it happens. That is the scenario that causes the greatest deal of concern but there is no evidence of what will even happen. That is just the scenario of the new and never-ending situation of constant chaos caused by only a claim with no support. It is that for which no hope can be granted. That shall be the day when all hell breaks loose. It is a way to get back into the confines of controlling nothing. But none of this makes a lick of any sense. It is all purely a case of what if it actually happened in this particular manner. It does not mean anything and it should not really mean anything. The rest could be history but that is the case of nothing. Everything else is a waste of time and decency.

Something more seems to be happening as Carina strolls down the streets of what looks like a deserted, abandoned, and disaster-riddled zone. It seems there could be a change in events but that is not even the bad part about the whole situation. It is only a case of something more sinister. No one wants that to happen but it could be too late if the process has already begun. So it would just be a lost cause and a waste of time to fix something that can't be actually be prevented if it has already started. And if people try to do it then they are purely idiots, but they don't know better.

As it seems now, every street is about the same and Carina has started to notice. She can't think of what is really driving this situation. She doesn't know what to do. All she knows is that she is stuck here in the middle of what looks to be some sort of abandoned and disaster-riddled area. It seems quite chaotic but no one is here besides Carina, and that is just the problem. People should be hiding or at least making an attempt to hide. They could all be hiding or could be elsewhere. But seeing there is no one else here then they could all be dead. Yet they all could be imprisoned as well.

As Carina is walking there is just something that doesn't feel right. Carina looks up at the sky and it is all dark and gloomy. It resembled like the sun is just about to set. It looks like twilight is just upon us and. The sun is indeed about to set but that is not even what seems to be bad. Everything seems to be very hazy as it can be. It seems like something bad is just about to happen. There should be awareness to everything and it should not be at the expense of anyone else. Carina wants to know everything but she can't because of what needs to be discovered. It is a time of disaster and chaos as well as with a case of what seems to resemble an apocalypse. It has all seem to have happened before but that is just the thing. It shouldn't happen again and it should have never happened in the first place. It is just the case of nothing.

Five minutes after Carina arrived she starts to notice a cloud of haziness. It resembles some sort of fog. It could even be smog. So far nothing seems toxic about anything. It is just getting darker and darker, for something that doesn't even make sense to anyone. It should all be a case for disaster so people should prepare for an apocalypse. But there is just no knowing if it is even an apocalypse. Everything just seems to be turning into a disaster. That is where the entire apocalypse begins. It all starts from there and it all resembles scare tactics in order to develop some sort of false pretense.

The cloud is just getting larger and larger. It is slowly taking over the entire sky. But the clouds are not even visible as being the normal color of white, and that could mean something else. It could mean that it is almost dark because it is probably almost dark due to it being twilight. That should just be the normal assumption of what is to be believed but not all will actually believe what they see. They want to see additional evidence that doesn't exist. It will all be a waste of time. It is a complete and total overcast across the sky. Nothing can be seen. There are just no clear skies. Everything seems to be hazy. It is not a mist because there are no water droplets. It is not a fog because there are no visible clouds. It is not a vog because there are no volcanoes nearby. But it could be air pollution such as smog or it could be a haze since it meets the basic criteria. There is just some sort of craziness going on and it is a type that is and will always be at the center of attention when trying to understand such a situation. It is at the course of all attention to which this must be figured out as quickly as possible. Nothing will be able to escape or it too shall be riddled with an atmospheric uncertainty of a mysterious factor.

Carina starts to notice the changings of the sky little-by-little. She looked at it before but did not think much about it. She thinks it is just normal but it seems it is not smog but a haze. There is a hint of dirt, dust, smoke, and finely grained particles that seem to be causing this sky to be less visible as it is normally. The entire sky seems to be entrenched in this thick orange haze that seems to resemble a mix of fog and smog. Not much can be seen in these types of conditions. The visibility is extremely poor and the only things that can be seen are up-close trees and houses. It seems to be only getting worse because the haze is growing larger by the minute. There seems to be a strange occurrence that doesn't last for this long at a time.

As Carina is walking down the streets she just notices the same things over and over again. They are just a pattern of repetitions. It all just looks all too obvious for it to be true. Everything looks and feels the same. It is like living in the suburbs, since the entire neighborhood Carina is in looks exactly the same. They are the same houses, the same types of front lawns, the same sidewalks, and the same type of design. There is nothing different about this place at all. Everything seems like it is just a copy of another but in some mysterious and strange way. But there is just this feeling nothing is right for some particular reason.

Electrical power lines line the street of the neighborhood with cars parked in the driveways and next to the front lawns. It is still the same and there is a sign of no escaping. It is just creepy because there is no sign of life anywhere to be found. It is just a sign of a larger problem. Something has to be done and it must be done now. This is just the time when it must be done.

The orange haze does not seem to be any bit dangerous but so far Carina is trying to see why no one is here. She rather be back in Mexico since that is where she can experience pleasure, luxury, and a type of world class atmosphere. It is all but inevitable but Carina might have to stay here a while and she does not even know where she is so that's a downer. And there is also the fact that she is tired of being alone and not knowing where other people are. That surely must be the life. But everything could actually be a dream, if there are people controlling everybody in some twisted experiment. If that was the case, then Carina might not actually be real. She could be just a creation of scientists in order to deceive people and the rest of society. That would be some twisted sort of tactic. But this is not that case, since there is not one shred of evidence this situation being some type of controlled scientific experiment. It is actual life and this is really happening. So, for the time being, Carina will just continue to walk the streets of this neighborhood.

Carina notices numerous things and other objects around the streets and it seems like they have just started to appear with no sign. They just started to appear out of thin air like some ghost or invisible being or entity placed them there. That is some very strange shit there and it is just something to see what is going on. There are sinks, toilets, scrap metal, and other common household items that are scattered throughout the neighborhood. It is just something that isn't part of life.

Trees and more trees start to appear and it is just another part of the neighborhood. It is getting to be narrower and narrower. Everything is just about normal as it should be but with a lack of people and a lack of life. There is still that hazy orange sky with a small chance of visibility. It is all too crazy and it does require something to happen. Carina is getting nowhere as she is seeing the same things over and over again. It seems like she is walking in a circle because everything is the same. Nothing is different and it just seems all suspicious. That is just how it is and it requires something different. It is a part of the reason why nothing is like what it seems and it is a constant problem. That is just how everything seems to be today.

Carina wants to get to an actual place or some safe building in order to see if she could escape this strange and crazy place. But the haze is just getting worse and worse. There is even more cloud that is blocking the sky. It seems there is a strange weather event happening but there are no people. It seems it is just an empty universe.

Fog is building up as now there are clouds that can be visibly seen touching the ground. It is a sort of a mixed weather pattern now but there is a sign everything is getting colder and colder. Or it could mean something else. But the clouds are getting even more visible but there is still this orange haze engulfing the entire city. It makes no difference whatsoever. But the clouds that just appeared are in addition to the cloud of orange haze. It just appears something is happening.

These mass clouds of fog are just engulfing the city by the second. Every second the cloud of fog just reduces the visibility significantly. Soon, there will be nothing left to see. Carina will probably need some type of specialized bright flash light in order just to see so she doesn't bump into something. It can get very dangerous with this fog around here. It is about as dangerous as a poisonous snake or spider to the extent that they actually sneak up on a person to begin with. This is just like that because this fog is a sneak attack. All of a sudden, the fog just got worse in a matter of minutes. Visibility has gotten so bad that Carina can no longer see. She needs to get out of this and needs to proceed with caution. It is about that time to escape. But just running will lead to accidents and tragedy. There is still some visibility for Carina to walk but she must be careful not to hit anything or she would risk something bad. There is just some type of thing that is going on. It doesn't even make sense anymore. Carina must escape but everywhere is just getting to be the same. Something is just not right here.

Within five minutes of the visibility getting worse by the minute, Carina is able to find shelter in the next street over after deciding to walk down a side street which led her to a main road. It seems that it is an abandoned warehouse. Carina quickly rushes to the abandoned warehouse after spotting the door is open. It looks like an old ammunitions factory but there is no sign of life. Carina looks around to see if it is a suitable hiding or resting place. She just doesn't know yet if it is safe. The only reason why she ever went inside to find shelter is because there was a lack of visibility and it is too dangerous outside. The fog has gotten so thick that the orange haze sky can't be seen anymore even though it is almost dark out. It just seems light never ends in this place. It looks like it is supposed to be getting dark soon because of the time, yet there is no darkness at all. It seems daylight is still in effect. But there is no reason why this is even happening. There is just a thick cloud of fog that it is keeping everything daylight. Or that could be the fact that the orange haze sky is still there and it is reflecting that so that is why maybe it is still light out as a way of the time. But that doesn't even make sense at all since it is supposed to be dark but there is no sign of the sun. There is only the orange haze sky that is blocking the darkness. It seems like it is a very sinister plot to prevent the moon from breaking out, which means night will never be here. Or it could be that there is perpetual twilight for some peculiar and strange reason.

Carina explores the abandoned warehouse and sees nothing that she likes. She chooses to stay here until it is safe. It just isn't safe to go out with this fog so thick because no one could probably see, including Carina. It's so bad that the entire city resembles an old bog that is constantly filled with fog because of the climate of the bog itself. Everything is just very strange and soon something else will happen. There is just something else. This fog is thick as a cloud of pollution that makes breathing unlivable in an open environment but

Carina isn't having any problems breathing. It seems the fog is so thick that there must be a mutation to it. But Carina wants to wait and see what will happen next. Meanwhile, the fog is just going to grow more. It won't stop until there is an utter and complete overcast of the sky. But it is just so thick that it looks like an over cast already. That is surely interesting.

Carina must find a way out but she needs some type of equipment like a bright flashlight that is attached to a hard hat or just a bright flashlight in general. She must look around in order to see if she can find anything. It will only be a matter of time until it will be safe again to walk outside, but seeing there is nothing to do here because of a lack of people due to everything that is happening. It isn't normal and it shouldn't be that way. The whole weather or climate thing with this orange haze sky and now this thick fog is just crazy.

What happens next is entirely up to Carina, but knowing her she will just see what she can do in what seems to be an abandoned warehouse. It is such a crazy situation but that is beyond the point of no return. Carina decides that she can't stay here for long so she has to see if she is able to look around for some type of bright flashlight. She is not guaranteed to find anything but abandoned warehouses are known to keep some very useful and strange items scattered throughout the building. It is just for that reason why it must be an adventure. After looking around what seems to be the lobby area, Carina sees that there is just a pile of junk scattered throughout the building. But everything else looks in excellent condition to say the least. It seems that there is just no hope but it will be here in a nick of time or some other crazy amount of time. That is just how things work around here, and to say otherwise would mean something is hiding to scare Carina. But, for the meantime, Carina sees another door to the far back of the building. It seems like it is locked from the very far distance but it isn't when she gets closer to the door. It is all an illusion to say the least but that is just how it seems. There is only a matter of time until Carina finds a way out and it should be sooner than later.

She is nearing the door but then all of a sudden she hears a loud noise outside. It seems like that the ground is vibrating and a volatile shake is going to ruin the building. That is what it seems like but Carina finally can reach the door knob and reaches to grab it in the midst of something dangerous that might be occurring outside. To her astonishment, the door knob turns and she is able to open it. When the door finally opens it reveals a small room and some type of metal or steel table with some tools on it. Carina can see a flashlight, some heavy-duty gloves, a hard hat with an attached flashlight, and some power tools. She grabs the flashlight and the hard hat. She then turns on the flashlight and it produces a very bright flash of light that is very powerful. She decides she is going to take it with her to see. Carina tries to see how to turn on the light but can't seem to find a button so she places it back on the table and then grabs the gloves for some reason and puts them on her hands. Carina then turns on the flashlight again because she thought she saw something.

She points the light and guides it toward a full spin around the room to see if she can find any sign of life or some way to escape. Carina sees something and she holds the flashlight in place. It seems that there is an invisible door just right in front of her and she can use it to escape. She walks toward it and tries to find the door knob. It is to her right and she sees it right away. She turns the door knob but it does not turn to the right. She tries to turn the knob to the left but it doesn't turn either. It seems that it could all be a show or just something playing a trick on her, but Carina can see this door because of the flashlight. It just seems so weird that a flashlight will be able to show an invisible door but then chooses not to open. It could be just that: an invisible door just placed in the building for display. But this door seems like it is actually a real working door so Carina tries again and pulls outward. Yet it refuses to open for her still, so she tries one last thing.

Carina tries pushing the door knob inwards and something is starting to happen. To her surprise, the door pushes out and she can see some sort of light.

Carina pushes the door forward again and this time it finally opens all the way. She can see that there is fog outside but there is a blue sky waiting for her to explore. It seems like it is daylight and everything is fine but it doesn't seem right. She looks back and is unable to see a building behind her anymore. It just vanished into thin air and now Carina is stuck in the middle of nowhere because she doesn't know where she is and how she got here. But from afar she can see a farm or what resembles like one, so she starts to walk that way.

The farm seems to be a plain corn field with no crop at all. Everything seemed so brown that the corn was either dead or was frozen. It could also be that the corn was not planted yet. But there is just nothing there. It is just a plain old corn field and it looks like it has been replaced by wheat. But it is not wheat even if it seemed like it, because everything was brown and looked if it was wilted. There was a small building that resembled a church on the same property as the corn field as well as a small building that resembled a house of some kind. Trees where everywhere and it seemed that it was a quiet countryside community, as it looked very rural.

The whole setting seemed very strange indeed, because of where Carina ended up. She didn't know where she was but she knew she was on a farm or at least in the countryside. It seemed that the world was changing for her but Carina was determined to find out where she was. Carina wants to see where she was so she raced to the church to see if she could go inside and see whatever. It is beginning to look like there was intent for the other building to lead Carina to this place but that could just be coincidental. That is the time and place for everything and it is at the height of what looks to be a new world order if Carina is the last remaining person on the planet. Sure, that sounds right but it is just speculation. No one would believe that type of information unless it was someone who was curious as Carina was. And then there was that whole thing about nothing.

Carina raced through the corn field but it looked like she was getting nowhere. It seemed as every time she got closer everything moved further away. That just could be her experiencing an illusion or a mirage or it could be a reality. She could most likely be experiencing an illusion or a mirage because she hasn't eaten anything in a while and she feels quite dizzy and lightheaded. So, that could be why she is seeing stuff that is moving away from or she is actually dreaming. It is just a race against time in order to see what this place has to offer to Carina, but it was the same exact thing over and over again. It was just about anything else. There was something hidden within everything that wasn't expected. It wouldn't show itself but it was probably just a figment of a person's imagination. That probably makes a lick of more sense since Carina needs to eat something before she dies. She probably needs water as well because she could dehydrate. And then, it hit her, she was just seeing stuff that was moving further away from her so she thought for a little bit and closed her eyes to see what would happen. She could be whisked back away to the beginning back where it all began in Winslow, South Dakota or she could be waking up from a dream but that is not the only reality that could happen. She could also wake up to nothing being false while all of the other stuff was history. But that is not the only real reality that could happen. Carina could also open her eyes and the church would be right in front of her for some mysterious reason. That would surely be quite magical but it might make the most sense at all or so it seems. Nothing could be known but it would be what is seen.

Carina opens her eyes and right in front of her she can see a church. The doors are open and she is so close that she walks straight in. She can see decorative maps of Italy on a plain old white background of paint and stucco. There is no one in the pews and the stage or foyer seems empty. It is still a sight to see but it feels nice even though it might be abandoned for some reason or another. But the church is not abandoned and it is a way out for some reason or another. It is the most perfect thing that could happen and it can be the craziest thing that could ever happen. Carina does not know what to think but she just looks around and sees that nothing might be quite like it seems. Or it could be something else.

Carina sees that everything is made out of wood and it seems nice inside that she doesn't want to leave. Suddenly, it seems a member of the clergy has appeared out of nowhere and he seems to be on his way to the room behind the altar. That seems strange that he didn't notice Carina or maybe he did and did not want to make a big deal about anything. That is just what it seems but everything is mysterious for the same reason about nothing. As it actually turns out, there is just something else but it could be that the rest of society is ruined for the sake of humanity and the human race.

The clergy exits the room from behind the altar and asks Carina to following him to some other room in what seems to be English. She is told to wait in that room until he opens it for security reasons. It is just crazy but she waits in the room so see what the clergy will do or say.

Chapter Twelve

Strange noises begin to happen but it looks just to be the wind. That is no problem but it could be the least of her worries. Carina is eagerly waiting in the room that the clergyman told her to wait. She is just in amazement at what will happen. But the clergyman could know everything, even the reason she is here in the first place. That should be very interesting to say the least but it would be at the sole discretion of the clergyman. Before something ever happens it must happen or else the rest would be history.

Carina waits for something that might be very important to finding out what could be happening. It is just something interesting and that is how it will be for the rest of life. As she is waiting in the room, Carina notices a desk and some office equipment but nothing else other than blank white walls. It is just plain and boring but that is how life tends to be so she just needs to wait until the clergyman enters the room for some mysterious purpose. That is something that is not to be trusted, but it is time to listen. That is how everything seems to be around. After a few minutes there is a noise. It sounds crazy but it isn't. Carina is looking at the walls in front of her and didn't hear what it was, as she thought it was near. Then there was another noise for some other reason. It was like a typical slamming of a door. Carina turned around and saw the door was closed. A few seconds later, the clergyman was sitting in a chair behind the desk.

He spoke.

"*You are here today because of something that has gone wrong. You were on a bus and met some very strange people as well as the bus driver and some person by the name of Sean Preston. You decided to get on the bus for some apparent reason and then arrived at some destination in the middle of nowhere. You decided to leave with Sean and the bus driver after all of the passengers got off. There was a rush to get off the first time but you, Sean, and the bus driver waited for the other passengers to get off the bus and then decided to leave.*"

"All of you finally exited the bus while the passengers went off to what resembled a mall. And then you, the bus driver, and Sean want to a much smaller building that could see what the passengers were doing in the much larger building. None of the passengers knew it at first but they would have a problem of escaping. All of the passengers were walking around what seemed to be a mall and they were enjoying their time. They were actually happy getting off the bus because they thought they were going to hit someone. Soon, they became all paranoid and believed police would question them or possibly arrest them for being potential victims, suspects, or even accessories to a crime such as murder. But that soon all changed."

"After the bus driver parked the bus, all of the passengers wanted to get off the same time but it seemed to have created some sort of commotion or some pushing and shoving. It took time for all of those passengers to get off the bus and the first building they saw resembled a mall, but the mall was abandoned, yet they had it all to themselves. Then, a few minutes later, you, Sean, and the bus driver got off the bus and went to a much smaller building that could see what those other people were doing."

"Now, back to what I was saying before." All of the passengers saw the time was almost near for them to head back to the bus but reality had another

plan for them. All of them pushed and shoved each other at the same time while trying to exit the mall and it was filled with chaos and disaster. In the end they all pushed and shoved each other, but they did indeed exited out of the mall. However, their escape was only short-lived because the mall soon collapsed on top of them. Then, you, Sean, and the bus driver unloaded their luggage from the bottom of the bus and left it on the side of the road or parking lot. All of you then boarded the bus."

"After the bus left, all of you were enjoying a nice bus ride and were expecting a new set of more passengers to board. The bus driver stopped the bus after seeing potential passengers. The new passengers claimed that they were headed to a convention near the US-Mexico border in California but they never said where. The bus arrived in the middle of the night or so it seems and everyone was still sleeping, so you, the bus driver, and Sean decided to leave right in the morning before the passengers wake up. Morning came and you, Sean, and the bus driver left the bus in order to find something in town. But all of you got lost and ended up some place crazy.

"You went back to the bus with the bus driver and Sean with the passengers all gone, who probably went to their convention. All of you then took the bus into town to get closer to the US-Mexico

border to find evidence of a convention but ended up going to a hotel for the night before it was too late due to it getting dark. At the hotel, you and Sean then sinned by having premarital sex, but no one cares about that. And in the morning, you, Sean, and the bus driver ate a gourmet breakfast in the hotel kitchen. It seemed like you never wanted to leave but all of you soon left the hotel to look around more. All three of you exited the interior of the hotel and now were outside standing right in front of the hotel property."

"All of you were in front of the hotel property now and soon saw something was about to happen, but you just looked around. You saw the beginning of clouds forming and then saw them turning darker and darker. And then you started to hear a wind that just started to pick up strength and speed. It soon caused a dust storm. The three of you saw a building and went inside and then all of you figured out that there was a security system that would safeguard the building from disaster. The security system was armed and all of you tried to find a way out."

"Then, you, Sean, and the bus driver found a way out and it took you to a secret passageway. You, Sean, and the bus driver opened the door to the secret passageway and picked up torches. All of you then proceeded to descend several flights of stairs

that took hours or about half of the day. And then it led to a new path of no more stairs. You continued to move forward until you came to a series of three new tunnels. You decided to take the middle tunnel, Sean taking the left tunnel, and the bus driver turning the right tunnel. But then something happened."

Sean and the bus driver managed to get into trouble by entering into traps that they couldn't see and eventually they fell down a set of trap doors, but they didn't die. You proceeded to walk without any incident and ended up in a luxurious Mexican resort in the Yucatan peninsula. You exited from a grotto and did not see it but you went inside of the hotel after a while and chose a random room. Now in your room, you look around to see where it is and find out that it is the presidential suite. You get accustomed to your room and take a look around just because you want to experience what it has to offer."

"After a while you decided to go and get into the sauna inside of your suite just to experience it and then you did something else. You decided to lie down in your freshly made bed to see how it would feel and then you woke up due to some rumbling noises and other commotion. Then, you saw a bright flash of light appear and decided to enter it. You ended up in what seemed to be a barren wasteland. You saw an orange hazy sky and a deserted city. Everything seemed like it was abandoned."

"And then you continued to walk the streets of a neighborhood and continued to see houses broken into and fire hydrants pouring out massive amounts of water. A cloud of fog started to develop and take over the entire sky, eventually blocking the orange haze sky for some reason. You wanted to see how to get out of this place because the fog was only getting worse and worse. You finally see a building you could probably deem as safe. You entered it and saw there was not much was inside. It was an abandoned warehouse and soon you found yourself trying to find a way out to see if you could escape. Soon, you go to a room and find some tools, and you pick up a flashlight. You use the flashlight and see it shows an invisible door and then you try to open it."

"Now, you finally manage to open the door and it leads to some place mysterious outside with the presence of fog. But you are here now. You see this church and corn field and a house near you and walk toward it. Then you enter into this church just to see what it has to offer. And that is where you are now, so you are thinking about finding about how to get back to your old life. But, we must begin training soon, since there is a war a coming, and if you aren't that well prepared you will be doomed. So sit back and follow me."

Carina paid attention to the clergyman and

was perplexed that he knew so much of what she had ever experienced. It is probably for the best but she just believed that he knew everything. It is just for that strange reason why something is strange here and for that reason it must be answered. That is just how it is and should be. So Carina follows the clergyman to a secure location beneath the church and it would be for the best. Carina does not know where she is going but it's probably for some reason to train for a war and then something could happen in the near months or years. It is just something that is above anything else in the midst of a crisis and it will be at the time of the plan to find out. That could just be karma if she says something bad before and ends up with consequences that she never expected. But Carina does not know if she will even fight in a war.

It takes Carina a while but she is thinking as she is following the clergyman. She is just following some mysterious stranger who seems to know too much information about what happened during the past few days. That is weird and creepy at the same time and possibly illegal if it is just stocking, but that is something else. The clergyman takes Carina to a staircase near the other part of the church and then opens the door. The clergyman turns on some lights and Carina follows and both of them descend about eleven flights of stairs. It takes some time but both of them are finally in the middle of nowhere or what seems to be the basement of the church. But it seems so large that it doesn't even make sense at all. It all seems too large for the church but if it makes sense then it must be real. But this basement, if it is even a basement at all, seems to resemble an underground bunker, but the lights have yet to be turned on so it is still dark. The clergyman finds the light switch and the lights start to gradually turn on. The space is larger than expected. It seems to be an endless space with no end in sight.

The clergyman spoke to Carina. "Here, you will train for the next two years; it is currently the fifth day of December of 1939, and on the next day you will be dispatched to fight in a war that will end all other wars," stated the clergyman. Carina thought for a few short seconds. It was a surreal experience that never made any sense at all, with the constant and never-ending threat of finding out that someone must train for war for two years. By two years, Carina should be properly trained, but this is going to be a war like no other. The clergyman never told what war Carina would fight in. She could be fighting the war against Hitler and his allies to defeat Communism, Socialism, and Fascism, but that is something to deal with.

Now waiting for the clergy to give her some instructions, Carina is patiently standing in what seems to be a very large room that expands to more than ten football fields long and wide, which might seem rather small but it is actually quite large, yet not counting everything else. When just that portion is calculated it is close to just over thirteen acres but the remaining areas are about two acres on each side and there are exactly five sides, which would make it seem to be ten acres plus the thirteen acres. That would be a total of about twenty-three acres but there is just more space such as storage space and other rooms and fields that make everything larger. So the new amount of total space would be approximately fifty acres of total space. That might sound large but that includes other rooms as well and not including any expansions to the main room where Carina currently waits. The main room can be expanded to a total of one-hundred acres, which is well above anything else. But that does not include the additional rooms and storage space, since all of them are separate. So now, everything totals up to be one-hundred and fifty acres, which is more than enough room to train and learn in order to prepare for an up-and-coming war.

Such expansions are proprietary but it could be known by the clergyman. He could know how to do the expansions or what switch to use to give a greater amount of space. There is nothing that could be wrong about him since he knew what Carina did all along. But everything about this clergyman seems rather weird and strange. On the other hand, nothing should ever be questioned or doubted. And in this case it is about war and how to defeat the enemy before some other event happens. But since this is about some sort of future war it makes everything crazy. Carina does not even know who she is going to even fight for or against. The clergyman just told her she is going to fight in a war in about two years from now and it could be over in Europe. However, that is the main problem to begin with, since no other information was given.

Anyway, the clergyman tells Carina about the size and scope of this entire underground facility and how it is meant to help her. And he begins by turning on more switches to reveal something additional, with the added benefit of security and space. So, that is how it seems but it isn't the end of the line yet, since everything is only beginning. That is how it was meant to be. But it is in the midst of a mindset and that is now and soon.

The clergyman spoke again to Carina.

"Here, you will soon find yourself in taking part in a twenty-two part military grade obstacle course designed to help you on the front lines. It consists of that many obstacles in order to test your endurance, strength, speed, flexibility, upper body strength, lower body strength, and agility. Some

obstacles you will find hard to navigate while with others you can expect to provide for a hefty challenge. You might not make it out alive but as you encounter each obstacle you should be able to develop an advantage sooner or later just to gain momentum. This won't be your only duty to accomplish because you have to participate in weight and strength training as well. This portion is strictly for physical fitness and endurance only just to make sure you are progressing well and that you have a good sense of adaptation."

"As you take part in each obstacle in each day you will find yourself in an easier situation. It will just get easier with each day. Sometimes you might face very compromising situations and might have to shred some clothing after completing certain obstacles due to the obstacle to begin with. That should not be a disadvantage to you but as a way to combat any and all possible challenges you might face in the front lines and real life."

"You will begin by climbing a low wall and then descending it, and then you will complete the dreaded tire walk and that is followed by stepping on solid cinderblock squares by demonstrating that you have the ability and capability of leaping as well as balancing yourself between an object. You will then enter into the rubble course in order to determine if you have the capability of vaulting and

ducking from any enemy combatants and then you will face the tunnel obstacle by making sure you are able to crawl in confined and small spaces without any difficulty whatsoever."

"After you have completed those five obstacles you will climb a rope wall and then descend it, then you will face the dodging obstacle in which you will have to prepare yourself to engage in lateral dodging in very confined or small spaces but to also make sure you are not detected by the enemy. After you finished those obstacles you will come face to face with the low rope climb in order to demonstrate your upper body strength and endurance. And then you will take part in the ditching obstacle in order to demonstrate your ability and agility to leap between long gaps between slopes and can also demonstrate being well-balanced and have the ability of landing safely between each of the slopes."

"For the tenth obstacle, you will take part in the monkey bar obstacle by demonstrating your upper body strength and that you have the ability as well as the endurance to swing your arms and body between each gap to appropriately judge distance. And then you will enter the corridor obstacle to demonstrate you have the ability to duck and hide between areas of low but restricted height. From there you will have to take part in the balancing

bridge walk by making sure you can maintain your balance, coordination, and jumping in order to avoid any obstacles that may pose a threat to your safety."

To complete your halfway mark you will take part in a swinging bar cross by first climbing a built-in ladder underneath the obstacle in order to swing from each broken bar. This obstacle is meant just to demonstrate if you can swing appropriately from large gaps but to also demonstrate your upper body strength can help guide you to the next bar by a means of having an excellent grip. You will then come face to face with a giant ladder wall in which you will have to climb and descend. After the giant ladder obstacle you will encounter a crawl walk underneath a mesh fence of barbed wire in which you will have to crawl very slowly and safely under a mesh of barbed wire while also navigating the wet dirt to demonstrate your ability, endurance, agility, and strength to be in confined and small areas but to also demonstrate you have an appropriate amount of upper and lower body strength."

"You will then proceed to a barrel run in which you quickly have to jump over each barrel and then proceed to duck and cover until you complete the entire obstacle. And this obstacle will demonstrate if you can hide, jump, and can handle confined and small spaces. After that you will face a

rope swinging obstacle in which you will have to climb a rope and then use your upper body strength to grab the next rope until you have reached the last rope in which you will proceed to climb down. Your next thing you will face is the belly roll in which you will have to use your body to crawl across several logs to demonstrate that you have strength and endurance."

"Next you will encounter an apex ladder in which you have to climb and then descend in order to demonstrate your ability of balancing while also maintaining distance and grip appropriately to avoid falling. Then you will jump through a window to ensure that you have the ability to make fast but well-informed decisions while on the front lines. You will then encounter a reverse climb obstacle in which you have to use your upper body strength by climbing from underneath the obstacle so you can propel yourself down when you finally descend. Your last obstacle will be to walk up a steep slope and to then jump, and this is to basically test if you can judge your distance and height when trying to jump to a much lower platform."

"After you have completed this twenty-two military grade obstacle course you will be able to rest for thirty minutes. This whole obstacle course should take you no more than two hours but on average it should take you no longer than twenty

minutes after you have mastered everything. Everything is up to current standards and you should do perfectly fine on the front lines if you succeed."

"Now, for the next two years you will live in the house next door and every time that you are not on schedule to complete a required task you should be in that house getting some rest or eating a nutritious but well balanced meal. To get to the house from here just follow the lighted path to your right and you should see a door right in front of you that will lead you to the house. You will also find a schedule in your room and it is there to keep you on track. It is not meant to dissuade you but to make sure you are ready to fight in a complex but dangerous war. If you need me I will be in the church. Your first round of training begins tomorrow morning at precisely 0430 hours and you will begin a rigorous regiment of training and physical exercises for the next two years until the seventh of December of 1941. Remember, I am just a few minutes away. Good luck!"

The clergyman left Carina and wished her all the best. She walks to the lighted path and sees the door and then opens the door. She enters into the doorway and continues to walk until she sees a set of stairs. She climbs the stairs and it leads her to the basement of the house. She then sees a sign pointing to the house and climbs the stairs and then opens the door. Carina is now in what seems to be her room and it is just spectacular. She sees that it is oddly familiar and everything seems like it has happened before. It is just a reminder to her memory.

Carina notices that everything looks exactly as her room back home in Winslow, South Dakota. It all just seems too surreal at first but maybe Carina is back at home but that might seem strange because it is just impossible to walk from one country to another if you are thousands of miles away. It is impossible because there are bodies of water separating the West and the East. The only possibility would be if someone went through a portal that links one country between the other. That is probably how Carina got here and it just doesn't make sense at all. But seeing it makes the most sense of all it must be true. And so, there is just nothing else to consider. Before long, everything will just disappear.

Chapter Thirteen

Intricate little details line the room with different types of patterns and shapes. Carina walks around the room to see what it is like, just to see if she can find or spot something she might like. An antique wooden oak nightstand sits in the corner next to a twin-sized bed, and there is a lamp reflecting a bright array of light throughout everywhere. On the far side of the room there is an antique wooden dresser in fine oak finish. A closet sits to the left of the nightstand with the lamp. Right in front of Carina is another door and it leads to the hallways of the house. The door can lead to the rest of the house on the current floor and can be a secret way out.

Carina makes sure the door is closed behind

her and it is, so she feels the bed and it is firm to the touch. The sheets are freshly made and feel as warm as a steam iron. So, there must be more to explore, or it could be something else, and then there is the rest of the house. Carina takes off her shoes and lies down in bed. She is going to think about what to do and if she really wants to train for the next two years. It is for that reason why everything must be important and to control the rest of society. That is what is up with the rest of society.

Carina falls fast asleep and tries to get a good night's rest or at least some rest until she decides to wake up. That is something that can be quite a bite in the ass but it happens. There is little time to waste and everything must be perfect. Without that precision-to-approach quality, Carina would be doomed and so shall the rest of society. It could change at a moment's notice and could be the difference of life and death, but that should not be of any concern. Time itself is just a waste of patience and time is the only thing that Carina has on her side. Something must be done and it must be done soon or else there will be a catastrophe larger than life.

Three hours have passed and Carina starts to wake up. She explores the house to see what it has to offer and she winds up in the kitchen to see if there is anything to eat. Carina opens a lead-lined refrigerator to see if anything is left. There seems to be a smell of leftovers and containers. There seems to be a sense of a smell of rotten eggs, but that could be due to the refrigerator itself being old in nature. And that might be a better explanation for everything. Carina sees a microwave and warms it up. She looks for some type of silverware and finds it in a drawer. Then there is a beeping noise.

Carina takes out whatever she warmed up out of the microwave. She wants to know what she is eating but it seems like it is ground meat that looks like a mixture of venison, veal, beef, and buffalo, as well as a hint of distinct spices. That is all it seems to be, a mixture of different grounded meats, which is just plain crazy. But at least it is food and has some taste. It is probably some type of hunter's meat pie or something similar like that. The only good thing about this meal is that Carina enjoyed it and she sees what else there is to do. She goes to her bedroom to see if she can find any clothes. It is possible that she might have to borrow some from other houses or buy some from a store, but that is nothing to worry about, since she can always train in the nude, yet that might seem a tad or even too unsanitary. So, Carina will have to find something suitable.

So, there is just one thing, and it is just the tip of the iceberg. Carina opens up the walk-in closet and sees it already has many clothes inside of it. There are dresses, shirts, pants, skirts, and belts hanging from the shelves. There seems to be heavy-duty jackets as well with specific patterns and designs that are meant for some reason. There are vests hanging and then there are different types of training uniforms to train for the next two years. Shoes are lining the bottom of the floor, with high heels and sneakers outnumbering sandals and flip flops. A wide array of special combat boots exists as well. And then Carina closes the closet to see what the dresser has to offer. But there could be something else.

She opens the dresser drawers and sees the most expensive and intricate lingerie that she could have ever imagined. Everything is lacy and looks as though it costs too much. Another drawer has some bras in it, while the third drawer has some pajamas, nightgowns, and other privatewear. She closes up all the drawers and walks over to the nightstand to find a note that she has never seen before. It just appeared out of nowhere.

She reads it and it is the schedule.

Your schedule is as follows:

***0400 hours**: Wake up and then proceed to report to the basement of the church for training. Do not take a shower or change your clothes. Wear what you are* *currently wearing. In other words, report to all of the sessions in your pajamas. If you didn't wear any clothes to bed there will be loose fitting clothes in the gym waiting for you. All equipment needs to be kept sanitary.*

***0430 hours**: Begin training in the gym. This should take about one hour. You will begin early morning physical fitness exercises. You will complete five sets of twenty pushups, fifty jumping jacks, three sets of fifteen lunges, a mile run or eight laps around the inside of the gym, and fifteen planks all in that order. This should be inside of the gym. You will know where to go after you arrive at the church basement. There will be a lighted path.*

***0535 hours**: You should be done with all of your daily morning physical exercises. Leave the gym and follow the lighted path to the weight training room. Be at the weight training room by 0540.*

***0545 hours**: Begin your weight and strength training exercises in the weight training room. You will do this every other day to help your muscles rebuild. This should take about one hour. You can complete all of the exercises in any order you want, but you need to complete the required exercises to help you in your training. You have to complete five* *squats, one round of fifty leg presses, one set of three deadlifts, one round of thirty-five leg extensions, three rounds of ten leg curls, one round of fifteen calf raises, three sets of five on the bench press, three sets of fifteen pullups, one round of twenty-five pushdowns, and one set of seventy-five crunches. You should not worry about physical harm because there will be a spotter on the premises, and it could be a real person or a robot, so don't worry.*

0650 hours: *You should be done with all of your weight and strength training exercises at this time. Leave the weight training room and follow the lighted path to the obstacle course.*

0700 hours: *Begin the military grade obstacle course by following the exact route. You are expected to be done within two hours, but overtime you should be done in about twenty minutes. It might be tough at first but it is endurance training as well as to train your upper and lower body strength, speed, agility, flexibility, and strength in general. You might feel tired and need to take a rest but that is expected. You even might feel cramps. Don't worry about this, as this is normal. The military obstacle course consists of twenty-two obstacles and they are all in order, so there should be no problem with completing the course.*

The obstacles are as follows: (1) low wall, (2) cinderblock leaping, (3) rubble obstacle, (4) tunnel obstacle, (5) tire walk, (6) rope wall climb, (7) lateral dodging, (8) low rope climb, (9) ditching obstacle, (10) monkey bar swinging, (11) corridor obstacle, (12) balancing bridge, (13) swinging bar cross, (14) giant ladder wall, (15) crawl walk, (16) barrel run, (17) rope swinging, (18) belly roll, (19) apex ladder, (20) jumping through a window, (21) reverse climbing obstacle, and (22) steep slope jumping.

Everything is in that specific order, so you will be going from obstacle to obstacle after you complete each one. You might find some of the obstacles very easy but they will just get harder and harder because of possible fatigue.

***0905 hours**: You should be done with the obstacle course by now. You have a thirty minute break if you complete the obstacle course by now. If you completed it in less time you will have more than thirty minutes. If you do as expected, I expect you will have one hour of rest if you complete the course by 0800 hours. But if you complete it in two hours you will only have thirty minutes to rest.*

***0930 hours**: Your thirty minute break, one hour break, or over one break ends. You can eat breakfast now if you choose in the house. It will be waiting for you if you are hungry.*

***1000 hours**: You have free time for the next hour in which you can do anything you want. You can explore this town more or you can stay here. It is up to you but you can do whatever you want.*

***1100 hours**. Your one hour of free time is over and now you should take a shower or you should have taken a shower during your free time. Either way, if you didn't take a shower during your one hour of free time, do not take one now. You should now be in the church basement. Follow the lighted path and it will lead you to an Olympic size swimming pool. You will be doing swimming exercises that should take about an hour.*

You will be doing the following types of water or swimming exercises: (1) kickboard kicks, (2) pikes, (3) tic-tocs, (4) flutter kicks, (5) dolphin kicks, (6) a 200 meter swim, and (7) vertical swimming in order to prevent drowning by treading water.

***1200 hours**: You should now be finished with your water and swimming training workouts. Now, you* *should take a shower if you have yet to take one, but if you have already taken a shower you should take one more to get rid of any sweat or perspiration. It is vital for you to be in good shape.*

***1230 hours**: It is now time to eat lunch so you can be well nourished. Go to the kitchen and you will find something is ready for you to eat. You might find it tasty or you might find it awful. You will get used to it so there is always time.*

***1300 hours**: You have two hours of free time starting now, so use it wisely. You can explore the town more or you can stay in the house or look around the church. You could also take a nap. Just remember that you need to be in excellent shape.*

***1500 hours**: You will begin three hours of military training techniques. You will be required to put on specialized gear on. Report to the church basement and then follow the lighted path to the end of the basement. You will learn how to use precision guns but will also learn combative techniques in martial arts. During the first week of training you will use rubber ducks or fake weapons, just so you will get use to how to operate it without endangering anyone or anything. During the second week you will start using real weapons and will also begin combative* *training to better defend you. Each week for the first five weeks you will learn something new, and finally in the sixth week and forward you will have completed the basic training course. From the seventh week and forward you will start regular training and will use all of your abilities and knowledge you have learned during the six weeks of basic training. For weapons training you will use fake weapons first and then will be introduced to the actual weapons. The weapons that you will be using will be the following:*

M1911 Pistol
M1917 Revolver
M1 Garand Rifle
M1 Carbine Rifle
M1A1 Thompson Sub-Machine Gun
M1918A2 Machine Gun
M1917 Machine Gun
M1919 Machine Gun
M2HB Machine Gun
M1903 Sniper Rifle
Ithaca 37 Shotgun
Boys Anti-Tank Rifle
Mk 2 Grenades
M1907 Dreyse Pistol
TT-30 Pistol
MP35 Sub-Machine Gun

MP40 Submachine Gun
Maxim gun
MG34 Machine Gun
Flammenwerfer 35

Some of these weapons might be easy to use while others tend to be difficult. But you shall receive all the proper training. Remember though, you have nothing to fear, so you will have nothing to worry about. There will always be someone watching you just so you will not kill yourself.

Now, you shall also receive combat training, and from the second week you will learn chokeholds, how to rappel down a high wall, how to properly use military knives and engaging in knife fights, elbow strikes, Judo, knee strikes, head-butting, grappling holds, joint locks, punching, kicking, sweeps, takedowns, as well as throws.

1800 hours: *Your three hours of military training has ended for the day. You will proceed to the house to go back to the house to eat dinner. When you arrive there will be food waiting for you to eat. After you eat, you shall begin your free time. You are expected to take a shower after you eat to refresh yourself and to get rid of any dirt, grime, or dust from your body. It should only take you thirty* *minutes to finish eating and then you begin free time.*

***1830 hours**: Your free time begins. You should first take a shower and then you can do whatever you want to. Your free time lasts for about two and a half hours and you will have to be in bed by 2100 hours.*

***2100 hours**: You are expected to turn off all lights in your room. This is when your curfew begins. This time begins a mandatory lights out session. You should now be sleeping because you will have a long day when you wake up again. It is important for you to get a well night's rest so you won't feel fatigued or even stressed out.*

Other Information

Remember that your training is fundamental to your success here. In many parts of your training you will be taking part in a live but simulated environment in order for you to get a better feel of everything. You will always be watched during your training and for certain parts of your training you will have a spotter behind you, in front of you, or on the side just to make sure you don't get hurt. The spotter could be a robot or even a person.

Good Luck!

Carina read the schedule and believed it to be very rigorous but she thought to herself for a minute or so and then realized it might be hard but she could actually handle everything. It might seem like there was something to gain but it was as expected and it too shall always be important to understand why she must proceed. Carina places the schedule back on the nightstand and looks around again. She just wants to see what everything has to offer. It could be that there is something to do or it could be the start of a new world. Either way, there isn't much to do, or soon there will be a reason for nothing. It is just some sort of reason for nothing.

Since there is nothing to do, there must be some other thing to do. Carina decides to put on a pair of silk pajamas and decides to rest for the night so she can get a good night's rest and doesn't feel fatigued or stressed out. It is not curfew yet but it is about 1800 hours. There is still three hours left until curfew, but since she is beginning training tomorrow she might as well start resting early. By the time she wakes up from bed she will be well rested.

Chapter Fourteen

Morning has arrived and Carina is already out of bed. A loud noise can be heard throughout her room and it sounds like a bugle horn. It sounds like speakers are near and there are speakers near. Carina looks up and sees there are intercom speakers on the ceiling and it is loud. The speakers are playing a song on the bugle horn as a way to wake up Carina. It is the first call of the day and it is meant as a way to get her up if she isn't already up. It is a good thing that Carina is up but it can still be heard.

Carina wakes up and reports down to the basement of the church. She sees the lighted path and follows it and arrives at the gym. It is still early but the lights are on. There could be someone here or the entire system could be automated, but that is just crazy to think of.

Then, it turns exactly 0430 hours and there is someone announcing on the intercom for Carina to begin her physical exercises. She begins to start the physical exercises. Before long, she is having fun doing the exercises. She likes them so much that she forgets the time but she does complete every task that is required to do.

Time flies when you're having fun.

So, with time to spare, Carina goes to the weight training room to begin her weight and strength training exercises. She follows the lighted path and she is there. She opens the door and then there is a sound coming from somewhere. A voice can be heard over the intercom system. It tells her to begin where she wants to. So, Carina begins the exercises based on what is required. She is just having fun again and is over halfway done. She still has some stuff to do and is on the verge of completing those tasks on time. It is good to be ahead of the game and it is good to make sure she keeps track of time. But that is the problem, as when Carina is having fun she can't keep track of time since she is busy, and that really applies to the majority of the people as well. That is just something that has to be dealt with, but she is almost finished with what she has to do. At long last, she has finished the last task on the posted digital board in the weight training room. But just to make sure Carina completed all of the tasks in the weight training room, all of the equipment had a censor on it and every time she had actually finished a task, well that task will be listed as complete on the digital board. All equipment in the room was connected to the digital board and vice versa, and even the equipment keep tracked at how many rounds or sets Carina completed. There was just no cheating allowed, and since that was the case, it also allowed everything to be more precise in a way that knew just too much. There were no people in the room, just robots and androids. The machines even kept track at how many times Carina did a single or multiple sit-up or crunch. It was just that advanced that it was scary.

After a few seconds of completing the last task, Carina was told to go to the obstacle course. She followed the lighted path and it took her a matter of only a few minutes. It was exactly 0659.59 and the voice told Carina to begin. Carina tried to complete everything as fast as she could but was told by the voice to pace herself or else she will become just too exhausted. Carina took the advice and slowed down and soon she would be at the center of attention or for some other reason. It was just for that reason why it was happening. Fifteen courses in, Carina was already ahead of the game. She finished those first fifteen obstacles in a matter of twenty minutes. She had only seven more obstacles to complete and it might look as though she will complete them in a matter of time, yet it was just twice as hard because of all of the exertion that had to be done. But Carina stood firm and she was not going to give up. She paced herself again and was determined to finish ahead of time. Time would be on her side or so it is said.

After pacing herself, Carina is able to complete the other seven obstacles in just twelve minutes. It was a sign of everything going right. But with short breaks in-between, Carina completed everything in a matter of just forty minutes. And yes, even the obstacles each had their own tracking system. The tracking system in each obstacle was connected to the overall automated computerized system in this place, and this is how the voice knew everything was complete. It just kept track of everything. If that what it's going to take to defeat cheating then that is how it is going to be for the rest of the two years.

The voice on the intercom told Carina that she could begin her free time now. So, she went on her way and followed the lighted path back to her room and it seems she is way ahead of schedule. The time is now 0745 hours and Carina is back at her room. There is still plenty of time left and Carina can do anything that she wants to. She probably should be eating some type of breakfast by now and so Carina has to decide if she wants to eat breakfast now. So, she thinks for a brief few minutes and decides that she will indeed and checks to see if any breakfast is ready. Carina goes to the kitchen to see that there is a plate ready for her filled with everything that she could have imagined that she would have never of believed she would have actually been offered.

There is a plate on the dining table and it looks very colorful. On the plate are pieces of toast cut in half, two eggs over medium, scrambled eggs, bacon, sausage links, black and white pudding, hash browns, sautéed mushrooms, half of one pan-grilled tomato, baked beans, as well as bubble and squeak. There was also a big tall glass of freshly squeezed orange juice on the side as well as a cup of some English tea on a plated saucer. It is a full English breakfast and it is meant to help Carina replenish herself after she has worked out and exercise for so long. The breakfast is meant to make sure she is well-nourished and if she had nothing in her then she won't be able to handle the afternoon sessions.

Carina eats the breakfast and she feels quite satisfied. She finishes most of it and then puts the dishes in the sink but then she sees what looks to be a commercial restaurant dishwasher. She puts her dishes in a dishwasher rack and then closes the hood of the dishwasher so it will clean her dishes. It takes a few short minutes to clean and then Carina goes back to her room. She can do whatever she wants but she now believes it is time to take a shower. She undresses and goes to the shower. It is an automated system that times the entire for conservation purposes and so the water and or electric bill won't be so high. It is a way to manage money. But Carina follows a lighted path to the shower buck naked. The door closes behind her and she enters the shower. It just takes about ten minutes and Carina gets some towels and then walks back to her room to put some clothes in. It will be something else.

Carina arrives back at her room in the buff and puts on some fine silk clothes and undergarments that are imported from very fine areas. Since she has eaten and has finished early, it is free time, and the time is now 0815 hours. With Carina dressed, she now goes to lie in bed. She could explore the town as well but she needs to rest. She could be doing other stuff but she wants to rest for a few minutes or so. There is still about over two and a half hours until Carina needs to report back for training. But for the mean time she will just think and wait for a short while. It is just that simple. And there could be something else to do in the midst of a crisis.

It has been only fifteen minutes and Carina has decided to go back inside of the church to see what it has to offer. She might have missed something or she just wants to see the inside again. There is just that type of uncertainty there. Maybe she is interested in that map of Italy again. Maybe she could have missed something. There could be something more there and she could have missed it. It's probably not that all too important but she will just go there in order to see if there is a hidden message.

Carina follows the lighted path back to the church and she sees that it is the same. It is just a very constantly dark passage of tunnels and several secret passageways that Carina has to navigate back and forth each time. It is not a problem but there is some light but it is dim as a way to keep the atmosphere and the ambience. It is meant for that way but there is just no problem.

She arrives and is back in the church again.

Carina is now in the lobby and heads to the sanctuary.

Now in the sanctuary she can see the map of Italy again. There is no one here but her or so she thinks. The clergyman could be anywhere by now or he could be just in his office. That is not unusual but it is part of something else. Carina could be on the verge of finding something out. She sits down in a wooden pew to see if she can notice something that she hasn't seen before. There could be something invisible in the walls that only could be seen. It is surely something that has not been noticed before but there is the time about everything. So, there is just nothing to do and only a short time left. That is plenty of time to figure out what the map means. It is sort of an awakening for the rest of society if they ever found what was really going on. And no one should be surprised about that to the point of no return. Surely, something needs to be known further, but no one knows at what cost it could be.

Not a scintilla of evidence exists about any of the things that have occurred but it is just a quagmire or something like that. Carina has nothing to do for the next two years except to follow a rigorous and possibly strict daily routine and schedule. It is always expected she completes everything on time but it is expected and recommended to finish anything and or everything earlier in order to demonstrate endurance, strength, and agility. So, there is something to think about and it might be near. That is the only thing that is needed. But no one can suggest that for some of the other reasons.

Then she looks further and sees that she is in Italy herself. The clergyman shows up and tells her that she is in British occupied Italy where nothing is controlled by Mussolini. Although it is a very small area, Mussolini doesn't even know it even exists, as it is in the middle of nowhere but also only certain people are allowed here. So, in other words, this place is basically non-existent to everyone else. It is crazy to think of but that is how it is. Something is just crazy with nothing to even know about but it is just the test of time. She sees the time and although there is still enough left, she goes back to her room. It is just the sort of thing that is crazy. Carina is just going to have to wait.

Back in her room, Carina just sits down in bed and does nothing else. She stares at the wall looking to see what she can do. There is not much and it is just the test of time and the situation. Carina might seem as bored as possible but that should be normal or it shouldn't be considered at all. It is just something that is crazy and it is kind of important to do everything with rigor.

Looking at the time again, Carina decides to go back to the basement of the church where she will train more. She follows the guided path and arrives at a very large swimming pool.

A voice speaks over the intercom.

"Please undress completely and then follow the lighted path towards the locker room, as you will put on the proper clothes that will be waiting for you," stated the voice over the intercom.

Carina undresses completely and proceeds to walk toward the lighted path. A door automatically opens for her. Now in the locker room, Carina is then instructed by the voice to put on the Lycra in front of her and then put on the Mark V Diving Suit. She puts on the Lycra and then the heavy duty diving suit with all of the amenities, excluding the helmet because the voice told her not to put it on. Carina then is instructed to go back to the swimming pool area and she does, and is then told to get in the swimming pool by going into the shallow side. Carina goes in and sees that there are objects for specific tasks. The voice speaks again.

Carina is instructed to complete each task as mandated by the voice. One-by-one, the voice tells her what task to complete and she completes them with ease and not too much difficulty. Before long, she is done, and she is instructed to take off the diving suit and the Lycra in order to take a shower to get rid of any dirt, dust, grime, sweat, or perspiration. Carina takes off everything and showers, and then is told to put on loose-fitting clothes by the voice. Having put on what seems to be loose-fitting clothes, Carina goes to eat lunch.

Back in the kitchen, Carina arrives and sees a plate of lunch waiting for her. She eats up and does not regret anything. Carina goes back to her room for some free time. She has two hours but that probably won't last that long since she has to put on specialized clothes on for weapons training. She might leave early just to see what she must do. And it is the crazy type of situation that will never end. That is the type of crazy that always happens. But two hours are almost over and Carina decides to leave fifteen minutes early in order to put on whatever type of suit or clothing she needs to wear. Carina follows the lighted path again and ends up in the weapons and simulation room, and then a voice speaks and tells her to strip off all of her clothes.

Carina strips again, but it is for the better because of training with weapons. She is instructed to put on a female jockstrap, compression pants, a sports bra, a t-shirt, a bullet-proof vest, heavy-duty trousers, a heavy-duty jacket, insulated black socks, and heavy-duty boots. The voice tells Carina that everything is in front of her. Carina puts on everything as instructed and is then told to look forward.

A screen appears and now sounds can be heard. Carina is told to get a rubber duck weapon that is located to her left. Carina picks it up and is told her to use it. She starts practicing with it. But Carina is told that this rubber duck has the ability to change to different weapons by using attachments. She is told to keep practicing. It is still only the first week so Carina won't train with real weapons until next week. That is the thing that matters most: to properly prepare her to use fake weapons first in order to learn the ways of the real weapons.

Anyway, Carina is instructed to train with the different attachments for the rubber duck, and she is just having fun. Before long, it has been three hours and it was time for Carina to go back to the house and eat her dinner. She follows the lighted path back to the kitchen and arrives back at the house. Carina sees that a plate of food is waiting for her as well as some tea and a glass of water. She eats and then goes back to her room. From there she undresses in order to go and take a shower. With free time starting, she is taking her shower and is finished within a matter of minutes of getting in.

Since it is now free time, there is just the crazy sense of freedom from everything else. Carina sits down in bed to see what she can do and she sees some type of new device in her room. It was a television but Carina could care less. It was big and bulky and made from fine dark wood. She turned it on but it seemed to not work. So, Carina believed it was just something to decorate the room with. She went to bed after an hour or so and she was ready to wake up for the next day to come.

Chapter Fifteen

Three months have passed since Carina has arrived in British occupied Italy. Her training is coming along great and her arms are very muscular. Carina is able to do stuff that she hasn't been able to do before. Now she is able to lift over 500 pounds of weight as well as bench pressing that same amount. She is so muscular that she is just too strong. But that is not really important now. There is still a long time to go and Carina is busy training for a potential war. Everything is going as planned and it seems that it will only be a matter of time until she goes to war.

While Carina is currently training, there are other things happening as well. The corn field still looks brown and dead but there seems to be growth nearby. Wheat seems to be growing next to the corn field and that could mean anything. But lately, it has been raining heavy. It could be that time of the season again. Outside, temperatures are mild but cool with a slight chill and breeze. Carina is underground and is not able to see this. She might be able to hear the rain but that is it. It will just remain something that shall not be spoken of again. As a matter of fact there is just everything repeating over and over again. And that must be crazy.

There is all sort of crazy going on now and it isn't going to get any better.

Days go by and soon weeks and months.

Soon, another nine months has passed.

There is only a year left of training and Carina is doing well. She closely resembles the frame of a professional bodybuilder but she is still slim, sexy, hot, and prettier than the rest of society. It is all a case of how it was in the midst of time.

Her long brunette hair can be seen from a mile away. But seeing there is very few people here, then that is something interesting. There is just no stopping her.

Since a year has passed, there is not much that can be done but train some more. She has grasped her weapons well enough and everything seems like it is a breeze to her. Carina is just in the middle of nowhere or what seems to be a small rural or countryside town or village in Italy. But it isn't known to that many people. It only exists for some crazy reason or to fight against crazy reasons. Carina can always be found but nothing will ever be invaded here.

The town is just invisible to the rest of the world, or so it seems because it is quite beautiful to live there but there is just a sense of emptiness due to what can be described as abandonment.

The whole town is the size of Rhode Island but it is not known to the public but there is just the type of craziness. Nothing is for that purpose the will of the people.

Everything is just nonexistent but it is just for the purpose to save humanity. It is not even on the map and maybe that is to shield the town from any and all possible destruction. Only the British knows that it exists while the rest of the world has never even heard of it.

There is just peace and quiet.

Since everything is empty there is no need for panic.

Everything will be fine. And it will only be a matter of time until something happens.

Perhaps the town might appear but that is still a problem for the rest of the world.

In a way, this mysterious town is kind of like an asylum for Carina. But the only other person here is the clergyman.

As a way of hope, maybe more people will soon migrate, but only if they are chosen to defeat the enemy. It is just something that is none other than a case against opportunity. That is just the way it is and shall always be.

The corn field is starting to grow after one year of Carina training.

It is a sign of hope.

It is a sign of opportunity.

It is a sign of everything going right.

Everything should be changing soon.

Soon, there will be some other thing to do.

There is just a year left to go.

Carina is just going to have to wait and it too shall be enriching.

Since it is the halfway point, Carina is told of a celebration to be held in her honor by the clergyman due to her still being alive and surpassing a wide array of challenges and successes.

Carina follows the clergyman.

The clergyman takes Carina down into a small hallway.

It feels cramped.

But after a few minutes they are in a larger room.

There is no one there.

It is only her and the clergyman.

There is not much to do.

Since that is the case, there is no point to even hold this celebration, but Carina might be in for a surprise.

There could be something waiting for Carina but she won't know it yet.

It could be a problem or it could be nothing.

That is just what it might be.

If something is indeed waiting, then there is a surprise.

And if there is nothing there, then it is just one of those lonely celebrations.

The clergyman tells Carina to wait for a few short moments.

He probably went to get something. Carina does not know what to think. She just waits there for some reason not knowing what will happen. It could be a sign or something but that does not sound like it is.

It has only been a few seconds and there is something happening but Carina does not know what to think still.

There is still hope.

And then there is Armageddon.

All is a sign of hopelessness.

Carina is hoping for something better and a sign that she will end up in a better place for some reason or another. There is just no hope but there is still a sign to live. It has only been a few seconds and there is still something wrong. She does not think for the future but hopes for something not too crazy. It is a lifetime of servitude. As there is something, then there is not. Carina is waiting for the clergyman to get back.

It is hope but there is none.

There is fire and passion but none exists.

The endurance is nothing.

Carina is devoted to train because she is stuck here, but she is too naïve because she believes some clergy person. The clergyman could be dangerous but Carina doesn't care about that since she feels she can trust him. That is just stupidity at its best, as no one should ever be trusted.

After a minute, someone arrives.

Carina is facing in the opposite direction.

She cannot see who it is. She does not know who it is.

It could just be all a dream.

Carina could be even awake.

But it also could be a lucid dream.

Hope might be returning but it is still a time of no return.

Carina does not know if she can return to her old life back home.

She does not know if Sean or the bus driver is still alive. For all she knows they could be dead since she has not seen or heard from them in a year.

That could be fate or it could be a surprise waiting to happen in a time of cowardice and fighting. It is a time of desperation. That all hope fails is something of the future.

Then something happens.

A person caresses Carina's shoulders.

It could be a sign of change.

Or it could be a sign of someone going to attack Carina.

She likes that feeling.

It seems all too familiar.

Maybe someone from her past has come back to visit her.

All might not be lost.

But usually there is something else to offer.

Carina does not know what is happening.

Someone could be here to visit her or it could be just a ghost. It could all be for a lost cause but it is something else. She just doesn't know what to think or how to respond. Comfort is all she needs and soon it will be here. There is just something else to respond to and that might be a cause for alarm.

It is all too common for this to happen. It is all too strange that this is happening right now. There is simply nothing that can be done or else it shall already be solved. That is how something might turn out if it suddenly turned south. No one wants that to happen and it probably will. So there must be something else that could occur. Or else everything will be lost and no one would care. But this is certainly the result of progress, at least according to certain people. But at the expense of everyone else, Carina still feels that she needs to turn around to find out who is touching her shoulder.

It could be the bus driver.

It could be Sean.

It could be the clergyman.

It could be a ghost.

Or it could be wind.

At the worst end, it could also be a demon spawn from hell sent to warn Carina or even help her for some reason. That is certainly a crazy feeling due to the craziness of the situation. There could be a case against humanity but that is not how it works since Carina wants to know more. It is all a charade and the person could be a figment of her imagination. That is probably what it is after all. As for the rest of that, well it might be her imagining something or someone but it might be an actual person.

Carina wants to turn around but she doesn't want to ruin the surprise, if there is any. If she looks back it could just be a disappointment, if there was never really anyone there who touched her shoulder. She is just going to wait for some sign or for when the clergyman arrives back, but that could take some time and it wouldn't be wise to wait. But on another note, Carina is fascinated with some artwork that she sees hanging on the wall in front of her. It just seems too beautiful to ignore. The work is just breathtaking and it can cause anyone to enter into a trance. That is just the way life is.

She feels someone touching her on the shoulder again and it is the same feeling as before, and she just wants to know who it is.

Carina thinks it's someone familiar and of course she desperately wants to look, but she is just so fascinated at what she is seeing. It is just something that is so fascinating and beautiful that no one would ever want to look away. It is an addiction. That is how bad it is. It mesmerizes people into thinking that they are looking at something great. It might seem great but it could also be a trap. That is why Carina should stay away from things and other objects that don't seem what they look like.

Everything is always the constant distraction and that is nothing new. That will be something for the ages or as it seems in the midst of a crisis in the time of war. But war is near and it could be that there is something more sinister.

Carina must decide for herself if she is going to continue to look at the artwork. But the other and more worrying problem is why the person touching her shoulders isn't willing to walk around and face

Carina. It could be that he isn't willing to see her again or that it is just not even a real person who is looking at Carina. She could just be imagining some type of mirage that only appears if a person has not consumed food or water in a matter of hours after being stuck in the heat for too long. That is the crazy part about dehydration, as it makes most people to see things that are not there. It will only be a matter of time until the person touching Carina's shoulder reveal himself if he is willing to accept the risk and that is what it takes. That is how it is meant to be and how it is supposed to look like. There is just clearly an enchantment on Carina.

Then something happens.

Carina is somehow not responding to any of the responses. She is dead silent and her eyes are just centered on all the artwork. It seems like she is in a trance.

There is nothing that can be done unless there is a secret way out.

The touching of the shoulders doesn't even have a response.

Carina felt something but by then she was already in a trance. She could have felt something while in the trance but she showed no response to any stimulus.

There is possibly a way out of this trance if that is what it is.

Whoever this person is probably needs to step in front of Carina and do something. Maybe a kiss will work or he could at least wave his hand in front of her eyes. It might be crazy and unorthodox but it could work for some apparent reason. And then there is the case about who the person actually is. That is the sort of thing that is crazy. Well, it could work, and it just might have some claim of being the best choice that will do the job.

But there is still the apparent reason why Carina was brought down here in the first place when she chose to follow the clergyman. She was told to expect a surprise celebration, but there is no one here in this room except for a mysterious stranger that Carina might know and Carina herself. The clergyman could be in the building or he could be the surprise himself. Or the surprise could also be the person who is touching Carina's shoulder. Anything is possible but there is a difference between mystery and just being plain creepy.

It should be as expected that there is a case to be known and then investigated that will further the reason behind all of this madness and it is especially infuriating that nothing can be figured out. As the world seems to be coming to an end or at least it seems to be because of a lack of people, there is still this case about why Carina is even still here. She is just in a trance and so far the mystery man is not showing his face. His face is completely covered in a black mask and only a shadow can be seen on the floor for some reason. It seems like he is invisible for the time being or he is just a ghost. The clergyman might know who he is but maybe the clergyman did bring the mystery man here to this place. Maybe this person is Sean. No one even knows anymore except for maybe the clergyman and he is nowhere to be found.

Sometimes people must remain secret because of a certain situation. This could be a certain situation because it might be a special circumstance due to what is currently happening. That is how something turns out to be when something is wrong and something is dearly needed to stop that from getting worse in the future or now. Since Carina shows no signs of any response something must be done in order to take her out of the trance.

The mystery person finally decides to walk in front of Carina and all he sees is just a blank stare. All he sees is Carina looking forward without moving an inch. He tries to wave his hand in front of her eyes but that does nothing. And then he tries touching her face with his hands but that does nothing either. It could be a case of something happening. And then he does what thinks might work. He kisses her on the lips but to his surprise nothing happens. That usually works but not this time. It is surprising that kissing her did not work. But it could be something that is actually right in front of his eyes. It could be that Carina is just in a trance for some other reason. That means that something is strange and it is maybe a choice to consider of taking down something. It is a case of something familiar.

If nothing else works then it must be right in front.

It must be a sign of something blocking the brain cells of Carina.

Something is blocking Carina and it is just part of reality.

The mysterious person decides that he is going to take down all of the paintings in front of Carina for some reason. It could work but that could just be too much work to do. And if it doesn't work then it would be all for nothing. That would be a waste of time if found to be true so some type of compromise needs to take place. The mysterious person was close enough to see something that looked sinister but be then tried to look back.

Just about he is going to take one of the paintings down he sees a button that looks as though would solve everything.

He pushes the button and soon all of the great paintings start to fade. It is just crazy.

The room turns back to its natural state of

mind and color, white.

Then, Carina slowly comes back to life or is at least gets out of the trance. She could be faking all along and it could look real. And then there is some sort of surprise. There is something that might turn out to be a real surprise.

The mysterious man reveals himself. He takes off his mask and it is revealed to be Sean. Carina and Sean kiss passionately. And then the clergyman shows up with a cake, drinks, cups, snacks, and other things and items to celebrate.

Chapter Sixteen

Hundreds of miles away, something is about to happen soon. No one knows what it is but no one seems to care. After reuniting with Sean, Carina is now training side-by-side with him. Although, Sean already has experience with this type of training, it might just be better this way. There are only three months left to go. It has been a long wait but time too shall make it case. As it might seem, there could be something else. And then there is just some weird feeling.

A few miles away there is something bad about to happen. It could be an explosion but it could be something more sinister. But there is a feeling of unpleasantness. It is a time when there is no exact time but there is a time of when it will occur. Besides, a potential explosion could mean the beginning of war and something that Carina is waiting for. But there is no sign of war. There is no sign of anything being in a present crisis. There is only something that looks as though life is disappearing. It sounds fascinating but any sign of war is dangerous. Nothing is known about the soon to be war. It could be fictitious or even quite exaggerated. No one knows who's fighting who. And the clergyman won't spill the details because he is just so mysterious.

That is something quite to say the least but no one should be surprised. Carina should not wait for anything to spill out. It should reveal itself when time is necessary. As time might say, there is something to go upon but it is up to no one, and in this case there is a time of uncertainty and a time of craziness in which everything might lead to a disaster. That is something to always worry about. It isn't about that being a way out, it is about not finding what is wrong. Carina just needs to continue the good fight or whatever she is even doing.

Since there is only three months to go there is only one thing that seems to be clear. There is a sign that something is going to happen because of events that are already set into motion. There is already an out of control situation and it is getting worse by the second. It seems nothing will stop it and even if they can stop it or engage in the war, Carina and Sean will grow tired. There is just no strategy until one is actually revealed. It might seem that the war is a lost cause but no one knows that. Carina only knows she is going to fight in a war because of what the clergyman told her. She has no reason to fight in the war but she had no other choice. It seemed like nothing was ever going to happen. Carina could be training for some sort of prize or something else but she has no clue what she is training for. That is just something that needs to end.

A cascade of events has already started.

Carina does not know what will happen.

The clergyman might know.

And so could Sean.

But Carina is kept in the dark.

Why is it that she knows nothing about anything?

Everything happens for a reason and that is the day of the century.

As events are made even clearer there is only one thing certain. There is only one thing that needs to remain true to anything. The war is almost here and she needs to fight hard. It will only be a matter of time until something happens. It will be a disaster if it isn't stopped in time. It will be a war to end all wars and it will eliminate everything in its path for no apparent reason but insanity. That is a case of why Carina must stop this unknown war and it should be applied to the rest of the world in order to demonstrate something good and peaceful. Carina must decide now if she wants to take on this war but with no other options, war is inevitable. It is apparent war will happen and it might be soon but it could already be beginning due to certain events that already have taken place. Without those certain events taking place there might be no war, but that is something that has yet to be revealed to anyone. There is just no other choice and Carina must fight in the war. There is just one problem and that has to do with Carina. She doesn't know how Sean found her. Carina thought Sean was dead since she did not see him or the bus driver after arriving at a resort. This Sean character could be an imposter or even someone sent from hell to ruin her plans. It could all be a ploy to end the world. But there is nothing that can be known yet. As it might seem, everything is just a disaster to begin with and it should be regarded as such because only certain people are kept in the loop about what might happen. That means there could be a cover-up nearby.

It could lead to a global catastrophe and there would be all-out chaos, yet no one wants that to ever happen because of what might happen next. And then people will start to panic because they don't know what to do but since everyone seems to be hiding then no one should even worry about anything. But there is also the threat of violence and destruction and that would be something far worse than anything else. It needs to be avoided at all costs because if there is even the slightest chance or appearance of disaster and violence, then everything will disappear into the near oblivion. As panic and chaos ensue, there will be nothing left. If people are alive they will be trapped for the sole reason of not being able to escape or due to the reason of not wanting to abandon their homes or hiding places. Surely, someone or something will be able to help them, but it will only be a matter of time until someone is able to succeed and stop the war, yet the war has yet to begun. So there is no need to panic and there is no reason to think of something sinister or bad. There is just this waiting game of uncertainty as a way for something sinister to happen. But that will not be the most horrendous of what might happen, No, that will be when something actually happens, and by that, it is what a person is most afraid of because of what might make them laugh. It will just be the sort of reason to escape.

Since the war has yet to arrive there is still hope for everyone and everything. But Carina cannot stop the events that will lead to the war because the war needs to occur. Without the war there might not be any peace and without peace there will be no end to war. It just needs to happen because chaos is just a way out and is always necessary in order to prove that something is always correct. Carina might be the only person not to know about what will cause the war. She doesn't even know why the war will occur. It is just something she knows she will have to face. She has been training for it during the last twenty-one months and it will soon come to an end. That is just how it is supposed to be.

As Carina knows no more about anything about the war, it is time for nothing more. There will be a new wave of events that will be happening soon and it will cause something more severe. It will be even more deadly than anything else. Chaos might be one thing and disaster and violence might be another, but terrorism is next and it will proceed to ruin and run the next society. That is why war must occur and that is why certain events must be escalated in order to protect the future.

There is no way out.

Everything will lead to disaster.

It will just be a matter of time.

And then suddenly, there will be nothing left.

Such events might cause sorrow but Carina is training for them. She might not know what she is even fighting for but she is willing to fight to the death or at least until she has given it all she has. It is just the sort of thing that should be encouraged and it too shall be known. Carina knows nothing more and needs to know only the basics. It can be dangerous out there and that is no place for a wimp. There will just be a time until it is necessary to find out the truth about why this war needs to occur. It is almost time to end the disaster and chaos about what is going on and it too shall be enough to escape. Hopefully, the war might be safe, but that is just no hope for anything to think about. War is imminent and the events leading up to it might have already occurred. That could just be a disaster waiting to happen.

Since there is only three months left, there is still some time to train. But all of a sudden, something is going to happen today and it will just make things worse.

About three miles away a noise can be heard but since this place is soundproof no one can hear it yet it is being monitored by no one. There seems to be a shaking in the earth. Everything seems to be moving and nothing is staying in place. There is just this noise shaking everything. Soon, everything will be impacted and people will become part of the problem. There is no chaos or panicking as of now but it might soon happen in a few moments. And that event that will soon to happen will not be the ground shaking because the ground is already shaking. To be clear, there is just something else.

The shaking is just growing. The earth is just colliding with each other. Grumbling can be heard and it is getting louder by the second. It seems like it is an earthquake because of what is happening. There is just this constant rumbling of the earth. It must be moving and that is something to worry about. There is just one thing to worry about: safety. It is not clear if Carina is safe or not. But there is a clear and present danger elsewhere that is in a constant bind if there will be any life remaining. And then a crack starts to appear in the middle of a road in a small countryside neighborhood. It is a small crack, but by each minute it just grows larger and larger. There is just no stopping it but it is just a part of it.

Each minute it grows there is something more that is going to happen. Soon there will be nothing left and that could be the end of Carina and everyone else, but that is just something she has to deal with. On the other side of town though, Carina doesn't feel a thing. It is though that nothing is happening to the church or the underground facility. Nothing is even happening to the home or even on the property it sits on. It seems that everything in close proximity to Carina is safe and that means nothing bad will happen to her. That is fine enough. But there is just something else that needs to occur because it hasn't occurred yet. It needs to be something soon but nothing bad should happen just because it needs to. That just seems strange since usually everything is affected. But on the bright side, Carina is fine and doesn't need to worry that much unless she goes further into town. And so far she does not plan on leaving this part of town in Italy controlled by the British yet. But, she will have to leave in the near future, yet hopefully everything will be fine by then.

The rumbling and shaking finally stops after a few short hours but there is something to be noticed. It is without a doubt the worst earthquake in the history of the world. There remains a very long and wide crater in the middle of the road for nearly a mile and no one is in sight. Soon, people who are hiding might show up and attempt to move. It is a sad day but there is nothing that can be done. It is all a lost cause and it remains that way.

There is just one month left to go and it seems that everything is just not changing. There are just more tragic events that are happening, and maybe that is part of the war or part of the certain events that will cause the war. Time will tell but the war or whatever it is will be here soon. There is just something to wish for and that time is now or as it seems to be in the way of the problem. That will surely help the war or as it seems to be a solution to everything. Yes, that is exactly what it is. The war is the only solution that will lead to better prosperity, freedom, and success, or as it seems to cause the chaos of disaster and violence in the midst of civility. That is just the way it is and it shall always be that way.

Carina is just busy training for one longer month with Sean. The clergyman only shows up when needed and he is such hard to find. That should be the end of nothing but the earthquake has left a mess near Carina about three miles away. Now, with there being a giant crater for nearly a mile, there is no knowing where it will lead. The giant crater could lead to the actual war or it could lead to someplace else. It is just a big and utter mystery. Surely it will lead to some type of place that will lead to something important or maybe it is just a diversion. That will surely be the end of the world but if someone closes the crater it will cost too much and maybe it will be good it someone doesn't close the giant crater because that might lead to an unexpected disaster that will cause certain events to cause chaos, disaster, and violence. But it is surely a concern.

Everything just seems so tense and it is for that reason why a war is actually coming in order to once again have peace. That is just the actuality of what is going to happen and it too shall be the rest of the land to be happy again. But with everything going on there is surely a price to pay, and that too might lead to the creation of a war that doesn't promote peace. That is just crazy, a war to end all wars in order to promote and maintain peace, that is just silly. But it can work and it will.

As it all seems that is the place to be and it is the craziest situation that someone will ever be in due to the situation of the moment. But that is just the new beginning. But it will lead to something more sinister to the end of the world and that too shall be in the wide array of a false hope. That is just how it is not supposed to end.

Nothing is lost to the cause of this future war unless it has already begun and if it has actually begun already then that war that is already in progress is the event or one of the events that will cause this war that will end all wars.

No one even knows but that is fine since it is just a rush of time.

It is the end of the day for now and that too shall pass.

Chapter Seventeen

Days, weeks, and months have finally passed, and there is only a little while to wait. Today is the last day of Carina's training and she has progressed well on her journey. Sean is something else because he has already taken this training course. But Sean just needs to brush up on certain skills. That is just as expected. Carina's progress is nothing short but a miracle but anyone who takes on such a rigorous type of military training course over a two year time period is surely a great person. That took on such a toll on her body, organs, and muscles but she was willing to take on something hard in order for the world to maintain and promote peace once again. It is just something new.

Since this is the last day, activities are going

to be different, and Carina is just going to complete the morning obstacle course and the physical training. It is still early but it has yet to reach the wake up time for Carina. She is still sleeping. It is almost time for her to wake up.

Carina wakes up to the usual bugle horn alarm over the intercom. She goes to the basement of the church and is greeted with happiness. She is ready just to complete the last day of her military training but it is not yet known of what is going to happen. But that should be revealed quick and fast for the purpose of what needs to take place.

That is for certain but she will learn soon and probably during breakfast or after she completes the military obstacle course. Either way, she will be briefed in a matter of minutes and that too shall be a surprise for the rest of the world. And if there is any certainty, everything shall be revealed because there is always a military plan of action to decide what must be done. That is how it has been done and that is how it will be done for the rest of existence. In just a matter of time, Carina will be ready to face the wrath of war or she will create the war.

It is almost over and everything too shall have a place.

Just now, Carina is completing her early morning physical exercises and she is almost done with them for the final time. It only takes her a total of twenty-five minutes to finish everything. It is such a very outstanding accomplishment. She has some extra time and she can rest for a bit. Carina rests for a few short minutes before she starts the obstacle course for the last time.

In a matter of few minutes she gets up and goes to complete the obstacle course. Now waiting for the intercom, she just waits patiently. At last, the voice over the intercom tells her to begin the obstacle course for the last time. She completes it in just a matter of ten minutes, which is a new record for some sort of reason. Carina is congratulated and is told to go to the house to eat breakfast.

Carina eats breakfast in the house and then she goes to her room.

In her room she finds a note on the nightstand. It is probably a military plan or something but she reads it.

Carina,

You have come a long way since you began your training here. It was a pleasure to help guide you in order to succeed in the future. You have clearly demonstrated that you are ready to go to war. It is very important that you listen to me so you won't get lost in all of this. Later on in the day I will be meeting with you. From there, the strategy will be discussed about the war and how you will get there.

If you don't already know, we are in a small rural community in the countryside of Italy, but that part is not important. The new information is that the place we are in can't be accessed by any outsiders. While you are able to be here, that is because you are supposed to be here, as you were chosen to fight in this war. You have all the skills and stamina to make it and will be an important asset in fighting in the war.

The purpose of the war will be described when we meet to discuss the strategy. But you might also have some questions. You might be wondering where all of the people went. Do not worry about that since most are in safe hands. While you might have saw people burning in buildings and houses back in South Dakota, those were not real fires. They seemed to be real but nothing ever turned to ash. It was like magic or a miracle from God. But the buildings never burned down because they had specific insulation installed in the building themselves to protect the structure and to prevent them from burning to the ground.

As it seems, the fires were intentional and were set by the enemy. But the enemy didn't know of this special insulation that was installed throughout the United States of America and many parts of Europe. It would be a surprise to them that the people in all of those buildings didn't die. All of those people in those burning buildings are safe now and they have been rescued. You might have seen mysterious people going into the burning buildings. Those mysterious people who were dressed in all black are our people sent by the allies and our people to save as many people as we can.

We prepared for everything before the enemy ever started to engage their plans. We knew what they were going to do because we had spies within all of their organizations and agencies. We know when the enemy will strike and we know their battle plan. We also know that they are getting ready soon to attack the United States but they might be delayed if some event occurred. The enemy was supposed to attack years ago but they got delayed by the certain events that blocked them from starting the war.

Every time a new event is created there is just a delay in their attack. And they must revise it, but then a new event comes along and blocks that. We are the ones behind that blocking by implementing those specific events. As for the people you saw, they are all safe and they are protected. You won't see them until the war is over. They are perfectly fine in a secure location. They know that a war is underway and want to stay safe. All of the people did not know what was going to happen to them and they were afraid when they saw the fire in their buildings. It was a natural response for anyone to be scared but they all accepted that they were going to die. So far, the only success that the enemy has had was very minimal. They tried to burn down buildings but did not succeed. It seemed that they believe their plan to burned down buildings in the United States was a success because the enemy thought a burning building would actually burn down and turn to ash and rubble. They were wrong because we protected those buildings.

The enemy doesn't know about us as a unit but there are many of us. You and Sean are only some of the many that have been trained by this elite unit here in Italy.

Sean has already left to go to the war and has been briefed beforehand. But when you reunite with him you will be working with many other members of our elite unit here from Italy. Some are actual people while others might be androids or robots. It is very important to distinguish a robot, android, and a person from each other and the differences shall be mentioned or highlighted in your briefing later on in the day.

Moving on, you will also find in your closet that your belongings have been packed for you in a small but deep enough suitcase. Everything that you need to wear has been placed in that suitcase but when you go to your new barracks you will have more clothes to wear. You will also find a duffle bag filled with weapons secured in their cases. You will bring this with this as well. But before I forget, there is also the required ammunition in that duffle bag as well, and each type of ammunition is in its own box labeled with the name of the appropriate gun or weapon. It is in very safe conditions as everything was perfectly placed in a secured setting. The duffle bag is meant as a tool to just combine all of your weapons and ammo in one so you don't have to carry too much stuff. But you might find the duffle bag quite heavy, yet you should be used to that since it will be no sweat for you to carry or handle it.

On a more positive note, you should do fine in the war. You have been trained properly and you will be well aware of your surroundings. The simulator has covered all of the environments that you will face or encounter during the war.

I will see you after lunch or 1300 hours in order to brief you on your new missing, when you will find out who you are going to fight against and learn everything about the war. Anything else that I didn't already explain will be explained then.

See you later!

Carina put the note down and thought for a second. But she realized she would be departing for an unknown war. In the meantime, Carina will see what she can do since she has additional free time due to it being the last day of her training. It is just as simple as that. She must decide what she will do but she must remain steadfast. That is what the goal must be or else it will be all for nothing. As it seems there is just some sort of precautionary events to calm the nerves but it is quite too early to eat lunch. And since that is the case, it seems Carina can only lie down in bed and think for a little bit. Yet that is highly questionable because it just is.

Carina decides she will take a shower now. It is better late than never.

She slowly slides down her pajama pants and then pulls her pajama blouse over her head. She walks completely naked to the shower. Her slim built body but sexy and muscular physique can be quite very satisfying to anyone. Her tight but slim ass matches her body perfectly, while her near-perfect round and fluffy 37DD breasts make her look amazing. It is just an all-out fantasy. Her long and straight brown but dark black hair is cut to a normal length and can be seen covering her breasts. Slender but muscular arms and legs are just another sign of her gorgeousness. It just seems like Carina is just the best girl to meet but it is part of life.

Arriving at the shower, Carina caresses the soap with her right hand and rubs it all over her body to cleanse herself. Soap suds are everywhere and it is just a sight to see. Water dripping down her body is like heaven. It is just so clear cut. There is just a pleasure of sensational stuff. It is nothing that has ever been seen before.

Slowly dripping down her body, from her sides and all the way down to her thighs, it is just fantastical to see it. The water has a pleasant feeling and it is like liquid gold. Her entire body is covered in soap, a view that can't be distorted. All 6'2" and 175 pounds of her body was completely soaked. It seemed as though it could only happen in a dream but it is real life. She is just a tall gal and is extremely gorgeous. Boys would be happy to see her completely naked but there are just none around. Sooner or later something will happen and it will be a mistake. Carina, on the other hand, is rinsing off all of the soap and suds from her sensual but pleasant and gorgeous body and structure. It is such an adrenaline rush but that is now out the window.

Such an exciting time for existence but that is not what it seems. Nothing is exciting about a war but it is necessary just to survive. That is how it is and how it will always be. Carina might enjoy war sooner or later because she is just used to the rigorous but tough training she completed over the past two years, and it takes a warrior to have those fine skills of being able to tough it all.

She turns off the water and opens the curtain

to grab a towel. Carina dries herself off and then walks off without anything on her back. She is walking back to her room and encounters the clergyman and he sees her walking back. "Nice body you have there; you should keep it that way because it suits you well and you have come a long way to fight in the war," said the clergyman. "Thanks, I really appreciate it, and I make sure boys are attracted to me," Stated Carina in the nude. "Well, it should, because boys will be stupid if they don't find you attractive," stated the clergyman to Carina. "It will be their lost," said Carina. "Yes it would, and see you after lunch," said the clergyman to the nude Carina.

It wasn't a strange conversation at all. Carina just embraced it. She didn't feel ashamed that she was naked. She didn't feel ashamed of being seen naked by another person. She did not feel ashamed of being naked. She did not feel embarrassed. Carina had no worries at all. She liked her body and believed that the clergyman was right about it. There was no negative experience felt between her and the clergyman. It just seemed that both of them embraced positivity. And that is just crazy talk. It could have been awkward but there wasn't anything embarrassing about the situation to begin with. Nothing like that even bothers her and so Carina arrives back at her room to get dressed but finds a note. She reads the note and it tells her that the clothes she is going to wear today are already on her bed. She looks at the bed and sees that the clothes are at the end of the bed. There was a G-string thong, tap pants that match the thong, a matching sports bra, a pair of sheer silk stockings, black pants, a sheer white blouse, black silk socks, a pair of combat boots, as well as a heavy-duty military jacket. It seems that it was all there.

One-by-one, Carina puts on her clothes. She puts on the G-string first, followed by the sports bra, then the tap pants, and then finally the sheer white blouse. Since it is still early, she is going to lie down in bed for a bit. It seems like it will just be too early to put on everything else.

A few hours have passed and Carina gets up and puts on her stockings, the black socks, the black pants, the shoes, and finally the heavy-duty military jacket, all in that order. It is now lunch time and Carina goes to eat lunch. She does not know what to expect since it's the last day. If it is the usual fare then it is worthwhile but if it's something new, well Carina would be eager to try it. Carina arrives at the kitchen to find it is some type of fancy meal when she looks at the plate. The lunch for the day is what she had at the hotel near the US-Mexico border. It was such a sign to see and experience. But there were also some drinks as well. There was a glass of sparkling water as well as an alcoholic beverage mixed with vodka, whiskey, rum, brandy, vermouth, gin, rye, hard cider, tequila, absinth, sugar for sweetness, ice, and a lemon and lime slice on the side for tartness. Carina didn't know what to think about that weird cocktail but thought she would drink up. She eats her food first and then will drink the weird beverage.

After finally devouring her meal, she takes one more sip of the water, and then she will take a sip of the cocktail. Carina takes a sip and likes it. She can taste a hint of fine liquor along with some pureed fruit such as strawberries and apples. She enjoys it so much that she can't get enough of it. Anyways, she is done with her lunch and all she can do now is to wait for the briefing.

Ten minutes later, Carina is still in the kitchen waiting for the clergyman. One minute later, he finally arrives.

The clergyman speaks.

"Here is the briefing for the military strategy."

"You will depart in one hour from now and you will bring with you what you're wearing on your back, the suit case, and the duffle bag."

"This will be a comprehensive overview so

remember what I say."

"First, we will begin with the differences between robots, androids, and humans. This might take some time but prepare to take some notes and or ask some questions if you find it necessary. Androids look like humans but they're not. They are part human and part robot. All of their organs have been replaced with electronics and artificial organs made of the finest metals that money can afford. Although they are no longer fully human, they still have their human brain but with some modifications done to enhance their intelligence. As said before, their internal organs have been replaced by electronic parts made of metal yet also rubber. All of their skin still remains their original human flesh. Their eyes are still the same when they were originally human but now contain metal parts and advanced electronics for support and to be able to develop artificial intelligence so they can be smarter."

"Now, for robots, they are completely made out of bare metallic metal. They don't have any flesh or skin to them and that can either make them hot or cold depending on the weather. Robots have no organs and no brain. They are fully-electronic and have artificial intelligence. That means no brains and or internal organs. Their eyes are fully

mechanical and so is their entire body. It is just a bunch of moving and non-moving parts all held together by metal, rubber, and plastic. Robots are hard to the touch because of what they are made out of, unlike androids which are soft to the touch because of them having human flesh from being a former human. You will immediately know if you encounter a robot."

"Humans, on the other hand, are completely soft to the touch like androids. But humans have real life organs. You and I are humans so you should know that already. But moving on the differences between humans, robots, and androids—humans are the only ones who can consume and eat food and beverages—which means that androids and robots solely rely on energy from electricity. Androids and robots do not need to eat or drink because it is not part of their system. But since we are on this topic you will be fighting on the lines with them, so you should just know the differences between robots and androids, as they are different."

"Moving on to the actual war plan in which you will fight in the war. You will leave one hour from now and then you should arrive safely at your destination. You will have to blend in with the crowd and make sure you can handle it. When you leave,

you will go outside of the church. When you arrive outside you will see a flash of light within three minutes. Ignore this flash of light as it is just a distraction by the enemy because they are trying to try to stop the blocking of them trying to win the war. They are trying to stop all of the blocking because they don't know about it but due to the fact they want to always know why they are not getting anywhere. To proceed, you will see a second flash of light and you will enter it and it will take you to the proper place."

"It will take three minutes to arrive at your intended destination. You will be going to Berlin and will remain at that location until your group is supposed to leave. You will be assigned to the Red Team when you arrive there. When you leave with the Red Team, you will be then divided again to Company 5. From there you will be divided into the Second Platoon. And then from there, you will be divided again into the 1st Army Squadron. There are other military units but you will be assigned to the 1st Army Squadron after all of the paperwork is finalized."

"Two days after you arrive, your squadron will be departing Berlin and will fight in the front lines in Poland. Your commanders will decide from there what will be done. However, you squadron will be

fighting with other squadrons from different teams and companies. Your goal in Poland is to engage the enemy when the least they expect it. Your squadron will build a trench in Warsaw in order to barricade yourselves from all sides. Then, in a few days, you will leave with your squadron to be transported to the capital of Belgium. When arriving in Belgium, you will be re-grouped into the Grey Team and then be placed in the 7th Squadron of the First Company. It is suitable to tell you that you will depart with your new Squadron to fight in Germany. However, you shall be kidnapped by someone known as Oscar Victor, and he will smuggle you to Switzerland in order to take you to our secret operations center there. Don't worry about Oscar, because he is with us."

"You will then meet your actual squadron at our secret military operations center in Switzerland, and you should also know that the previous military units you were assigned to were enemy units. You had to gain acceptance into the enemy lines in order to fool them so that Oscar Victor could track you down, and so that you could be with our military unit of the highest caliber. You will spend a few days at the bunker here before you shall depart for a secret and classified location."

"After you arrive at the secret location, you will be serving as a military adviser to the front lines of our soldiers. You shall also join as a soldier but you won't fight regularly, only at off-peak times, which is when there is a slow down during the day and into the night. It is expected that you guide your military units to the proper areas as described by the high command in the daily update letters. Each day is different and you shall be briefed before you head out to the next scouting location."

"You will come face to face with the enemy and you will have to fight in the front lines whenever you deem it necessary, as in when it is getting bad out there and you need to aid your fellow soldiers. Now, there are different possible outcomes."

"Outcome One: We win and then you shall be back in South Dakota to begin your senior year of high school at Prep Stone Academy. You will know about what has happened but your classmates won't. Sean will know and so would I. The enemy will be obliterated off the face of the Earth. And then it will seem like it was only a memory of your past."

"Outcome Two: The enemy will win. In this outcome, our team will be endangered of being captured but we won't be captured, just the other

allied units. If this is the case, it is because the enemies outsmarted all of the allies. It was the plans of the allies that caused the war to be lost. And if this happens, then the enemy will create an alternate universe dystopian and totalitarian in nature all around the world."

"Outcome Three: This is the last possible outcome and in this outcome the enemy will call to a truce in which the enemy will surrender. However, if this is the outcome to occur you should be aware that the enemy is just fooling the allies. The enemy has actually found a way to go back to the past in order to change certain events so that everything shall return to the medieval ages. In this outcome, most everyone will be peasants or commoners and certain members of the enemy will be part of everything. This would possibly be the worst potential outcome because everything will be reversed back to simplistic times when someone with high power could determine if you died or survived. There will be cruel punishments and public squares, but that is not the bad part. The bad part is that justice will be corrupt because only the most wealthy and powerful shall win. While the medieval ages were a time of prosperity for some or many, in this alternate time line it too shall be a dystopian society and there will just be lots of wars and battles."

"It is impossible to determine which outcome will happen but just be aware of everything. You will have to blend in. I will be watching from the side lines and from the secret operations center. Good luck to you and your unit."

The clergyman left and Carina went back to her room to stay for a few minutes or until it was time to depart for the second flash of light. With about ten minutes to go, Carina gets her suit case and grabs her duffle bag and then leaves the house in order to go back outside. It takes a few minutes but Carina is now in front of the church. She will just have to wait for some type of flashing light or a flash of right. It could transport her to the necessary place but it could take her to an alternate time line. Although, Carina did not know what it will be, but it should take her to the place she is needed the most: the enemy lines in order to blend in and learn their secrets. It will be something that is skillful and necessary.

There are still a few minutes left and Carina does not see anything. Time will tell when something shows up. There is just a smell in the air that seems like burning brush and it feels very close to the house and church where Carina is currently at. The sky is just normal with not a cloud appearing. It is all a clear sky with nothing but the clearest weather. All seems well and it just reflects the day of the year or a very pleasant day. It is surely something Carina might never encounter again but the outcome that is bad will probably happen.

Carina must fight hard and must blend in well with the enemy lines. She needs to feel at home and not uncomfortable. If she was found out by the enemy to be their enemy, then something bad will happen, but if it does happen everything will be compromised in a bad way. The enemy will use her as a sex slave and she might submit, but she will persevere through the entire time. There might not be any hope but there will need to be. It will all be for a purpose and that too shall be courageous.

The first flash of light appears and it just sits there. There is no knowing what will happen to it and it seems like a disaster is waiting to happen. It is just a menace and that is not good. Something will soon be in the works to happen but maybe it will be for the better of society. The first flash of light disappears into thin air like it was never there. It seems the enemy has lost this round and might lose in the end but they could actually win and change history for the rest of eternity. That should not happen but if it does then it will be the end of civilization.

After a few short moments, Carina sees a

second flash of light. This is the light that Carina must enter or else all hope is lost, as something bad might happen. Or it could all be a trap for some other type of reason. Carina enters into the flash of light and from there she awaits what will happen to her. It will just be an adrenaline rush.

Chapter Eighteen

Flashes of light spit her out into a place of disarray. It all looks hazy with smog or fog. It is not a nice day but it is apparent something is in the works. Carina is trying to find the exact location but she does not know what to do. Then, all of a sudden, something appears right in front of Carina's eyes. She is in Berlin now and it took some time for time to catch up. It was just part of it. In front of Carina, she sees a building and it resembles military barracks or headquarters for the enemy. Carina walks forward and she is greeted with open arms. Her unit commander assigns her to the Red Team after he saw and looked at the paperwork.

Carina is then assigned again to Company 5

and is told that she will be part of the Second Platoon and will then be split into the 1st Army Squadron when he submits the paperwork for approval. It is surely a case of luck but the clergyman was correct all along in everything. She just needs to relax and not risk being exposed. It is all a game and it should be noted as that due to something evident.

The unit commander comes backs and he tells Carina that everything was finalized and approved. It will take a while but Carina must fit in. Carina is also told in two days' time her unit will depart for Poland in order to fight the enemy. But the enemy she will be fighting is the allies, yet she already knows that so it shouldn't bother her.

Time is a crazy thing but Carina has nothing to worry about. It will soon be all over and it will be the center of attention again. However, there might be a surprise waiting for the rest of society. It will be the ultimate betrayal but no one is even listening to their commanding officers probably.

Carina is told to go to the Red Team military operations center. She is told that it is only one block away and from there she learns from the commanding officer that she will be sorted according to the just recently filed and finalized paperwork that was now approved. She takes her suit case and her duffle bag outside and walks for one block to enter what looks like a prison camp. There is just nothing but a metal fence surrounding the entire perimeter of the building with sharp razor wire on top as well as near the bottom of the fence. That's probably to make sure that no one gets any ideas about deserting or just to make sure the enemy does not try to break in and then kill the enemy.

Carina approaches the gate and she shows the security guard the identification card given to her by a commanding officer. The guard opens the gate and lets her in. The gate closes behind her and then the door to the actual building is opened for her by some other security guard. She is greeted by another one of the commanding officers and is told to strip down in front of him. She obeys as she doesn't want to cause a scene. Carina is then told that stripping just to her bra and underwear is not enough because she needs to be completely naked. Carina obeys the commands again and is given a new uniform.

She puts on the new uniform only to find out that there is no bra, underwear, or other type or form of undergarments. It is just the standard issue military uniforms for females of the enemy troops. Now since that is finished, Carina is ordered to go to Company 5 of the Red Team, which is right down the hall. Carina goes down the hall. She arrives there and is then told just to stand at attention for a few short moments. It takes about fifteen minutes for another commanding officer to come out and he tells her to drop the suit case and duffle bag. Carina drops the suit case and the duffle bag. The commanding officer tells her that she will be sorted into the Second Platoon of the 1st Army Squadron. The commanding officer then tells her to go down the hall and to the left and to pick up the suit case and duffle bag while looking at her nipples poking out of the military uniform even though there is a built-in bra and she is also wearing the standard military jacket as well.

She just does not care.

Carina goes down the hall and to the left with the suit case and duffle bag in tow. She sees that she is nearing her location because of a sign. She arrives at the location and is greeted again by another military commander. She shows him her identification badge and is told to go to her barracks. Since she is only the second female to be part of this specific unit she is told she will have separate living quarters from the men, as the enemy feels it is inappropriate for women and men to mix in the same barracks. Carina is also told that her living quarters will be right across from the men's barracks of the Second Platoon of the 1st Army Squadron but also there will be one other female soldier staying there. Carina does not care who she bunks with and she goes to the female living quarters of the Second

Platoon of the 1st Army Squadron. Carina meets her roommate and she has the same exact features as her. It could be an exact copy of Carina. Her roommate introduces herself to Carina as Svetlana Pierreovay-Noirresors, a Russian spy who is on a mission to destroy the enemy. The two get along really nicely and become friends instantly just because they like each other. Both of them are very beautiful and seem equivalent, which is nothing new, but Svetlana already knows that Carina was also sent to fight the enemy.

For some strange reason, they decide to kiss each other passionately on the lips for a few seconds but that is it. That could be some sort of secret code or something. Meanwhile, Carina and Svetlana are busy with organizing their beds and since both of them are on the same team then there is nothing to worry about for just being on the same team.

Two days have passed.

It is the early morning of deployment.

There is an announcement over the intercom.

The message orders all soldiers regardless of being male or female to take showers in the same locker room but to also strip down for a strip search before entering the shower in the locker room. And that is nothing unusual.

Carina and Svetlana arrive and they both strip in front of a drill sergeant. They are told to spread their legs in order to reveal their rectum and vagina just because it is required to due to the fact that there is a drug problem going on. It is an unpleasant and uncomfortable feeling but no drugs are found within their bodies. They go in the big open unit shower stall that can fit up to 250 soldiers. There are mostly other men taking a shower with a few other women, and then there seems to be a couple having sex in the middle of the stall as the other soldiers are egging them on.

Carina and Svetlana feel disgusted at what is happening. But they don't bother to care as they just ignore what is happening around them. They see it part of the old system and the old guard and just want to not get caught. After some time, they get out of the shower and put on assigned military uniforms in front of the male soldiers. Svetlana blushes for a few short moments and so does Carina, after a few other male soldiers made comments about their asses. They did not feel ashamed but quite puzzled because of what has occurred in the shower stall. Still, that was just a crazy situation.

Now dressed, the entire group is ordered to go back to their quarters and to get ready to leave and then to report back when ordered to the mess hall after eating breakfast.

It is just the last day of excitement and there is something to enjoy. It could be something but there is a reason to consider everything.

Carina and Svetlana go to their quarters in order to get ready to leave and so that they can just sit and talk or do something else. It should get very interesting but that is just the craziness of what is currently happening. Carina was not even aware that another spy was embedded within the enemy that was engaging in war.

A few short moments later and then there is an announcement over the intercom. The announcement orders all soldiers to report to the mess hall so that they can eat breakfast in their assigned units. Carina and Svetlana go down to the mess hall and they go to find that it is a self-serve buffet. It seems like all of the food is freeze-dried but maybe that could just be how it is cooked.

The scrambled eggs look real but seem it is just from powder. Although it is cooked and feels soft to the touch, it seems the eggs are cut into cubes. And then there are the sausage links, which look as though they are over cooked. The toast looks too under done because it is not quite brown enough. The sausage and gravy looks fine while the biscuits look like that they had been made in a factory.

Everything else just looks gross or extremely unappetizing. But if that is what is to be eaten, then Carina has no other choice. Carina just got here a few days ago and Svetlana got here one day before

Carina for some strange reason. Carina and Svetlana get a tray and then grab plates and some tall cups. They put the food on their plates that they might like the most and then go to a machine to get some orange juice or whatever beverage it has to offer. It takes some time but they find their table that is assigned to their specific unit. It is marked with the Second Platoon of the 1st Army Squadron.

They sit down and begin to eat their food.

Other soldiers start to look at them.

It is just some sort of crazy situation.

Carina looks at some other man while trying to eat but he doesn't care. He just looks at his food as he does not care about her or any other soldiers. Carina goes back to looking at her own food.

Svetlana just looks around when she is eating her food.

Thirty-five minutes have elapsed and now an announcement was made saying that breakfast was over.

Everybody finished eating, though they just remained at their assigned tables.

Another announcement is made over the intercom,

This time it is about departing the mess hall to go fight on the front lines.

It is ordered that each group line up in their appropriate places.

And so, with the push of a button, all of the tables disappear to the side and now everything is just a big open space in the mess hall. Carina and Svetlana line up with the Second Platoon of the 1st Army Squadron and their commanding officer tells them that they will be going to Warsaw, Poland. The Second Platoon of the 1st Army Squadron is told that they will get on a military cargo transport plane in a few short minutes. The commanding officer tells them that they will be fighting for the goal of communism and fascism in order to promote a government-controlled society with nothing but a belief in authoritarian and totalitarian perspectives.

It is for that reason why Carina and Svetlana came here in the first place because they were instructed to engage with the enemy in order to be accepted by the enemy.

The commanding officer gives the orders and a single file starts to form behind him as they start to leave.

They walk to the airfield just a few blocks away.

There is a plane waiting for them and it is large and wide, or that is what it seems.

The Second Platoon of the 1st Army Squadron board the plane via the air stairs in the rear loading bay or what seems to be the cargo hold.

Carina and Svetlana are the first to board the

plane and they get the best seats in the cargo hold in which they can see the commanding officer. The last person boards the plane and it will take a while but the door closes. Now it's just a waiting game for the plane to leave and it will take a while.

The plane needs to get approval to depart.

It is all for a good cause according to the enemy. But there are some doubts if it will even work, so there is something to better understand. It is always about that. But Svetlana and Carina do not know if they will see each other again. They don't know if they are going to be kidnapped at the same time. That is still unknown. But Carina does not she is going to be kidnapped and so does Svetlana, but they don't know if each other is going to be kidnapped. It is just unknown.

The plane gets approval for takeoff and it lifts off the ground.

One hour and forty-five minutes later, the plane lands on the runway and the cargo door opens. The commanding officer orders everyone off so they can prepare to battle on the front lines. There is only a sense of intrigue.

Carina is the last to get off because she was the first person to board. Svetlana is right in front of her and then the plane just waits there.

Other enemy units were lined up to Carina and Svetlana and were ready to fight whenever it was in the best wishes of their commanders. It was the sort of thing that was crazy but there is this and then there is that, which doesn't make sense at all. It all stems from the point of no return or what seems to be the most things feared and that would be war or being found out the enemy has found a member of the allies has just now infiltrated their units.

While that has happened, it is certain that they will not get caught, and that is the way it is meant to be.

Waiting for the order from their commanding officer, each military unit stands at attention, just to be sure something is in the works of being achieved.

As for everything else, there is just little to do with this.

At long last, the commanding officers finally give the orders to line up in formation all as one unit so they can fight together. Carina, Svetlana, and the other members of her squadron will be teaming up with different units from different enemy bases and that is how it is. But once they get into their assigned positions on the front lines, the units will all separate at different ranges.

With all units in single formation now and a commander separating each line in order to guide their squadron to the designated position all commanders agree to begin the march over from the airfield to the grassy dirt fields. One-by-one, each section leaves and follow the orders from their commanders. As they leave the airfield and approach the grassy dirt fields, the squadrons begin to separate from the main unit into individual lines. Carina's unit is the last squadron to separate but they are also the furthest ahead so that they can see who is on the horizon. Plus, Carina's unit is to construct a trench all around them in order to prevent the allies from winning. It is just a way to stop the blocking if possible from the allies, but there is a reason it might fail.

The commanding officer of the squadron gives the orders to dig a trench with their bare hands until he can find some shovels.

Thirty minutes later, the commanding officer brings back shovels and rakes in a wheelbarrow. Each one of the squadron members grab one and start to dig or even rake the ground.

There was some dirt but much grass but they could still dig the dirt with their bare hands. When the shovels arrived, then they start actually digging into the grass. And then once it was deep enough they would rake the dirt to make sure it was leveled or even sturdy.

Carina's squadron started to build the trench, not knowing how big it would be. In a few short hours all of the soldiers in the squadron built a trench twenty feet wide by fifty feet long. It was an enormous feet to do, but they still were not done. Three hours later, the trench is now fifteen feet deep and it would be able to hide everyone in the squadron without the allies ever finding them. But the members of the squadron could also effectively fight using weapons while having a place to easily duck and cover. So far there is no one in sight and no allies can be seen but there is just some sense of worry by the commanding officer thinking that his squadron isn't safe. The commanding officer sees something and knows it's a wild animal of some kind but he begins to shoot at it until it dies as he has a feeling that it might actually be an allied soldier in disguised as a wild animal.

The commanding officer orders his entire unit, with the exception of Carina and Svetlana, to fire their weapons at any animals they can see.

Carina and Svetlana are told to keep digging the trench deeper.

There is just some type of paranoia with this unit commander.

It seems that all of the officers believe that any wild animals are allied soldiers.

Paranoia is at its best right now and there is nothing that can be done.

Carina and Svetlana continue to dig the trench but they can dig no more because they fear there could be a water table being breached soon.

So, since they can't dig anymore, they decide to pile the dirt around them in order to make a secure dirt fort.

It takes five hours to complete and now it seems to look everyone is safe. There seems to be a sense of calm but the other enemy soldiers keep on firing at any wild animals they see intermittently, as a way to protect themselves and the remaining unit. It is all a sense of compassion.

Night falls and the unit commander assigns a few soldiers to watch the field in front of them. It is only a short while but each must take turns in order to make sure a wild animal does not get pass the trench or else it could be doom for the other squadrons. It is just a part of why it must be reasoned. There is just the craziness of paranoia.

The next morning arrives and it is the last day it will be spending here. It goes quickly with nothing being quite the opposite. Everything was just the same as yesterday.

And then night falls, so there is just a sense of this paranoia again.

The next day arrives.

The commanding officer says it is time to leave because there mission is done.

All of the members are told that they shall be re-grouped into the Grey Team and then be placed in the 7th Squadron of the First Company.

The squadron lines up in formation and enters the rear air stairs. They are told that they are going to be re-grouped when they arrive in Belgium and then they will travel to Germany in order to fight. It is just a sign of change. Carina is not going to make it to Germany though, as she will be kidnapped in Belgium by some mysterious person. And that will surely be a sign of nothing.

The unit commander tells the squadron that he shall remain their commanding officer when they are re-grouped into the grey team.

A few short minutes later, the plane takes off for Belgium.

It is just the sort of thing that is so crazy that nothing will happen. But that is not true, since Carina will be kidnapped, yet she does not know how she will be kidnapped. And that is the main point of nothing in the idea that everything always makes itself known to the rest of society.

It will take a few hours to arrive in Belgium but it is just a boring flight. Everyone is just stuck in the cargo hold of a military transport aircraft. There is nothing that can be done because it seems there is just a lack of enthusiasm. All remains to be quiet because that is how it is.

No one wants to be treated like dirt but that won't happen. And yet, there was really never any reason to shoot at the wild animals thinking that they were enemy agents in disguise. That was just paranoia getting in the way but it seems to work. But there was really no real reason to ever go to Warsaw if the goal was just to shoot at wild animals and then do nothing from there. That should at least be considered a waste of valuable time because it just distracts from the rest of the war. There is just nothing to do on this plane to Belgium, and that is just as usual. Everything is just so cold with so little insulation. Nothing is ever so warm and it seems that is the way it was meant to be. It is just a waste of time. And that is something for the rest of society.

It only has been thirty minutes since the plane took off from Poland and it already seems like forever in a land of hopelessness. Everything seems to be in the middle of something more important, like there is a delay or something. But being a soldier, Carina is used to that kind of stuff already, with the hazing and other rituals that take place during training. But she never actually faced that in training because she went to some place special that not many people knew about for some reason. Everything feels like it will be a very long day. That is how everyday turns out to be, as the climate is to blame. But that is just a load of crap and lies because it is just how a person feels, and that could translate to the day or week being boring to the extent that nothing can be done. And that is just a waste of time.

It has been a little over two hours and there is still about thirty minutes to go. It must be a really slow and old plane or the pilot is just slow. That's probably what is happening but no one cares. The soldiers just want to make it to Belgium in order to begin the next phase of their deployment. But something will be waiting for them once they land, yet Carina and her new friend Svetlana might end up somewhere else due to some miraculous event.

No one knows it yet but some people might be saved while others will end up dying. But that is just how war works. It is such a sinister situation that not everyone can escape its consequences such as death and misery. People need to learn how to live but there is such propaganda waging that no one will ever find out the truth.

There still remains that problem and then there begins another. Maybe propaganda is the way to go at the center of the universe but then all hope might be lost to time since there is uncertainty if that will help win the war. It is all a sign of something sinister so that nothing will end this war. That is just the way it is and it shall remain that way forever and eternity until there is change.

The plane is closer to its destination.

There are only a few minutes left.

The soldiers can feel the descent.

It seems like it has been forever from the

moment they left Poland and arriving at Belgium. It is just surreal or it might be fate.

Everything shouldn't go to shame.

It should only be a time of thinking during a time of sorrow. That is just the way of life but it seems to be just a complete waste of time. Until there is that time of unity there is just no hope. It is lost to the eons of lunacy.

Everyone else though is idiotic.

The plane is preparing for final approach.

There is a sense that everything shall be fine.

Well, then there is something else saying doom is approaching everyone not named Carina, Svetlana, and a person named Oscar Viktor.

It could be exactly like it sounds.

But there is just no proof to any of this.

Everything just results in madness, so it is a way to make up excuses.

That is just how life is.

But then there is reality and what must come to an end.

The plane lands in a deserted airfield in the middle of nowhere in Brussels, Belgium. It seems as though there is something missing and then there is some place to hide but then there is a problem to be known in case of an emergency. It is without a doubt one of the more common situations that have ever been on the horizon of the truth. At least that is what the problem is.

The rear airstair opens. And then the unit commander tells everyone to remain calm so that he can be sure that nothing is wrong. He probably will know what is coming next or maybe he is part of it and will make sure the enemy wins. Or it could be the exact opposite or something else. That is just what is needed.

The unit commander gives the all clear and tells everyone to line up in formation. So, that is just part of everything usual.

It takes a few minutes but everyone is now in correct formation.

There is a sense of quietness and intrigue but then there is something else.

The unit commander takes a look at all of his soldiers. He sees that there is nothing wrong but he just wants to make an example of something. But he just doesn't want to have favorites. So, he must make a decision.

The unit commander goes down the line of the formation to check if everything is in order. He wants to check for uniformity and neatness.

It could be a trap because everyone is in the correct formation.

Every one of the soldiers is following the unit procedures of military action in times of war.

That is just a face to make an example of

some people.

Then, he notices Carina and Svetlana and how attractive they are, and tell them to follow him to stand in a corner near the front of the plane. Carina and Svetlana follow the order of the unit commander and are now away from the rest of the soldiers for some type of unknown reason. It is just getting a bit crazier by the hour. But that sounds normal or it is due to something else that is not evident to the extent of how it is happening.

Carina and Svetlana remain at the front of the plane as they wait to receive new orders. They don't know what will happen but they have a reason to think that they might be kidnapped soon. But it is only a hunch of what might happen. And that is just how it seems. Nothing is like it wants to be and in this case there is a case to enter into a false reality. That is just the core of it.

The unit commander orders the other soldiers to march forward towards what seems to be a bunker on the other side. The soldiers march forward without their unit commander because they believe he will meet up with them soon, but it is just a trap and there is something sinister. There is just this sense of irony that nothing good shall happen from this situation so it just looks suspicious. That is just the basis of it and will be at the end of nowhere. It is just so there is just a fantastical piece of nonsense.

As the soldiers are marching forward, they await for their next orders when their unit commander arrives. But he might never arrive. It is just the crazy sign of something sinister.

Then, there is just something strange that is about to occur. Someone approaches Carina and Svetlana from the back with a black ski mask and dressed in dark clothing.

Carina and Svetlana don't even hear or see anything as they are facing forward and standing at attention. They are just facing forward and do not care what will happen to them. It all seems like that there will be a kidnapping soon and that too shall be the new normal. Then, all of a sudden, the masked man approaches Carina and Svetlana. He places a piece of tape over their mouths in order to prevent them from saying anything. And then he places a bag over each of their heads so that no one who sees who they are. It is all a case for something other than torture but they figure they are being kidnapped. They scream and shout but no one can hear them. It is all something that is all too clear.

They are being kidnapped by someone by the name of Oscar Viktor but they have yet to see his face, so they don't know who he is. It is just something that is not clear at all. Then the masked man takes Carina and Svetlana to a smaller plane and puts the seatbelts on them and locks the doors from the outside so that they can't escape.

Meanwhile, the unit commander arrives at the location of his soldiers but the soldiers are just facing forward and waiting for new orders. They don't know what is coming next but they are doomed. The unit commander grabs some grenades, removes the pins, and then throws them at the soldiers for some reason or another. Then there are explosions after explosions since each of the grenades touches the ground or the clothing of the soldiers. The unit commander sees that it is a large explosion but that isn't enough, since he believes they might still be alive. He grabs a machine gun and shoots straight at their backs. He wants to make sure they are dead. The soldiers all fall down from being hit. There is no more but that is still not enough.

Carina and Svetlana are waiting in the much smaller plane and they can hear everything. It is just something that sounds awful but necessary, so it must just go on. The unit commander sees a few cans of fuel and wants to get rid of much of the evidence as he can so the enemy doesn't find out. But he must find some type of long detonation cord so it doesn't kill him, Carina, and Svetlana. He finds detonation cord long enough and wires it near the end of the cargo transport military plane all the way to the location of where the deceased soldiers are standing. He rolls out the detonation cord and makes sure it will be good for the mission. The cord is tight now and he pours all of the fuel on the deceased soldiers. He gets a match and goes to the other end of the detonation cord. He then lights the other end of the cord with the match that is near the end of the military plane. And now all he has to do is to escape. It is just something that is in the necessary steps of proper procedure. That is just the proper thing to do.

Then, the unit commander runs back to the much smaller plane and gets into the cockpit.

The plane takes off and is off the ground, and now there is something else.

The unit commander speaks.

"Hello girls! My name is Oscar Viktor and I will be taking you to Switzerland today. You might already know me as your unit commander, but I am on your side. I have been told to take you to our secret operations center in Switzerland. We will be arriving in Berne in about a few short hours. You can also take off the bags off your head as well as the tape over your mouth."

"It will be quite cold there so there are a few jackets and sweaters on the seat next to you. Please be aware that the enemy does not know about us being part of trying to fight against the enemy. I have been here embedded within the enemy forces in

order to see what they are doing. And I have also been creating all of the events that block the enemy from winning. They don't know about me being part of the group to defeat them."

"Just let me say one thing to set everyone in here straight so there is no confusion. We are not with the enemy and we are not with the allies. But we can be called partners to the allies that will make sure that the enemy loses. Yet, we are also the good guys and we mean no harm. It is safe to say that we have a great chance of winning, as the enemy does not know who we are. The enemy believes we are part of a small group of allies because we have the same goal in defeating them. However, they are making a mistake since we don't train with the allies. It is just a type of conspiracy they developed because of paranoia, as they believe that all militaries have this secluded team of soldiers with superior training. While this can be true in some instances, it is not entirely correct due to the fact that the allies don't know about us either, so that is something."

"They only believe we are part of the allies because they swore they have seen us fighting, but they are probably hallucinating and delusional, since no one knows where we train. They could be dreaming as well. So, that leaves us to all of the soldiers under my command while posing as an

enemy officer. Well, they were all part of the enemy forces but they never suspected me or any of you. Those enemy soldiers believed I was one of them and they never thought I was crazy. They also believed the animals that we shot at were actually allied officers. All of those soldiers under my command are now dead because that was just the easy way out to get you girls out of the enemy lines and take you to Switzerland. And if they ever found out about the plan, well then they might report me and possibly you girls to the higher authorities in the chain of command of the enemy forces. This way, it is better."

"And if you are wondering about the enemy now, we are all safe. I removed the transponder when I put you girls in the seats of this plane. The enemy can't track us and they believe that all of us will be in Germany. Just sit back and relax."

Carina and Svetlana just sit back and relax for the next few hours. They take off the bags off of their heads as well as the tape over their mouths. It is just a sign of hope that everything will be fine. That is just the way of life.

Sometime later the plane descends into a small runway that looks like it is part of an airport. But it isn't an airport. There is just a runway and it is only a façade.

A few minutes later, the plane taxis into a hidden hanger that suddenly appears right in front of them. It was probably there all along and that they were just paying attention now. And then the door of the hanger closes. Now dark, there is nowhere to go, and only Oscar knows what to do. He tells Carina and Svetlana to both stay in the plane while he gets out in order to push a button. That is certainly crazy because it is just so strange. And so, Oscar gets out of the plane, goes to a corner of the hanger, sets a timer, and then pushes the button.

Oscar gets back in the plane and tells the girls in a few seconds they will be in the secret operations center soon.

It seems like there is a chance for hope but that is it and it too shall lead to progress. That is about what is happening now and it seems there is a sign the enemy might be defeated. Carina and Svetlana have to know what they must do before they end up doing some sort of crazy thing. It is up to them but they are not the ones who will win the war. They are not part of the allies. They are part of an underground group of the resistance that is better than the allies in order to stop the enemy.

The plane starts to descend as the floor is now moving lower and lower. It is too soon to know what will happen. Soon they will be in the secret operations center of the resistance and it will be up to them to fight alongside the allies in order to see how to keep on blocking the enemy. But it won't all be fun and games for long.

At long last, Carina, Svetlana, and Oscar arrive at the secret operations center. They wait for a few brief seconds until it is fine. Oscar tells Carina and Svetlana to follow him, so they follow and he leads them to the lobby. From there, they meet someone all too familiar. The clergyman greets them to the secret operations center of the resistance, and then he tells them what will happen next.

"Hello girls! You have already met one of my advisers Mr. Oscar Viktor. Now that you have arrived here, I will tell you what will happen next, just in case you forgot about what I already told you."

"Both of you will stay here for the next few days in this secret operations center. Both of you will become military advisers to our soldiers, otherwise known as the resistance armed forces. From there you will be advising them, but you will also be fighting on the front lines whenever necessary."

"When you are acting as a soldier you won't fight regularly, only at off-peak times, which is when there is a slow down during the day and into the night. It is expected that you guide your military

units to the proper areas as described by the high command in the daily update letters. Each day is different and you shall be briefed before you head out to the next scouting location."

"It is expected that this might take you four years to complete this mission. Don't get discouraged but you have very difficult jobs to do. The resistance armed forces are not expected to win or lose because we are trying to defeat the enemy by blocking their abilities to win. We use conventional warfare as well as non-conventional warfare. What the resistance armed forces does is to severely restrict the ability of the enemy in order to carry out their duties. That is about as easy as it gets. But, the enemy still thinks we are part of the allied forces because they sometimes see people in the middle of the wilderness doing some pacing and or even patrolling. They think just because we have the same weapons as the allies that we are one and the same with them."

"However, they are dead wrong, because we are not affiliated with the allies. But, if you are asking about who is responsible for everything, well that will rely on the allies. If the allies do something wrong or fall for a truce, then the enemy would win. But if the allies win and the enemy is defeated, then the enemy shall be defeated and will be held accountable. We don't know how everything will

turn out in the end but we do know that the enemy must be defeated."

"Here are the following outcomes again."

"Outcome One: We win and then you shall be back in South Dakota to begin your senior year of high school at Prep Stone Academy. You will know about what has happened but your classmates won't. Sean will know and so would I. The enemy will be obliterated off the face of the Earth. And then it will seem like it was only a memory of your past."

"Outcome Two: The enemy will win. In this outcome, our team will be endangered of being captured but we won't be captured, just the other allied units. If this is the case, it is because the enemies outsmarted all of the allies. It was the plans of the allies that caused the war to be lost. And if this happens, then the enemy will create an alternate universe dystopian and totalitarian in nature all around the world."

"Outcome Three: This is the last possible outcome and in this outcome the enemy will call to a truce in which the enemy will surrender. However, if this is the outcome to occur you should be aware that the enemy is just fooling the allies. The enemy has

actually found a way to go back to the past in order to change certain events so that everything shall return to the medieval ages. In this outcome, most everyone will be peasants or commoners and certain members of the enemy will be part of everything. This would possibly be the worst potential outcome because everything will be reversed back to simplistic times when someone with high power could determine if you died or survived. There will be cruel punishments and public squares, but that is not the bad part. The bad part is that justice will be corrupt because only the most wealthy and powerful shall win. While the medieval ages were a time of prosperity for some or many, in this alternate time line it too shall be a dystopian society and there will just be lots of wars and battles."

"Just remember that you might come face to face with the enemy because of your position. Now, both of you are responsible for many squadrons in your path. You will advise the individual soldiers if they need any help. But the most important job both of you have is to advise the commanding officers in the resistance armed forces. You will always have to provide daily updates to the commanding officers in charge of each unit. You will get your daily briefings from high command and then you shall update all of the commanding officers."

"Now, all of your belongings are in your assigned rooms in this underground facility. You will each have your own room. This facility does have the same training rooms as the one in Italy but since it is larger there are additional rooms and spaces that can further improve your training. You are not expected to take part in additional training but both of you may see what it has to offer. In addition, your rooms are so large that they can fit about seven families in each of them. Each room is basically a presidential suite with its own sauna, hot tub, two full size bathrooms, one extremely large walk-in closet, a full size kitchen with a gas stove and oven along with a walk in freezer and a normal refrigerator and freezer unit, as well as a parlour, living room, ten bedrooms, five guest rooms, and a pool. This might all seem too much but just remember one thing: you don't have to use or visit all of these rooms or areas within your suite. It is only so large of a suite because of your position within the resistance armed forces."

"Now, if you follow Oscar, he will take both of you to your suites."

Carina and Svetlana followed Oscar to their suites for the next few days.

They arrive.

The doors to the suites are next to each other.

However, they are separated and a wall is also dividing them. But one suite is to the left while the other is to the right. The doors aren't all the way to the end but in the middle, making it seem like the space will be small inside. But this just means that the rooms are extremely large because of how everything is set up according to the blueprints.

Anyway, Carina and Svetlana enter their own separate suites.

Oscar hands them their keys after the door is opened.

And just like that, Oscar leaves them to go and complete some paperwork. The girls enter their room and close the doors behind them. It is as if there is just nothing to worry about. But that is how it always was in the beginning. Carina likes what she sees and she just wants to experience everything. Svetlana just wants to know more. In just a few days they will be leaving Switzerland in order to become advisers to the resistance armed forces.

That is something fantastic as well as crazy for some other reason.

They must be trusted.

They must provide accurate information.

They must persevere.

It is not all an act but it is part of life and it must be in the mindset of who will be where and when it shall occur.

As Carina and Svetlana look around their own separate suites, both of them are amazed, and they see that it is worthy to stay here. They only have a few days to stay here and that shall take some time as well due to the fact that nothing is normal around here. It is just crazy. There can always be fun and games but that is also crazy. Nothing can escape the truth from the resistance armed forces but then, they just know too much information. It is just something that is not even known but if it matters then it must be true or the fact that nothing is relevant anymore. That is just the price of life for eternity.

Half a day has come and gone already but there is still some time left. Carina and Svetlana see the time and try to find something to eat. It is just something but then they find meals in freeze-dried packets. It is probably terrible but they taste it and it seems decent.

They finish it and don't seem to hate it for some reason.

In a few days, Carina and Svetlana will go on a new mission to a classified location. It is just the sort of thing that is crazy and delusional.

But it just might work.

Chapter Nineteen

Electrical flashes of light are appearing out of thin air in the midst of a crisis outside. No one can see them but it is not out of the ordinary. It must be the enemy or it could be the resistance. No one actually knows to the extent of anonymity. There is just the chance maybe someone is trying to escape or the resistance is trying to block the enemy, but it could be the other way around as well. Maybe it is a tad bit possible for the enemy to have figured out the flashes of light thing. But if the enemy has figured the flashes of light thing, they need to know what it is in order to proceed.

It could be luck or just a case of spying on the allies or even the resistance. But the enemy is still not aware of the resistance as they believe the resistance is just another name for the allied forces. But the enemy is surely something else because of what they see as a threat to their existence. It is why they must win so that they can control everything. Yet, the likelihood of the enemy winning is slim because of too many events that blocked them from succeeding on the front lines. If there was anything that could save them it would be time travel, but they have yet to master that, or they are just experimenting something with lightning or some crazy thing like that.

The flashes of light are supposedly strikes of lightning but no one might believe that if they start to question science itself. Or it could be the reason to just start worrying about the future, due to the fact that there might be something sinister happening or at least something that is about to happen. That is the problem though as there is just a simple-minded mentality in the hope that individual liberties will be repealed due to some people who refuse to accept freedom. It is just the case of timing but that does not mean anything to the rest of society. There is just hope and change but it is not in the best interests of society. It is for that one and only reason why everything is false. There is just a center of no return.

Everything outside is not as it seems as there

is just a case of bad weather.

There is just an abundance of snow outside that it might be too harsh to go outside. And it is just the beginning of everything. It wasn't snowing when Carina and Svetlana arrived here but things do have a tendency to change. That is just normal and it is like a ghost is messing with the rest of society. Nothing will be in the result as it should be. Carina won't care and the same would apply to Svetlana. It would just be a waste of time.

Then there is a loud pounding of some kind on the roof but that is difficult to believe unless it is from the hanger. The noise seems questionable because the secret operations center is completely underground in order to stay hidden from the enemy. And even a case of evidence is irrelevant. That is the case that gets to the problem the most. But, before it is needed, there is something is just about to happen. That is how it will all begin.

Sirens start going off without notice. It is just throughout the secret operations center. It is just so loud that no one could escape it. But there is just a case of uncertainty. Carina and Svetlana are already up and they could depart soon. It could have been a few days already but then there is something that might have gone wrong. Or it could be that this is actually happening right now. There is just this type of conspiracy.

At a time of disaster, there is just this kind of new nonsense.

There is the enemy and then there are the allies who seek to defeat the enemy. It is sort of this crazy analogy that doesn't make any sense to the crazy and type of system that does make sense. It is all to the whole extent of craziness.

There should be more time left.

And then there is a new theory.

It all happens for a reason.

And then there is a case of uncertainty to the extent of nothing. It is all for a cause of deceit. It is all for the case of decency. That is how it was meant to be in a case of inefficiency. But there is nothing new that can cause any more harm unless somehow there is a truce. Everything that is always wrong has gone wrong but only in the beliefs of the people who have a glorifying review.

It is too soon to know what will happen but then there is just something that needs to be known to the rest of society.

Carina and Svetlana report to duty in the lobby of the secret operations center.

From there they follow Oscar Viktor to an undisclosed location and it all seems dark from the building or place they are going.

It could be that it is time to be deployed but then there is something to the extent of what might go wrong. Besides that, there is just this uncertainty of evil. It is all about the craziness of society to this new and violent theme of rage. It must all be a dream since people will start to riot if the enemy loses. It is about the craziness of the brain as they believe the enemy is the solution. The people who support the enemy just don't listen.

Carina and Svetlana arrive to a much larger and darker hanger.

It is time to leave.

But the location is still a mystery.

It is about that time again but that is how it is in the craziness of society.

The rear airstair opens.

Carina and Svetlana are briefed about what is going to happen.

The briefing lasts for fifteen minutes but it does not include the location of the mission. It is just that secret that it isn't worth spilling the beans. It is for a good reason: to make sure the enemy does not get any idea if they are listening in. But that will probably never happen because the enemy doesn't know about the resistance armed forces. It is all for the precise and crazy reason to protect the future of the people. And then, it is time.

Carina and Svetlana board the plane.

Oscar leaves.

Then, after a few minutes, additional

members of the resistance armed forces join the girls.

Carina and Svetlana are strapped in and are just behind the bulkhead. All is still very quiet and it is like something bad is going to happen. Then there is a sound of happiness, besides the clicking of seatbelts by the members of the resistance armed forces. It is just something better but it could be the last time that gets noticed.

Then everything turns to dark, as the rear airstair closes. It is time to depart but the doors of the hanger are still closed. It is just that crazy but it is the time of the season.

The doors open and it is just about time to leave.

The engines fire on and it is just a very loud propeller noise.

The plane departs the hanger and is ready to taxi to the runway.

There is no other plane leaving and it is in the dead of the morning.

It is still quite dark but it is time to leave.

The plane is sitting at the end of the runway and is ready to leave.

It is cleared for takeoff.

Everything is just in code to disguise it from the enemy. Even the transponder is blocked from the enemy's eyes.

The plane leaves and it is headed to some place that is still unknown. That is crazy but it will just have to do.

It reaches cruising speed at about 25,000 feet in the air and there is all but waiting. It seems that it is all for a good cause and that is how it is meant to be in the end.

There is nothing but silence.

And then, after a few hours, the plane is about to descend into a secret military base.

The plane lands in Spain in a secret site that is not occupied by anyone.

Carina and Svetlana are told to depart first so that they can get started on the mission. They are told that it will take up to four years to complete their new mission.

And then they are told that they are in Spain in order to aid the resistance armed forces in order to try and stop the enemy.

The soldiers of the resistance armed forces get off and disembark from the plane.

Everyone departs the premises and go on two buses to fight on the front lines by using a set of many underground tunnels to get around the enemy. That is how it's done.

The buses arrive at the battle ground of where all soldiers shall stay for the next four years or until there is a victory or loss by the allies. The soldiers of the resistance armed forces set up camp and then it is time for Carina and Svetlana to go to the headquarters of the camp site.

Carina and Svetlana are briefed about what they will do and then they start to begin all of the advising to the military command of the resistance armed forces.

Carina and Svetlana are in the midst of the war as they can hear enemy and allies battling each other. It is just that serious in Spain.

There is just danger everywhere and it feels like nothing can be done. Something is about to go down and that will be like nothing else. It is just the sort of thing that will just appear to be crazy. That is the whole point of it. Mortar fire can be heard from every point and then there is the situation between the allies and the enemy. It seems like a never-ending war to the nth degree for some stupid reason. They are fighting like crazy and the resistance armed forces have yet to assemble in the necessary formation. This will just go on for too long and it appears nothing will be the same.

This is the start of something bad and it shall take some time to get used to it but the soldiers on all sides have nothing wrong with any of it. Everything is just fine and dandy. That is something that is not crazy because it is just life in a time of war. The soldiers in the resistance armed forces are still setting up camp so they can eat, sleep, and rest when they are not fighting on the front lines. But when they start fighting on the front lines they will be hard to identify from the allies as both the allied soldiers and the resistance soldiers are wearing the same military uniforms and Carina and Svetlana are wearing the same military uniforms meant for advisers that the allied military advisers are wearing.

So, that is probably why the enemy soldiers can't tell the difference between the allies as well as the resistance soldiers. It is all meant to blend in with the crowd to confuse everyone. That is just the same type of crap that gets people killed, but Carina as well as Svetlana also has the same military ranks as all of the other military advisers in the allied forces. They are all lieutenant generals and that is just the thing that is crazy. But that is how everything turns out to be as there is nothing but simplicity.

This isn't Switzerland anymore but there is the smell of defeat and victory in the future.

The resistance is just in a secure area that is closed off to everyone and there is barbed wire as well as an electrical fence surrounding the entire perimeter. It is good but it will have to do.

Carina and Svetlana begin to attend another new briefing because of a new strategy by the enemy has been found out.

The end is near but it is just the beginning to take down the enemy. It sure looks like something is going to happen and that is it. That just sounds like a cryptic message. Nothing will ever come of it and will just be the epitome of hope and civilization. That is the price that people will have to pay in order to properly defeat the enemy. There is just that case of what not to do.

Danger is more apparent than ever and it seems like nothing will stop it. There is just nothing to be scared of. Soon, there will be a revelation of what might happen to the enemy. But before then, there is just no solution to anything if something happens to the crazy thing of humanity. Carina and Svetlana are done with their briefing. They go to the soldiers of the resistance armed forces and tell them what the enemy is going to do.

With a change in plans, some of the soldiers of the resistance have to scout the enemy. It is just sort of crazy and due to some new strategy by the enemy in order to see if it is necessary. That is as far as it gets in order to understand it better.

But there is just this strategy that likes to creep on everything else because of the enemy. Soon there will be enemy fire everywhere but not before there is a case against the allies.

The soldiers of the resistance are ready and it is like a carnival of emotions out here. There is just a lot of rapid fire coming from both sides. It seems to be a non-starter but there is this ongoing debate of what will happen to the rest of society if the enemy is the victor in the end.

As everything evolves, it begins a new day of hope, a new day of change, and a new day that there shall be a victor. That is what is needed but the enemy and the allies are just fighting each other on the front lines.

As the mortars keep on firing there is not a whole lot of surprise what is happening. It all seems to be a case of stupidity. There is just something that is in the place of uncertainty.

Crazy as it is, there is just something that is in the realm of possibility.

But everything is just a drag.

Chapter Twenty

Mortar fire is continuous. After two years of being on the front lines in Spain, it seems like a never-ending war is eminent. It seems like the enemy has become a very strong foe to the allies. Every time the allies make a change in their plans the enemy seems to find out. It would seem that the enemy is trolling the allies or it could also be that the enemy probably embedded spies within the allied forces. The latter seems more logical and might be a way to win the war, or at least the portion in Spain. It is all about strategy. Carina and Svetlana often fight on the front lines when they are not advising, but it does not all seem that way. It seems that everything is changing constantly and that will mean that all of the plans have been sabotaged or are not sufficient enough to defeat the enemy. That is, the allies always change their plans because they believe their spies within the enemy forces are saying that the enemy is changing their strategy. That could be a way to distract the allies in order to fool them. It is all about defeating each other in a war of the worlds. Nothing seems like it is going to stop. As it seems to always be, there is just a repeat of history.

Then, there is a change of plans again, for a sign of uncertainty exists.

It is just uncertain how the vast majority of soldiers can keep up with this constant change of action. Nothing is the same and it looks like there will be a case of something sinister happening. That is how it shall be and that is the case of what it means to the rest of society. Soon, there will just be a past that was considered right and too old to prosper, but that shall be replaced by a bleak future. No one wants that to happen and it would just lead to a disaster being the only possibly outcome. Everything would belong to the enemy and the allies would end up being sent to prison for losing. It would be something that would not be good for society. That is just the idea of the rest of what could happen.

But it doesn’t end there. Carina and Svetlana

would end up as sex slaves and they will be subjected to the enemy for many years to come. It would lead to a disaster of epic proportions. That is just a theory but it could happen. There is just an unnerving outcry to the rest of the world.

The enemy is gaining ground on the allies and it seems all but inevitable that the allies will lose. It is such a sad day if that happens and it shall lead to the rise of chaos and destruction.

Soon, it will lead to violence and then it shall lead to the end of what was once a prosperous society in the entire world. The enemy wants that to happen so that they can control everything in their grasp. It is a sign of the times and it is necessary to decide if any threats exist in the end. Carina and Svetlana are just as culpable to anything and that will be a time of when the whole world knew the enemy attacked from the other side.

And then, it all seemed too surreal, because there was just attack after attack. It seems that the enemy is just getting more powerful by the minute and that is not good because the allies are starting to win some battles but it could all be a little too much for both sides to handle. That is just as crazy as it was meant to be and it seems like something is about to go down. That will be the end of the war if it seems like something is imminent. It will be a cause of inaction by the allies if they lose the war in the end. That is about how it ends if it is true. That is how it is meant to be or else there is something. Nothing seems to be in that place of desire for the allies and it seems that all is lost. As the tide turns, there continues to be non-stop chaos and destruction on both sides. It is all for a reason of insanity.

Then, out of nowhere, it has been learned at the last minute that the enemy wants to agree to a truce with the allies. There is nothing that can be done to prevent this as it is believed that the allies will just accept it because they want the fighting to end and that is the worst possible outcome. Nothing will ever be safe again and the world shall turn to chaos in the middle of something strange.

So, looking back to the outcomes that could actually occur, Carina has a flashback.

Outcome One: We win and then you shall be back in South Dakota to begin your senior year of high school at Prep Stone Academy. You will know about what has happened but your classmates won't. Sean will know and so would I. The enemy will be obliterated off the face of the Earth. And then it will seem like it was only a memory of your past.

Outcome Two: The enemy will win. In this outcome, our team will be endangered of being captured but we won't be captured, just the other allied units. If this is the case, it is because the enemies outsmarted all of the allies. It was the plans of the allies that caused the war to be lost. And if this happens, then the enemy will create an alternate universe dystopian and totalitarian in nature all around the world.

Outcome Three: This is the last possible outcome and in this outcome the enemy will call to a truce in which the enemy will surrender. However, if this is the outcome to occur you should be aware that the enemy is just fooling the allies. The enemy has actually found a way to go back to the past in order to change certain events so that everything shall return to the medieval ages. In this outcome, most everyone will be peasants or commoners and certain members of the enemy will be part of everything. This would possibly be the worst potential outcome because everything will be reversed back to simplistic times when someone with high power could determine if you died or survived. There will be cruel punishments and public squares, but that is not the bad part. The bad part is that justice will be corrupt because only the most wealthy and powerful shall win. While the medieval ages were a time of prosperity for some or many, in this alternate time line it too shall be a dystopian society and there will just be lots of wars and battles.

Carina thinks for a moment and she thinks the enemy will strike a truce with the allies to surrender and give up. But there is just something wrong with this scenario. It is all a sham from the beginning that the allies and the enemy agree to the truce because the enemy would have already defeated the allies in the past.

The allies believe they have just won the war after the truce is signed but it will take some time in order to finalize everything. That will be something interesting to watch because the allies would believe they have the advantage when the truce will be signed and agreed between them and the enemy. It is all for the rest of opinion to survive but the third outcome will just wipe out progress and turn everything back to the medieval ages. No one wants that to happen but it will happen soon because there is something in the need of the enemy to take place. It will be hard to turn back time to the way it was before because the enemy will control the whole world. That is just the case to be occurred.

As time goes by there is just this déjà vu of a thing that was forgot. It will be the thing that caused everything to go wrong but that is just the case of the history of sarcasm. That is just the basis of what will happen.

A few days later, the high command of the

enemy and the allies meet in a secret bunker nearby a grassy knoll. No one knows where it is but today is just the time of something that never can change back once over, unless people decide to build a time portal back to the past at this exact moment in time or before the enemy announced they wanted to seek a truce. It will be something that is just a rush against time. That is something very bad and it should be a warning sign in the near aftermath of destruction. All hope would be lost, as everything turns back centuries. There will just be chaos and simplicity.

With all of the hoopla that is going on there must be a delay and then something will be agreed upon in the near future. That is just as it was meant to be. Nothing would be able to decide what will come next. That is possibly the worst outcome to end up in a situation that is hard to reverse.

And then, it happened.

The high command signs the agreement first and then the allies sign the agreement.

Something happens and it is a surprise to the allies.

They thought they have won but it is just a case of deceit.

The enemy claims victory as everything turns back centuries.

It is now the medieval ages once again and

there is no going back.

The time warp claims everyone and everything and soon it changes people dramatically.

With this being the outcome, there is just a loss of hope for humanity. The situation is dire and it is a case of disaster. Something bad has occurred and it is not the fault of the resistance but of the allies. The enemy has successfully bamboozled the allies due to a crazy plan that was unheard of. But there is just this new and crazy thing of not being at the center of the world. Something is just wrong and it will be at the center of nothing.

Buildings start to disappear and soon the allies start to become peasants and commoners.

Carina and Svetlana have escaped but they are hiding in a secure location, only going out incognito to fool the enemy who now controls everything. It is just the case of disaster and that remains to be the course of time.

The enemy is in charge now and they call themselves Hällstadftß or Haellstadftss in English. It was now the dawn of that new political party. It is the reason of how they came to power.

Chapter Twenty One

Bloodshed ensues as there is just too much chaos everywhere. No one knows what to do. It is such a mad house in here that people are panicking because there clothes all of a sudden just changed to old garments that resembled what was worn back then in the Medieval ages. Everyone seems to be a commoner or worse a peasant. That is just the situation of the moment but it won't change anytime soon if certain people don't figure out how to change it. People are running away in all directions because they do not know what is happening. It is just a day of sorrow because they never were interested in the war in the first place. Something just doesn't seem right to them and it is a cause for concern because of how the truce changed everything. The commoners or what many can be referred to as peasants didn't even know of any truce agreed upon between the enemy and the allies. They didn't care about the war because all they wanted to do was to live their life and make sure that no harm was done. What happened to them was very surprising. It was something they thought was never even possible. Nothing makes sense for the purpose of a con.

But how did it all happen?

How did it get to this?

There are just too many questions to answer but they shall be revealed with time. It is just the sort of thing that is based upon the case of the situation to change everything. Something might happen but it is up to the rest of humanity.

No one knew this would happen and it seems that there will be a case of evil.

As time goes on, it will just lead to the type of situation that is not deemed possible.

Someone needs to do something soon and it must be now.

As the tension heats up there is just a rush to judgment. The people are scared. They don't know what to do. They have never experienced this type of situation before. It is now a time with chaos. There is violence and destruction. People don't know what they're doing. It could be a cause for concern because it is a concern. There must be a way to solve this but there isn't. It is a good thing Carina and Svetlana are in a safe place now.

The buildings have changed to what it was like back then. Churches were everywhere and it seemed as though there was something better. Hopefully, the people will go there to pray in order to try and return it back to what it was before. There is just this case of what it must remain.

The Latin cross plan is something that was at the moment in religious medieval architecture and that is true again now. There was a nave, transepts, and an altar. It was all there as it was just a common design back then. It resembled the glory of God and what he represented to humanity. And that what is happening now again. It was just another typical day in what now seems to be a modern medieval day. There is just this crisis of what will happen next and that will be the day of something new.

Then just as people are trying to settle in, there is just more chaos. More violence breaks out and that leads people to trample upon each other in what seems to be the public square.

It was a melee and looked like it wasn't going to end soon.

Soon, war broke out and that would lead to the outcome of what the Hällstadftß wants to accomplish. It is the reason for why there is something bad here and that is bad. The Hällstadftß is just an example that wants to promote chaos. They knew what will happen and they just enjoyed what they're seeing. It is for that reason why it is not good.

Carina and Svetlana are nowhere to be found but maybe they are in an alternate universe. There is just something wrong here.

The Hällstadftß is a party that demonstrates law and order or it seems to be. It is a false type of law and order promise because they rule over everyone in this current age. The Hällstadftß have created a new type of kingdom that promotes corruption and war in order to engage in outlandish tactics. They engage in unethical practices but that is just common. They do the devil's work themselves and they know that not everyone is guilty.

On top of that, the Hällstadftß makes up their own evidence in times of criminal and civil trials but they like to turn civil trials into criminal matters. It is how they roll. The Hällstadftß have executed a plan that is so crazy that nobody has ever heard of it and that is because it is now just happening. They thought about everything and no one saw it coming. It is a time of chaos and destruction and that is what the Hällstadftß wants. As it turns out, there is just the case of everything. That is just how it seems to be and that is not what it means.

The Hällstadftß is starting a war and that will cause something that is more sinister than it sounds because it is just like that. They are planning to start the war soon and it too shall be the epitome of evil in the end.

There must be something to do and that would be the case of something in the middle of nothing to the fuller extent. As it turns out, there is just nothing wrong with anything but of society itself. And in this case this has happened.

The goal of the Hällstadftß is to promote a new agenda of dystopian chaos in order to make people the weakest members of society. There political party is just like that.

And then there was something after all.

It has been years since the enemy or what they call themselves now, the Hällstadftß, have taken the control and advantage over everything.

A war has broken out and the peasants are engaging against each other. It is a war that seeks to destroy everything and it is all for entertainment. That is what it seems.

For seven days, it was just infighting. There was no peace. Everyone was waging war against each other. No one knew what to do. There were no orders given. There was a lack of leadership. It was just a way to promote chaos. People did not know what to do because they just organized based on some opinion of rumors. With this lack of leadership, there was just a sense that everyone would assume themselves as the true leader in charge of the war. It would surely be a sign that something went wrong but everything has gone wrong. People are taking it upon themselves in order to take action. With everyone claiming to be in charge, there is no clear chain of command. There are just idiotic orders given by people who just do not understand war. They are causing chaos and that is leading to violence and destruction. No one has died yet but there is a lack of discipline. It remains to be seen if something is happen for the better of their once great society. But that is what the Hällstadftß wants so that they can cause divisiveness as a way to control the narrative of what is necessary. The Hällstadftß do not care about the people because they only care about remaining in power.

It is a case of a dystopian society so that there can be the start of something bad. Everything already has gone wrong and the people just don't understand that that is the main problem. This lack of leadership is causing something not short of disaster because that is what it will lead to. The start of this war will just lead to further outrage as there is something to the extent of cowardice. So far, there is no sign of the war decreasing. It is just growing more and more unsafe and dangerous by the second. That was always the true intention of this new war, as it remains to be seen as something inappropriate. That is a case of how and why everything is inconsistent with the rest of the society being fooled. The war is just heating up now for some sign of new intentions. It is a growing sign that the populace is becoming more aware by the hour that there is a lack of command. They are finding it is hard to lead because they are just peasants and they know they won't win if they continue on this path of chaos and destruction.

After a month of disorganized fighting in the war, the peasants decide to elect a leader to lead them to a righteous victory. They want to win but they have to know what to do. It is especially crazy and then there is a surprise. Someone needs to step up to the plate in order to act courageously so that the peasants can defeat the Hällstadftß. The peasants know of the Hällstadftß and they do not like what happened after the end of the previous war. The end of the previous war just made things worse.

But no one can seem to understand why this has happened. None of the peasants seem to care how the Hällstadftß came to power, as many of them have a sense that nothing can be done. It is weakness to say the least, but it could also be that they don't know what to do. The people have never faced this situation before and now that they are peasants they demand that something be done. Yet, nothing can be done, due to the fact that this is something new. The Hällstadftß must be pleased at what is happening because all of the peasants don't know what they are doing. And the Hällstadftß also likes that it is war amongst all of the peasant classes. It is certainly a crazy time but one has to know about the primary purpose. There seems to be the time of the century.

At long last, someone finally had the courage to become the leader of the peasants during this time of war. She looked familiar but not many even knew who she was. She was courageous for standing out in the crowd and since she was the only one who could do the job. But no one knew who she was. She just appeared out of nowhere yet she fit in nicely with the rest of the crowd. It was like a dream come true and all seemed like the bad things will end. Yet, there was no sense of approval for this sexy but beautiful female who just appeared out of the blue. That is the thing with this problem. Everything is just a part of life and it shall end with nothing better. However, that time has yet to come, because there is just something that must be figured out.

This brave heroine steps up to the plate in order to lead the new peasant army. It is a sign that will cause the Hällstadftß to shake in their footsteps and will make them to rethink their plan. It was a time of confidence.

But who was this mystery girl.

Nothing even makes sense.

Yet, all of the peasants went with it and then they started organizing their new military of armed villagers or peasants. It was a glorious day for all of humanity.

Her name was Carina, and she was with the resistance, and yes it was that Carina. But she hid in order to escape the wrath of the Hällstadftß. She knew of the perceived outcome so she knew what she had to do.

Carina was right for the job of being the one in charge because she had the ability. She didn't care for the politics but she wanted to demonstrate confidence for the rest of the peasants. She herself wasn't even a peasant at all because she embedded herself within the hierarchy of the Hällstadftß. It is part of the plan in order to see if the Hällstadftß can be stopped but she also had the help of Svetlana who was also embedded within the hierarchy of the Hällstadftß.

Carina stood up and declared herself as the new leader for the peasants in military and battle to take back what is right. Everyone cheered as there would be new hope. It was a sigh of relief for the rest of the peasants and it seemed like something is about to get better. That is just the beginning and it shall be the rest of society.

It was an all-out plan to defeat the Hällstadftß so that they would no longer exist. Carina organized a plan of how to win but it took some time. She used as much information as possible in order to reshape her new peasant army. It was a longshot because the entire army was in disarray.

They had no organization. They had no type of military structure. And they had no type of military strength. It would seem like a lost cause because they were just so weak and did not know what to do. That is how weak they were. There was just a lack of any discipline and it seemed that it was a good thing since they had no idea what they were doing. Carina asked each of the peasants to declare an oath that they will help fight against the Hällstadftß so that the rest of the world can return back to normal. It would be a very tough decision but something must be done in order to instill proper discipline within every part of this new peasant army. Carina just appeared right in time, as she would have seen an utter disaster if she waited for the Hällstadftß to disappear without notice. Luckily she was there in time.

Carina declared that today was a new day that was filled with hope and change and that this new form of government will topple. "The

Hällstadftß shall be removed from power, and they shall pay for their atrocities against humanity," Carina said. It was just the type of leadership that was needed and it was like the thing that appeared just in time for a proper use of their time. Nothing will be the solution if there was a sense of sorrow but Carina saved the day. She said that she was willing to day for the purpose of making sure the Hällstadftß was defeated. She wanted to know if the peasant army would do the same for her so that she can count on them to save the day if she ever got caught or killed by the Hällstadftß. That was the thing that mattered the most and something needed to be made clear once and for all. It just needed to happen now or as soon as possible but the peasants needed to train as well or else there would be victory after victory for the Hällstadftß. Carina knew something had to be done so they had to make sure they were well-trained. It would take at least three months to train the peasants.

She wanted to make sure that the peasants will be able to defeat the Hällstadftß without any hesitation for the purpose of humanity. Carina asks the peasants a question if they were against are or are with her. The crowd chants they are with Carina. That is a sign of new hope and it shall stand with time until there is a resolve. But Carina asks another question, as she needs an assistant to help her lead the new peasant army. She wants to know if anyone can possibly help her lead the way to defeat the Hällstadftß, so that she doesn't have to do it alone. It is just so that everything can be better organized.

No one answers at first because they all have a sense that they are not experienced enough to lead a war against the Hällstadftß. And then, out of nowhere, someone steps onto the plate to save the day. It was just in time but someone finally saved the day in order to help Carina. Her name was Svetlana and she is that same Svetlana who battled alongside each other with Carina to fight against the enemy. Svetlana just came out of nowhere, as this was the perfect time to appear when she was needed.

Carina knew this would happen and so did Svetlana as well. It was no surprise to them but it was a sense of hope for the rest of the peasants. It was a sense of reform and bravery to attribute to the higher power of the institutions. That was the case to begin with in order to remove power from the Hällstadftß so they shall be defeated. There might be hope for now but it could end all in tears. It is the sense that there will be responsible leadership and well-disciplined leaders and soldiers. That is something that is part of the duty of war. For the sole purpose of whatever is needed, it just seems this is the last chance that the peasants can afford.

This won't be the final straw but the peasants

might believe it could be. They just detest the entire hierarchy of the Hällstadftß and they want to defeat them so they can return back to normal. It is just a sign of progress. But the Hällstadftß doesn't see it that way because they believe they can stay in power. It is just so backwards of what is happening throughout the world. It isn't something new but it is just about the time that is needed because there is a certain piece of mystery that is always required, especially in many situations such as the one that is happening right now. It is just how it was meant to be.

Carina and Svetlana unite the entire crowd of peasants. They all declare an oath to defeat the very powerful Hällstadftß. And then Carina tells them that their three months of training begins now. It is just the sense of pride that offers hope.

Chapter Twenty Two

Three months have passed since the peasants did not know what to do. They can begin the good fight and challenge the Hällstadftß so that they can be no more. No one knows what will even happen but it is just like it is. They must form in order to defeat the Hällstadftß. A strategy must be in the works by Carina and Svetlana so that the army can defeat the allies of the Hällstadftß. It is a very strange and complex situation that involves two strong and independent, sexy, beautiful, and gorgeous women leading the fight against the Hällstadftß. That should be outlawed.

A plan is developed and it involves the peasant army surrounding the Hällstadftß and then trying to take out the hierarchy all throughout the buildings that belong to them. The plan is finalized and it involves the peasant army surrounding many of the buildings at once in a strategic formation. And then the hierarchy shall be killed on order by mass destruction so that no life will be loss for the peasant army.

Carina and Svetlana advise their peasant army about the strategy and then they all unite in order to begin the attack.

It is starting to look like a plan, as the peasants believe if their two leaders have the courage then they too shall have the courage to succeed. It might sound far-fetched but the new peasant army could win. It is just a sense of pride and passion and there might be the case against the winning side of the other side of the aisle. That would be the Hällstadftß, as they still believe they are above the law. The Hällstadftß has a sense of too much pride and they think that they can defeat anyone because they are the ones in power. It just resembles a sense that they are delusional due to the fact that they can win at everything. But they could win in the end but something might happen to them that would lead to something else. It might be their last fight so they need to believe that they will win in order to stand their ground. That is just the way that might lead to destruction. Time too shall pass as a way to stop the war. This is just all temporary so it has to be with the best interests of the peasants to fight with a vengeance. There will be times when it won't be easy and then there are times when more battles shall be necessary and are caused by the primary war of origination. It is all a ruse to gain the upper hand in a delicate situation. It is in part a way for the hierarchy of the Hällstadftß to gain political momentum as a way to succeed.

The new peasant army hears the plan and they support it. They find it scary at first but they are happy to die for their movement. It is a movement to instill the faith of smaller government while the Hällstadftß demands and promotes a much large government that seeks to control the decisions made by people. That is such a travesty because the government believes it has the right to take away a person's freedom because they believe they can decide what is best for the rest of society. That is something that shouldn't exist but it does. And so it begins.

The new peasant army marches on towards the headquarters of the Hällstadftß in order to surround it and several other buildings that belong to them. It just might take a few hours or a few days but they hold their heads up high. It will be a cause in the right and future direction. The Hällstadftß is just a corrupt and defiant organization filled with hateful people, due to the fact that the high command demands the peasants to follow the government. No one should follow what the Hällstadftß should say because what they want to accomplish is just a revolution that leads to the rest of society being brainwashed in order to promote a very extreme and radical element. That must never happen and so it begins.

Carina and Svetlana lead the new peasant army to the buildings with armor in hand so that they can fight the Hällstadftß. It is just the beginning and it will lead to hope if their plan succeeds. That is just the point of everything. It is all of the same and it is part of the new agenda. That is just the way it must stand in order to recede.

The new peasant army is taking its time as they need to get it right the first time and they see it as a way towards something interesting. There could be many legal consequences but the new peasant army is willing to accept them.

It has been a day since the new peasant army left and it seems like they are getting nowhere. There seems to be something very wrong with this plan. It seems that there is a lack of buildings. The peasants have an idea that something is wrong and that it is part of the Hällstadftß's plan to defeat the new peasant army. They are just trying to find the headquarters and the rest of the buildings that the

Hällstadftß own and or use but it is just impossible. It could be that there is something strange going on here because there is just this funny feeling that someone is misleading them. It is just an opinion yet they do not suspect that Carina or Svetlana are misleading them. They suspect that the Hällstadftß can see anything and everything, which will result in every building they use or own turn into an invisible object. That is possible but it is just too early for all of those scientific experiments. It is just a fact of life that nothing that elaborate can take place in the medieval ages. But it is a long shot, so they just have to wait and see. That is just the point of all of this craziness.

It could all be a ruse or the Hällstadftß is just watching everything. That is potentially why nothing can be seen because there is a state of the art security system only known to the Hällstadftß as a way to do the evil things that are being committed. That is the whole idea of something like this happening to the creation of something. As it is a long-standing and an extremely well-known position, there is just the same old stuff that keeps on happening. The new peasant army is just waiting for the right time but there is just nothing that can be done. They will have to wait but they know it is a bad plan because the Hällstadftß is just watching them until they leave. And then there was just something else to consider.

It could be that the new peasant army is just in the wrong place, as no buildings are present. It is just all dirt and some grass here with frequent gravel and concrete walkways and roads.

That might be the current situation but it is all just something interesting. It is just about the current state of affairs so that there is just this situation with no resolve. Carina and Svetlana lead the new peasant army in a different direction forward so that they can find something. It is almost clear that something will be found but it is just further down the road. That is just what it is.

The new peasant army finally approached what appeared to be a building, but it seemed to be out of place with everything else. The army wasn't in any type of desert but they just saw a giant pyramid right in front of them. It was certainly a surprise but it just could be the nerve center of the Hällstadftß. It was like a puzzle was just solved. That is just how it feels like to the rest of the peasants but then there is the sight of the pyramid. The new peasant army can see the pyramid from afar and it is just grand but old and golden yellow. It seems very aged and like it needs to be repaired. But concrete will always show that type of aging because of its structure.

There is no one in sight and the new peasant army is just waiting to approach the pyramid. It is all but a fantasy but it could be a mirage. Something must be done and it must be quick, so that the Hällstadftß can be defeated. It is just something that is needed in the time of hope but that is completely silly. That is just how it seems. This is the beginning of a new and prosperous revolution or what just seems to be the end of the new world order. That is the type of crazy and incoherent situation that has ever been stated and it makes no sense at all. So there is just this little and complex problem about everything else and it must be the time to end everything else as a manufactured crisis. That is the point of everything so that a war can commence. Or else there will be nothing to fight for in a sea filled with dirt.

The new peasant army moves closer and closer at a very slow pace in order to make sure nothing bad happens. As they get nearer the new peasant army can see more buildings, both large and small, including at least seven basilicas. There is just craziness to all of this, as there seems to be no one here. It all deserted in a sense that no one is here or it could be for that exact reason why there are only buildings here. It could all be a trap because the Hällstadftß could be expecting the new peasant army. There is just something that is needed to be made clear. That will be the time when all hope is attracted back to the center of the known crisis.

And then something happened.

There was nothing more that can be done.

As the new peasant army approached the main building at the center of all of this or the pyramid, they had to know something had gone terribly wrong in the sense that no one knew what was going to happen in the first place. It was just a disaster waiting to happen in a time of hope and change and as a way to try and defeat the idiotic narrative of everything else. It is the only way to describe such a thing.

Buildings started crashing down and it all seems like the end.

First it was the pyramid. And then it was the basilicas. After that, the houses started to crumble down piece by piece. There was nothing but rubble on the ground. No one knew what has occurred but it was just disaster. The members of the new peasant army all survived the disaster but they were almost harmed by the incident. It was a surreal situation that meant the Hällstadftß was not happy. It was a sign that there was a sense of hooliganism in the sight of the crazy and almost uncertain future. But it wasn't at the time of day. It was a crazy situation that was just in the type of situation that was just puzzling and it should not scare anyone that this is happening. That is just the case of action and it needs to be made clear or there will be more tragedy.

There is just a sign of disarray in this moment of silence after the new peasant army is trying to see how to regroup after a scary and frightening situation in a time of disaster.

Then, the new peasant army moves forward, trying to get pass the rubble of all of the buildings. It seems like these buildings were just a trap and it was all a set up to warn the new peasant army, but the new peasant army. But they did not care because the trap just made them stronger. It is all the time in the world that is needed. No one even looks back at the rubble as the new peasant army just moves forward. They are just fine and dandy and it seemed that there is just a new sense of hope. Nothing will force them to go back now because the new peasant army wants to defeat the hierarchy of the Hällstadftß but they know that they are going to face obstacles. It is a sign that it will be extremely difficult to face. There is just this type of new system that is unheard of and that is just the start of new revivals. It is all unheard of and it might stay that way forever or as long as the Hällstadftß remains in power. That would be a bad sign and it seems no one is willing to give up for some type of higher than average political power. No one will give up but traps might be in place.

And then, more events start to begin that are just so strange. The earth starts to shake and this just leads to the dirt turning into sand. There is just some type of barren wasteland. And it seems that the new peasant army has been transported as a time warp in order to be defeated, but they do not give up, as they start to move forward.

Everything is just a barren wasteland and it seems to all be a backwards society. It is the sign of the times but there is some type of the times in order to perceive as a new order. It is just the time of the new beginning. It is time for the waters to recede in a time of strengthening and it is meant for the readiness of a situation like the new peasant army is facing in a time of war.

No one even knows what will lead to the case of the Hällstadftß being defeated. The new peasant army has been transported back to a time that hasn't been seen for centuries upon centuries. It is just a sign that something is about to happen. It is a sign that there is readiness but the new peasant army is about to be surprised. Someone or something will be waiting for them but it could be the leader or the hierarchy of the Hällstadftß. That is surely something that needs to be seen or else all hope is lost.

It seems the new peasant army has just been magically transported back to the biblical times due to the triggering of the buildings crumbling down after they moved forward. There is just something that is needed to be made clear but now the new peasant army is in the heart of Israel during biblical times of after the death of Jesus. There is something waiting in the crosshairs for the new peasant army and it is just in the nick of time.

The new peasant army arrives in the public square of biblical Jerusalem and it is just spectacular in a strange situation. There, they wait, until a sense of hope arrives or when they see something they must act upon. Everything was present and nothing seemed to be missing. The appropriate buildings were in all directions. Nothing seemed astray. Although, the new peasant army wanted to know why they were in the ancient city of Jerusalem, they thought it was due to the Hällstadftß trying to get rid of them. It was the best possible explanation because the new peasant army believed the Hällstadftß had some type of new or old mechanism or device that could send people to other places. The new peasant army figured that the Hällstadftß was hiding something because it was only a matter of time until the Hällstadftß would be found out. But the new peasant army has no evidence of that due to the fact that they are now in Jerusalem and the new peasant army doesn't even know where they are in the first place. It is all a mystery to them and they are just something that is apparent that there is the case of something more sinister. It was all there and seemed to be part of the whole picture. That is just the point to be made.

The new peasant army waits for a sign so that they will know what to do. This all resembles the sign of a disaster. The people will know when something is going to happen and it is believed to be part of the ill attempt of the Hällstadftß to subvert everything to the rest of the world. It is just a sign of the times and a way to ignore the truth. It is just propaganda and the sign to recite what is right and what is wrong with the rest of the population. That is about as good as it gets with all of this nonsense and crazy shenanigans in the sense of the ability to know what is wrong and what is right.

Just in the nick of time, there is just a new type of plan to be adopted. Carina can see that the climate is changing so she decides to tell Svetlana to move the new peasant army to the north. Carina can sense there might be a new storm. It looks to be a dust storm and a very large one at that. There seems to be a case toward the back end of the ancient city. It is all for safety and that is what is needed.

The new peasant army advances to the north in a matter of minutes and they are just waiting for a sign of what will happen next. It is too soon to tell but they are just advancing to the point of no return and it just all seems wrong. The new peasant army advancing is probably just another trap for them because they will be sent somewhere else so that the

Hällstadftß can be hidden without being noticed. So far they see nothing within a mile. After advancing, everything just seems to have disappeared with no trace. It is not surprising that this is happening because there is an agenda on the loose. And the agenda is to make sure that no one finds out the location of the Hällstadftß because the Hällstadftß doesn't want to be known, as they believe that they are a classified organization that likes to cover up illegal actions. They have been funding the terrorists, fascists, communists, Marxists, as well as socialists in a bid to turn the people of society into a people who support big government. This idea has worked in many cases but others have seen past it, as it is just an attempt to make sure government will be in control of everyone. That should be a surprise to no one and it appears that there is in action for the time being.

The Hällstadftß have advanced their agenda ever since they started to fight against the allies in the war. And it started before then as well, as it was an eager attempt to use and promote widespread tools of propaganda to promote an ideology of hate and other divisive rhetoric against the supports of freedom and liberty. It worked to some extent but there was just the tone of incompetence to say the least. The Hällstadftß knew they were wrong but they proceeded to just do the bidding of their benefactors. It just all falls into the right place when something is about to happen, and that is just something.

As it stands out, the Hällstadftß is only the new beginning of the new world. It seems there is cycle of new revolution being promoted against transparency and it also seems that propaganda is being used to get rid of essential liberties that were once granted by the notion of a God.

It is all without cause unless it is due to the Hällstadftß.

But the Hällstadftß is about to do a thing that will outrage its opponents even more, to the extent that nothing is made clear.

There must be a way out of all this mess that is turning into mass hysteria of people not understanding what really is going on.

It is all a political ruse for the purpose of government for the government and government against the people of society.

That is well versed and it seems no one will be able to challenge that, unless people rise up and show a strong disbelief for dictatorships. It is only a new opinion.

There is just this crazy thing that must be in the works and it is about time to use that in order to eliminate the problem.

There is no weakness; there is just the

growing sign of possibility as the new peasant army advances to find and then defeat the Hällstadftß.

It could all be over soon if the Hällstadftß shows themselves and gives up but that is not what they will do. It might be a long battle. It will take some time and it too shall be at the end of the new world.

Chapter Twenty Three

Water has turned into blood and resembles red wine. It almost looks like it has been dyed by some ill mad man who seeks to destroy everything. But this is just something more sinister. While the new peasant army was advancing further, the Hällstadftß decided to use another time wrap and take them further into time. Now it is the new goal of something to hinder detection. It is the time to focus.

The new peasant army is now in ancient Egypt and it is all a bad sign. They advanced pass a body of water and it all seemed to be polluted with disease and pollution. Thc water is just contaminated and it must be avoided at all costs. It is just apparent that the Hällstadftß is messing with anyone who is trying to find and then defeat them. That is such a plan to make sure they stay in power. It all has a cause and it shall remain that way forever. As the new peasant army is advancing further into ancient Egypt they just see the familiar signs of a corrupt pharaoh who just refuses to listen to God. He believes he is above the law and is a power-hungry leader who demands it is his way or the highway route. That is pretty typical of him because he sees nothing wrong but he might be worried about the future of his people.

The new peasant army arrives at what seems to be the Nile River and they see that it too is red. That is a very disturbing sign as it is now contaminated. It is a thing of the present day.

Dead fish can be seen floating on top of the Nile River. They look contaminated and dangerous to eat. It seems it is a curse upon the people so that the pharaoh and people can get the message that no one is messing around. The new peasant army is not even a wee bit frightened at what they see. They perceive it as a threat by the Hällstadftß who wants to end them and anyone who despises their hierarchy. It is a good call but it shall not hinder anything. All is in the case of the natural being. Nobody is frightened but there is just a sense of chaos. The people of Egypt do not know what is happening to them because they believe they are being attacked due to their pharaoh. It is just another sign of incompetence. It is a sign that there is a lack of solid leadership from the leader of the state of Egypt. Therefore, there is just something that is in the works.

Suddenly, frogs appear out of nowhere, as it seems they are attracted by the smell of dead fish, but there is something wrong with that. Then, it is now known why they appeared in the first place. Hundreds and even thousands of flies can be seen flying towards the new peasant army. It now seems that the frogs are attracted to the sense and smell of the flies. But, there is just no end in sight.

Members of the new peasant army are now being bitten by these ravaged flies because there is just no end in sight. It is just a trap set by everything in order to make sure no one succeeds in capturing the hierarchy of the Hällstadftß. The new peasant army does not give up. They try to escape the wrath of these flies but there are not many frogs. It will take too long for all the frogs to eat all of these flies. And besides, the flies are just too high for the frogs to jump. It is just something strange. This usually doesn't happen but it did today. As there seems to be a narrative of how to confront this, there remains something that is ever needed in a time of chaos. This is war and God is attacking the new peasant army, or the new peasant army is getting attacked because they are just in the path of the flies. So, there must be a decision be made in order to stay away from the flies and the frogs, as it is just strange. The frogs smell like swamp water while the flies are just everywhere. It seems there is nothing that can be done. But there is just this case of the crazy situation that happens. The new peasant army moves forward while trying to fend off the wrath of the flies. It is just a harsh attack by these flies, as they could be the dangerous ones with all of the crazy diseases that can cause death. That is just the case of the indication of survival.

The new peasant army finally is able to avoid the wrath of the flies. And then like that, there was a strange smell that could be sensed. The Nile River is just near them and it just all seems too familiar to the common man. There is now a smell of rotting fish from the Nile River. It is such a heavy smell that no one wants to go near but they have to move forward in order to find the Hällstadftß. It is a sign that there is a new symptom of what is to be in the mindset of the overall character. And just as the new peasant army passes the flies, there is a new menace. A dust storm has just begun. There is now rapid biting of everyone and everything. No one can see anything and it is just a mystery to be found out. The new peasant army is being bitten by an invisible pest during a dust storm to cover up their real faces. It is just causing everyone to itch badly. Soon, their skin starts to turn red and bites show of everywhere on their skin. It is just a nuisance that this is happening and that is the purpose of why it is a notorious thing for harming the body. There is just the itch that hurts the most but it is just non-stop in the systematic way.

The culprit is a mix of lice and fleas. It is such a drag on life that everyone wants to get out of the way in order to stay clear from the culprit. They need to find a hiding place soon and it must be near or they shall face something more sinister. It is just the end of time but they must find shelter.

The new peasant army sees some type of small building a few minutes away in front of them and they all decide to walk towards it in order to find out what it is. They get close to it and see that there is only a solid concrete door. It is just how it seems to be and it remains quite strange. That is the whole thing and it seems quite small. Carina opens the door and it leads to some place they have probably never gone. It is just a surprise but they must enter it in order to get out of this desert trap. They all enter in a single file line in order to fit with Carina and Svetlana leading the way to the end. One-by-one, the members of the new peasant army enters the door and it looks quite dark but there is some indication of light. There are some wooden torches on the walls of the inside of the structure. The inside is quite large and spectacular, even if it looks small on the outside, but that is due to the fact to lure away grave and tomb robbers. That is just common but strange as no one will know to the extent of where it will lead the new peasant army to. As the last member of the new peasant army enters into the building, they close the door and then more torches decide to magically light up. The new peasant army sees stairs in front of them and they will have to decide if they will descend them. It has been decided that the new peasant army will descend the stairs, not knowing where it will lead them.

The new peasant army descends the stairs so that they can go seek shelter or can find a way out. It might take some time but they will eventually find the way out.

So far, the new peasant army has descended at least seven flights of stairs and there is still more to go in order to get to their destination. They have no idea of how they will get there. It just seems like it will lead to the center of the universe. As it seems there is something out there to get them but it is the sign of the times. The Hällstadftß is just the enemy of the day and they hate the new peasant army because of the new idea of others. But just as it turns out successful, there is something else to consider. And that is about the rule of the stairs, which is something that is at the center of attention.

The new peasant army finally sees the last flight of stairs in front of them and it might seem like a drag it is not because there is just this sense that they are almost done. They could be done but it could just be a trap. They could be considered grave robbers even though they are clearly not grave robbers. It is the will of the demise. But there is just this goal in the attention of society.

At long last, there is some applause, as the new peasant army has just descended the last stair in this crazy building that leads nowhere. It is just crazy but then they see there is only one way to go. They have to turn left and so they turn to the left and see that they have to climb stairs now. This is not a surprise but it is quite the place to take shelter, even though there is no place to hide. It is just the sign that something is awry in the face of death but that is nothing new, and so it is fine and dandy. Svetlana can see the light at the end of the tunnel and Carina sees something ahead. It is the last flight of stairs and then they must see how to get out of here. There is a door but they don't know if it will even open. It is such a crazy ordeal that no one knows what will happen, so that is just crazy. It is just that in the times of need that this will happen or there shall be death.

There is just this sense of time but it is in the

hands of nothing else. Alas, Carina and Svetlana reach the door to the potential exit. It could be the exit or it could be something else. That could just be it and it shall lead to something else. That is just the thing to do but as it turns out everything could be a trap just to fool the new peasant army. Now at the door, Carina opens it and can see the light outside of this strange building or tunnel. It seems like a tunnel but it could be something else but it is an enclosed tunnel that is just crazy. And then Svetlana follows Carina to the outside. The new peasant army then follows Carina and Svetlana and it just seems so grand. It is just the type of situation that is needed but it is the test of time in order to advance something.

The door shuts behind the last member of the new peasant army just like magic. It is just like it seems but there is just something crazy and strange about what is happening. There is just a cloud of thick smog or what seems to be fog and then there is some type of smell. It is the smell of dead animals and it all stinks. The smell of the dead animals is so rancid that everyone wants to die but the new peasant army must think about implementing a new plan that will try to avoid the stench of the rotting dead animals. And there is just one plan. The members of the new peasant army must cover their noses in order to avoid such a rancid smell of rotting flesh. It is the only plan that is able to work because the nostrils will be restricted to a point that it can't smell everything to a certain degree. That is just how it works. It was such an ordeal that it was a very bad experience. The new peasant army had to get out of this place before anything else happens in the foreseeable future. Granted, this is not as bad as the sand turning into biting insects as well as frogs and flies. This is almost the same as the smell of rotten fish from the Nile River. But it is worse than smelling the rotting fish because that is such a normal smell in the fish markets. But this smell of rotting dead animals is just putrid. It is just so painful to experience that it is resulting in people wanting to die. There is just one thing about rotting animal flesh that is different when it is killed by a person. The difference is that a person will kill the animal and then prepare it so it can be eaten within a number of hours and that usually means it will have to be cured or cooked. But with this dead and rotting flesh, there is no person who will eat that, as it was killed in unnatural circumstances, meaning it just died because of pests or it being attacked as prey by some more dominant animal in the wild. And then it will be unsuitable for consumption because no one wants to eat that except for the flies, maggots, and the birds.

The new peasant army can see that there are

many flies and other insects flying around the dead and rotting animals. No birds can be seen hovering over the dead carcasses, as it is too early or it is not their time yet. There were just dead animals in all of the directions. It wasn't a surprise because the new peasant army believes the Hällstadftß was trying to stop them, but it failed to work due to the new peasant army is just too tough to give up. It is just a sign that nothing will lead to the death of the new peasant army or something might happen. The Hällstadftß is just the enemy of everyone.

It takes a few hours for the new peasant army to get out of the valley filled with the rotting and dead animals. It is just the beginning of something else but they are finally out of that place that seems to be in the past. And then there is just more bad news. It is just the beginning of the purges or what seems to be the time when people are going to be harmed in more of a severe and chaotic manner. There is just no way out of this madness, as the Hällstadftß continues on with the wrath of their hatred for anyone who wants to topple their regime. It is such craziness but the Hällstadftß is not going to stop at anything. They will just continue until all of their enemies are dead. The Hällstadftß do not care if it takes a millennium because they have all the time in their world according to them. It is just the thing that they will do to hurt everyone in their path as a way to gain more power. It is just the time of the new future. It all remains to be seen as a way out in order to do nothing.

Now all of the hoopla is about what will come next. It could be more rotting animals. It could be the returns of the flies, fleas, or lice. It could also be the return of the frogs and the dead fish. The new peasant army just doesn't know what will be next. It is all a complete mystery until the surprise is revealed by the wrath of the Hällstadftß or Mother Nature. That is just the beginning of everything. Or it could be that there is a time for everything. Nothing can be ruled out until there is a sign or something that reveals the potential of the impact.

Then, something happens. It is just another sign of a potential impact. There is now no more sand or dirt. It is now a small village. This might be the last place for safety but it is for the best. The new peasant army can see the small village a few miles away and it just looks so gorgeous. It will be night when they get to the small village but it shall be worth every step of it because it might offer safety from the Hällstadftß. It is a sign from above or it could be a trap as well, but that could be just normal as the time passes. Nothing is in the direct interests of the Hällstadftß. It is all for their reasoning to stop their enemies but it shall not be the last of the new peasant army.

The sun is about to set and it will be dark in a matter of a few minutes. So, the new peasant army is worried they might get attacked if they don't find any type of shelter. But, even if they find shelter, then it is possible to expect a trap as well. That is just the result of insanity for the purpose of everything other than the facts. It is just like something from what seems to be a very complex situation. Before anything happens, it is just something that is needed, but it is just in a manner of time for everything to take place. It is for just that precise reason why no one is in control of the situation except for the new peasant army and the Hällstadftß, as both somehow have survived. And by now, it is just the result of nothingness.

The new peasant army arrives in the small village and they see it to be quite a delight of natural wonders. It is the most beautiful sight they have ever seen and it just seems to be getting better. There is still light out because the sun is still setting but there is the sense of new hope. The locals are out and about and are getting ready to close up shop in order to return to their homes. Then, there is the sense of something new that could occur. It is just on the nose of the heels of the new peasant army.

Then darkness sets in.

There is only the moon now and it can be seen by everyone.

All of a sudden, there is another dust storm that can be seen a mile away. The new peasant army finds a large enough building to hide in and then the doors are shut along with any windows. It is a sign that the Hällstadftß won't give up. This is just the new beginning. Something is about to happen because of this dust storm. There is nothing that is known about this situation because the wind just picked up speed in a matter of minutes and then there was sand being picked up by the strong wind. It is such a mystery that it seems like a crazy situation. There is just something that doesn't make any sense at all. It all seems like a pre-meditated plan by the Hällstadftß using a new very advanced electrical machine that shouldn't even exist at all in this time. Everything is possible but it is all part of life. There is just this feeling of déjà vu that this isn't the first time this dust storm started and it all seems to be all too familiar. And then there is the very belief that this dust storm might ruin all of the existing infrastructure and other buildings. It is such that there is a thing to be considered in order to acknowledge the details of everything.

Everything just seems so suspicious in the sound of everything. There is this feeling that this is only the beginning of the dust storm and it won't be the last time that the Hällstadftß will try to end the new peasant army. It is all for the cause of something that is not needed but it is still occurring in the midst of a crisis near the top of the clear certainty of how to do the opposite of the Hällstadftß. It is all the same and this dust storm is nothing new. Therefore, it is the creation of the new peasant army to force out all of the corruption by doing exactly nothing. That is just the thing that is nothing new for the purpose to be in the citations of history. But it is always right, so there is ample opinion on everything. That is just the truth and how it stands, but the dust storm is about to happen in the midst of something else. That is what it means and is part of that situation. As it takes the position, there is just something to think about because there is a skill set to survive this crazy weather. Nothing will be in the crisis of civilization.

The storm picks up speed and there is just this crazy type of situation now. It seems like there is a bunch of buzzing as well. It could be more insects or it could be bees deciding that they want to attack the rest of society. Or it could be a trick by the Hällstadftß in order to promote chaos and destruction. That is just the whole point of everything. But now as it seems, there is just something more interesting, because it is just a sticky situation that makes no sense at all with this dust storm.

There is now nothing but a whirling wind in

the near distance. It silences everything else and it is just part of the further existence that the Hällstadftß is after the new peasant army. This will not be the final straw, as it is just the beginning for everything. It is still what is needed. The sound is just getting nearer and nearer, and it seems nothing can be stopped, due to the current speed. It is all a spectacle in order to intimidate people in chaos.

That is just something in the perplexity of the whole situation. A few minutes later there is just silence.

It seems that the whirling wind has passed but then a few moments later there is another sound that can be heard. It is just too much buzzing but it could be a massive amount of insects that are flying closer and closer. There is just nothing that can be donc.

It is all a sideshow and there is just no proof of the opposite. That is just how it folds and how it takes place.

Then something happens.

The insects reveal themselves.

It is a massive amount of locusts and they are flying into the small village in order to attack all of the villagers.

There is no way out of this one and it is just the toll of predators. That is just how it seems and it is an act.

The locusts stop at the doors of the buildings and try to damage every part of them. They attack any people that they notice.

It all goes dark from there.

Chapter Twenty Four

Darkness is everywhere. The locusts are still out there. But the wind just came back. It is just madness out here and nothing will even end it. Everything is just a catastrophe. The lights turn to darkness as the wind picks up speed with the sand and dirt. People outside are being bitten by diseased locusts and it all seems something is just crazy in an attempt to go forward. There is just no more light in the buildings. It is completely dark. People are scared but the new peasant army is standing strong and they vow never to give up. It is such a disaster that no one wants to go outsides. And if people are already outside they are doomed because of the crazy locusts who want to destroy everything in sight. It is just the sign that everything is wrong and turning against the people in society. It is for that reason why there is one last effort. Nothing will be able to help the people now as it is all done.

Hours after the locusts and whirling wind has arrived it is safe to assume that everything has now disappeared. The new peasant army goes outside to see if it is clear to escape but they find a surprise to see that the people on the streets and roads have all collapsed. There are locust bites on all parts of their bodies and it seems that there are no survivors. It is just something very bad. But there is just something wrong with the locust bites. The locust bites seem to resemble boils and they are just all over the bodies of the people. People are dying and it seems it is due to the locusts and the dust storm. There is just dust in all directions.

The new peasant army looks to see if it is safe and clear to leave, and it is. They leave this devastated small village in Egypt and they leave before anything else bad will occur. It is just the latest in attempts by the Hällstadftß and now the pharaoh is outraged and wants to do something but nothing can be done. It is such a travesty.

It takes a few hours to leave the small village that was left devastated but the new peasant army is now finally out. There is nothing left for them here and they never look back for fear of a reprisal. It is just something that is crazy but it might work in the end. Then, out of nowhere, a time warp appears and it transports the new peasant army to someplace else. It is just something more interesting.

The new peasant army is now in first century Rome and they see it is quite amazing. It is just very spectacular but something isn't right here. It seems to be a trap or something. They are just in the center of Rome but it is just spectacular.

The new peasant army looks around and it is just amazing.

Suddenly, there is commotion, and this could be something interesting. It is just so loud but that is not really important.

Trumpets can be heard and this could be the start of something sinister.

It is just the beginning of the end.

There could be an event that will end all other events and that might turn fruitful.

No one knows and it is only the beginning.

That is just the end and that too shall pass with time on heated angels. It is just the time to outrage the whole population but that is just the whole point of the hit job on the rest of the world. The Hällstadftß is only the beginning of the end and that shall be the sole and primary purposes to promote what is currently in the works of the rest of society. As a matter of fact, the sound of the trumpets does mean something that is very meaningful but it is actually about something sinister. No, the sound of the trumpets means that there is an event going to happen right now or it shall be in the near future such as now. It is all or nothing now but the new peasant army is just waiting for a sign. Maybe it will reveal itself but there is just the case against humanity. None of them even know if the Hällstadftß exists. It could be all imaginary or they could be the brothers of the allies. But that doesn't even make sense, so there must be another reason why the Hällstadftß haven't shown themselves yet, and that might be due to them being the epicenter of the world that has yet to arrive. It could all be a type of situation that the world is ending but there is just a sign that it is just hours away. That is just something that needs to be explained.

As the new peasant army waits for a sign there is just anxiousness awaiting everyone. It is just a part of the waiting game in order to see what might occur in the near future or now. But that is just how it seems to be. Everything is not what it seems and it too shall be wrong.

Then, more trumpets are sounded in the heart of Rome. There must be a competition nearby because it is just so loud. That is nothing new with gladiators fighting for their lives to escape slavery if it is their time to be set free once they win their final match. It is all the same. But the new peasant army moves forward in order to scout out the location of the trumpets. They just want to know more about what is happening, so who could blame them for being curious. It is just a sign of wanting to know more. That shall be the case of all deceit.

Meanwhile, on the other side of Rome, there is some mysterious man going to different churches. He has been to four churches already to speak about the true word of God or what seem to be very old as well as new specific problems that might be occurring in the different communities surrounding the churches for some reason. Those problems are just plaguing the members of those four churches but he is not done as of yet. There are still three more churches in which the mysterious man must visit. It is not known yet if he will finish preaching to all seven churches in the same day but anything is possible. It wouldn't be a miracle for this to be finished in one day but it will take the rest of the day to travel to all seven churches. It is just that thing with ideology. Far too long, there has been an uncertainty of doom, and that is why the man is going to the seven churches to preach about specific and reasoned concerns. It is all about strategy so it is just the beginning.

The new peasant army moves forward after it

sees something that doesn't seem interesting at all. It is nothing new but they head to the Coliseum to see if that is the location of the trumpets being sounded by some mysterious being or person. The new peasant army just wants to know where everything originated from in order to solve a problem or issue that could be prevented in the future. But that is just something that will be in a crisis if it ever happens. That is just the new beginning of everything, so says the rest of the world, and so says the Hällstadftß. It is just the precise reason to forget.

The new peasant army arrives at what seems to resemble the Coliseum. It seems to be grand but it is so spectacular that they just want to leave. It is why it is a wonder of the world. The new peasant army hears some noise from with inside and they suspect that it is just another sporting event because of what they were taught in school. That is pretty typical but it is such a sporting event, as there is loud cheering and people are waiting for death to kill the challengers. It is such an amazing feeling and it is part of everything in the time of need. The new peasant army decides to enter the Coliseum just because they want to and then they all find a seat so they can experience the world class atmosphere in a time of chaos and uncertainty but they also want to experience violence and gore in the way that promotes the execution of justice. It is just why it must be watched.

Alas, the mysterious man arrives at the seventh and final church to preach after a full day explaining what must be done to promote the better things in life and society. It is almost dark but the man must preach to the seventh church about not promoting sadness and sorrow by investing in things that make people of the church to become miserable. And if the members of the seventh church don't listen, then they shall face the wrath of misery forever and eternity. It is not that very good news. In fact, it is frightful, scary, and can lead to a dark meaning, and no one wants to hear about that. People want to experience excitement and joy in order to be happy.

And then there is the hope of unity in order to promote peace and prosperity. It is just something that is a part of the whole world of change and it is easily an enjoyment of society.

Three days have passed and the new peasant army is still in the Coliseum. They slept there and it seems nothing ever gets old.

There is just the waiting of more events.

It lasts for days at a time and there are breaks in-between to make sure everyone gets needed rest to fight and or watch in a real sport.

The new peasant army left the Coliseum, as they saw what they needed to see.

Meanwhile, the mystery man can be seen now going to the other side of Rome with. The man enters some temple in order to see what must be done in order to help the rest of society and prevent something sinister from occurring. It is just something that must be done because if it isn't prevented then time itself shall bring the end of days in a time of war when there will only be shame, doom, and darkness imposed on everyone. It will be a time of calamity and deceit, as there will be someone waiting to offer a bad deal to all who exist and thrive on life. People shall be deceived and then they shall be stuck in a state of confusion and sorrow. It could cause suicidal thoughts but that will just be the end of society. Or it could be the beginning of a new world controlled by someone who wants to decide what is right and what is wrong but that is just the end of the beginning. As there is no time to spare, there is just pain and suffering. There is just pain that will never go away and the suffering shall be at the hands of an evil person or being. It is just the same type of narrative given before and that is just how it seems to be.

The new peasant army leaves the Coliseum and they move forward in search of a temple to find the exact location of something mysterious. It is just something strange.

The man is now inside of the temple and he

sees a throne with a rainbow positioned over it and the person sitting in it is revealed. That throne was just in the center of the temple and it was so bright that it can blind anyone if they look at it wrongly. And from that point on, twenty-four more thrones appear with elders all appearing in ancient Roman garb. The elders seem to be just sitting there waiting for something, as there could be something that will reveal itself within the next moments or so.

The elders are all crowned and looked well for their advanced age.

There must be a meaning for all of this since it might lead to something being prophesized. That then could lead to an almighty decision being made so the notion of prosperity for everything can be answered but there is just something not right here. There is the sense that everything has already happened and that this can be déjà vu all over again. That is just the main and proper reason everything fails. But then there is just that notion about why it always has to occur in this particular way.

This could all be an elaborate hoax but there is no confirmation of that as of yet. It remains to be real until it is revealed to be fictitious in the heart of what actually is true. That is not really what it means but the presence of twenty-four crowned elders sitting in thrones surrounding a being of high power is nothing that should ever be ignored. It is just something that is part of community or so it seems and that is just how it was meant to be. Everything is just so powerful in what the man is seeing right now but he is just amazed at what he is seeing because he is in awe. It is just for that reason that everything is just crazy for nothing that is powerful. It will be a time waiting for the rest of the world to wake up, and once they know the rest of the world shall emerge at this temple to worship the epitome of greatness to celebrate a dystopian society in the sense of curiosity. That is why the mysterious man is here, in order to reflect from his own beliefs in order to decide how the world must proceed. It must be a sign of prosperity for the future or it could be the rise of something evil. It is not how it seems but it is the time of the century.

The man then sees something else and he sees it as a reflection of what death and hopefulness will bring to society as a whole when death is near and when people are forgiven for what they have done. It is not a crisis but it is part of the race to understand the precise measure of quality.

Now there is a question of certainty and a sigh of relief.

It is a sign that reflects where people will go when they die.

That is just how it seems and it is just about the crisis of the situation.

The man sees four creatures with six wings each and they all seem to be living and breathing in the sense of humanity. They all have many eyes but each is different. One has the face of a lion, another has the face of a young bovine, while another seems to have the face of the man, and the last is the majestic bird known as the eagle. It is just the beginning of that time and this presents a claim of reality and a sense that there is a place for forgiveness in the sense that everything is fine.

At this time now, the new peasant army arrives at the same temple as the mysterious man.

The new peasant army enters the temple and they find themselves seeing twenty-five thrones all in use. They view it as a sight to cherish forever but they bow down before everyone. The four creatures begin to speak and warn them all about bad events that will happen if something isn't done. They warn the man as well, for he might be the only reason to live. Then the four creatures bow down to the center throne in order to offer gratuity.

And then, from afar, the man can see a book with seven seals.

Chapter Twenty Five

Ornamental designs decorate the book that is held by the greater being sitting in the center throne and it can be seen as a sign of grander importance. It is a sign that all can be forgiven but that is just what it means to decipher the word of evil. It is a sign of how evil must be stopped and a way to see if there is a way out. It is all but a step in the direction of inferiority. Everything is unique and it remains to that way but what comes next is just as crazy as before. It is just like that and remains boring. That is just how it is in the end.

The new peasant army and the man move a few feet closer and they see that something is just not right. It is a sign of something sinister and it is a sign that something is about to take place now or in the near future. It is a time of resurgence and it is a time of anonymity and deceit. Out of nowhere, when no one is looking, someone steals the book, and then the new praises begin.

The person who stole the book can nowhere to be found and the four creatures are now worshiping the person who stole it.

The person breaks the first seal and now the creature with the face of the lion has released a white horse with a crowned figure with a bow in order to conquer.

The person breaks the second seal and this time the creature with the face of a young bovine sends a red horse with a figure that has a great sword to engage with.

The person breaks the third seal and now the creature with the face of a man releases a black horse with a rider who holds a pair of scales.

Then, the person breaks the fourth seal, and this time the creature with the face of the great eagle sends an ashen horse who is nicknamed death with no one following him but Hades. The fourth rider has no weapons because he is death and he shall be the last one to see everything in the cause of chaos and danger to the extent that people shall die for the purpose of a war.

With all four horses released there is nothing

that can be done now.

There is just a case of uncertainty now and it is a cause for concern. And then it happens again, for the sole purpose of humility, courage, and bravery. It is all for the cause. With the fifth seal broken, the souls who have been slain for supporting God's word are now in the presence of humanity once again. It is such a very glorious time that there is no time to cheer. It is just the sign of the times.

But now, the sixth seal has been broken and this time it causes destruction in the form of a giant but violent earthquake. The sun turns black as hair and the moon turns to the color of blood. The stars fall to the ground. The sky breaks apart. And now the islands and mountains move away from each other. It is such a moral disaster but in the temple, everyone is safe and sound, because there is no sign of concern. The temple is just invincible to everything in the path of the seals being broken.

After the sixth seal is broken, everyone who is not safe hides in the caves and mountains in order to acknowledge that God is here and is ready to resume his control over the world as well as the wrath of the person who stole the book and broke the seals. It is just the beginning of the end. And then, the servants of God make themselves known to the rest of society as a way to promote transparency. It now seems to be the end of the world or the beginning of the new world, or so it seems. That is just the question to ask in order to recite the true meaning of what shall happen to the rest of society. There is just something that is not even in the philosophy of everyone else. It is so to convince the reason behind everything. That is just the crazy type of situation that is needed and it is part of the world to gain back society or so it is known and that is something to be made known without being tested in the first place.

The new peasant army and the man are still in the temple and are safe from everything.

But the servants are representatives from the twelve tribes of Israel.

And then the great tribulation occurs in which a number of them appear wearing white robes and holding a palm branch in each hand.

It is the time for war and the time is almost near.

And now, the seventh seal is broken by the person who stole the book.

It will only be a matter of time until the end is near. Something is about to happen and it is still a big surprise to all.

The new peasant army and the man are still in the temple but they do not know what is happening on the outside. They do not know of the events that are even occurring. They can only see what is happening inside of the temple, which is practically nothing but the practice of worshipping and sitting. There is also the prospect of waiting. Everything is just so quiet in all directions of the temple. Outside though, it can't be described the same. The outside is just chaotic with the people running.

It is just a disaster waiting to happen, as there is the presence of something evil. And then there is the sense of something good being in the presence of all people. This is a really bad situation bad it might not ever happen again. Time will tell and that will be the surprise for all.

The inside of the temple remains the same, being quiet but filled with many people.

There just seems to be this waiting game for the purpose of uncertainty. It is only part of the thing that will be a part of the rest of history.

People are just standing around, sitting, or even bowing down to the person who stole the book in the first place. Everything is just divine and heavenly inside of the temple but that can't be said about the things happening outside. On the outside there is just the act of chaos. It is turning into a disaster and it is just out of control. People do not know what is going on and they feel like they are going to die or will be stuck here forever. That is not a very bright future due to everything that is happening right now.

Chaos is causing violence to occur.

Chaos is causing mayhem to occur.

Chaos is causing people to panic.

Everything bad is happening in the presence of the epitome of what seems to be a disaster. It is just the time that remains neutral. Soon, the outside will just turn to ash. It shall be destroyed by people doing the thing that is wrong. Everything will turn to dust and dirt because people are destroying everything. The city of Rome will just burn and there will be nothing left but the remnants of buildings. That is no way to lead a country.

It has been thirty minutes since the seventh and final seal was broken and now there is the presence of some noise.

A bright golden yellow altar appears out of nowhere. Everyone in the temple can see the altar and it is just a spectacular sight. The new peasant army is in awe and then there is a bright white light. They just want to appreciate it more. And then another throne appears before it, like it was majestic. That is just the type of situation that needs to be.

An angel flies down from above and bows down to the new throne. It is a sense of gratitude as well as something that means there is a time of action in a time of need. The angel offers prayers to all those saints who live to serve a holy being. It is just the type of situation that is part of everything. And then there is the presence of smoke surrounding the altar and the throne for no known purpose. The new peasant army and the man can see the smoke but they are not subject to its effects. It is just there for some reason or another and its primary purpose is to reflect for the better of society. The smoke starts to fade as it begins to ascend towards the greater holy being. It is the time to begin everything and it too shall pass in a time of the situation. The smoke has disappeared and now it is just a distant memory but the angel uses his powers to light up a censer with fire and then he throws it to the side of a temple into a small opening. It is just the will of his aptitude for the will of the people but that is just the beginning of the end or the end of the beginning. It is just something in the world around us and so it is for that reason why there is punishment. That is just the beginning of everything, as the end is near and it is time for justice.

The angel causes thunder to be heard outside. There is lightning, noises, and the presence of what seems to be an earthquake. The ground outside is in the midst of a crisis. There is nowhere for people to go and it is such a bad situation. That is just how it seems but there is a presence of his holiness.

Inside the temple, everyone is safe, but on the outside there are storms galore. On the outside, there is a dust storm, a lightning storm, a thunder storm, and a giant earthquake ruining everything. It is just that for which all shall be destroyed. That is just how it seems to be in the presence of nothing but greatness. It is why everything must be destroyed. The world is about to end and that is the glory to all who worship at the hands of his feet. It is a symbol for unity and a way to demonstrate platitude. The world must be destroyed in the sense of rebuilding it. There must be a new set of living conditions.

Soon, it will all come to an end and that will be the time to live and prosper. It is all but a dream but it is real. It is actually happening and nothing can stop it to the extent of war. That is how it seems to be and that is everything.

The angel then disappears and now there is only a waiting game.

A few moments later, another angel appears and he sounds his trumpet. It is the first trumpet to be sounded. Everyone inside the temple was safe but the same can't be said about those outside. It is just the time of destruction.

After the first trumpet sounded, it caused hail and balls of fire to fall from the sky. Blood started to appear and then the grass turned to brown. The green grass was now completely burned while the plants soon died off. It was the beginning of an epic disaster with no end.

Then the second angel sounds his trumpet and now mountains started to burn with fire deep inside and the fire launched into the sea. The sea was now the color of blood and everything and everything in the ocean started to die. But anyone in the temple is safe. It was just a disaster outside but no one would seem to be safe. It was all that could be clear in the presence of danger.

The third angel sounded his trumpet and now a star fell from the sky. The star poisoned the water in all directions, from ponds to oceans.

After twenty minutes, the fourth angel sounded his trumpet. The sun and the moon dimmed to the point of complete darkness. It was just something that was frightening to everyone outside.

Then, a mysterious angel appears and sets the tone for what shall happen in the future or after the time of his disappearing.

A few short minutes later, the sky is now dark and all is pitch black outside, with the exception of the burning fire and a small patch of sunlight.

The fifth angel sounded his trumpet and now the first woe has been signaled. A mysterious star falls from the sky and a bottomless pit appears. The pit opens up and then the smoke billows up towards the sky in a sense of ascending towards immortality of hoping to live forever and eternity. The smoke causes the sunlight to fade to darkness and the air becomes a state of emergency. Locusts appear out of this smoke from the bottomless pit and a dark angel appears and commands that anyone who is out and about to face the wrath of evil and torture to be tormented for the rest of eternity. It is just something that is out of touch with the rest of society and that is practically why it is not what it seems. This is the start of a new world and the future doesn't look bright.

The sixth angel sounded his horn just after the evil angel of the bottomless pit and darkness tells the locusts to attack anyone they see. The second woe now is released and it just begins a catastrophic event that is evil. The four angels of the Euphrates turn from stone back to their true living form after centuries of being cursed. They are now living again and begin to fly over the earth to recruit a massive army to kill all in sight. It is just the beginning of evil and darkness as well as a new war.

Then, the seventh angel appears before the man who stole the book with seals with a small book in hand, and he screams and cries out while there are seven counts of thunder who sounded their name. It is just something to think about. And then it happened to the extent of nothing else. The seventh angel tells the man to seal the book so it can be closed forever but not to scribe anything or else there will be doom for all and eternity. The man listens and he is then told to burn the smaller book so nothing bad further happens to anyone. He burns the book and is instructed to seek shelter in the nearest temple.

An hour later, two witnesses are sent to view the carnage for forty-two months in order to set the tone of the future. It is just something that isn't worth it but it is part of life. A beast appears out of the water in order to spread fear and to kill the witnesses if it can overpower them. For months, the beast cannot seem to find the two witnesses and it already started to torment everything and everyone it sees. The beast does not give up and eventually forty-two months later the two witnesses finally die off and members of a local tribe in Rome cheer for the defeat and the deaths of two olive trees and two lampstands. It is just the time of that, but that is just the beginning of what will happen.

An earthquake occurs five days later and there are many dead that belonged to this local tribe. And then, the seventh trumpet is sounded, marking the third woe. There is a loud celebration in the sky that is filled with applause. But down below there is war, a war that is never-ending on the grounds outside of the temple.

Somewhere in Rome, a mysterious woman

gives birth to someone who will watch over everyone and everything, but someone or something tries to destroy the new baby so that good will vanish for the rest of eternity. The plan fails. The earth eats up the flood water and returns it to the oceans, seas, and rivers for gratitude. The woman flies off because she is done with her mission to promote peace. It is a sign of nothing new. But now, the beast from the sea is wounded and a beast from the underworld of the earth replaces him. It is now or never but the people of Rome are doomed. It is such a sad situation but there will be more chaos, war, and death, leading to the rest of the world ending in catastrophe. People of Rome try to kill the beast but they are killed instantly by the sheer force of his strength. The beast grows tired of this and decides to harvest the rest of Rome in order to take control over everything.

There are people still fighting outside due to the war of chaos caused by destructive events. It is just a disaster waiting to happen, and the beast tries to harvest the people of Rome.

Seven angels suddenly appear outside all in Rome spreading plagues to all who witness these events. People start to worship the beast because they have nothing else to do. The worshipers and followers of the beast start to develop boils all over their bodies as a type of punishment.

And then all seas surrounding Rome and Italy turn to blood with the rivers turning to blood as well after the water overflowed into them.

The worshipers and non-worshipers of the beast start to burn up after a deadly heat wave. It is just the beginning or the end.

A short time later, darkness plagues the city of Rome and then the Euphrates dries up in order for the good armies to prevail.

An earthquake around the world occurs a few moments after darkness plagues Rome and there is just lightning, thunder, and a hailstorm for all to see and imagine. Then, as people thought it would be all over, there is just something new. A harlot flies in on the beast and reigns over everyone and everything in Rome for the next seven years. But seven years later, the people of Rome finally had enough of her, which results in her death.

And out of nowhere, the mysterious man uses a sword to kill the beast with all of his strength. It is just something. However, Eastern Rome falls to the beast.

The new peasant army is told that they must leave the temple now in order to fight the remaining evil that still remains. They ride out in white horses in all white linen.

Chapter Twenty Six

Clouds of black and white start to appear and it are all but a memory of what has yet to come. There is just a crime of the century waiting to happen. It is all for the best but it shall occur. The new peasant army arrives to meet their new cavalry. It is a heavenly dream and it remains to be seen. There is just a new world to be discovered in all of this mess and it seems to be loud and clear. There is just the end of time and it is to remain.

The white horses unite against evil.

The red horses unite against good.

They all meet in the center.

The new peasant army and their cavalry of soldiers on white horses meet in the Western portion in the center of Rome while evil is waiting for them on their red horses on the Eastern portion in the center of Rome.

It is now or never but it is not a mistake. The war that will end all wars must occur and it shall begin today or everything else shall fall to evil. That is just how it is.

Chaos ensues.

The two sides charge at each other.

The horses in red are the followers of the beast and the horses in white represent the good. It is just the time of every situation.

Chaos is everywhere.

Evil is trying to make a comeback.

Darkness is still upon everything.

It seems this war will never end but it must end now or it too shall get bad.

The new peasant army engages the mark of evil but evil is just so strong because their hate is part of the beast.

It will take some time but it is a challenge for the world to appreciate.

And then it is about time.

There is just this uncertainty of doom.

Storm clouds can be seen spreading lightning as far as can be reached. Thunder can be heard as loud as the beast itself crashing down upon the buildings. It is not a good sight to see.

Evil tries to pick up speed by trying to worship the defeated beast. They try to wake death to avenge their souls.

It is just crazy but it fails to work. There is just something that isn't how it seems. There is the case at all prospects.

The new peasant army chases down evil.

Lightning strikes the weapons of the horses in red.

It blasts their weapons to pieces.

There is just an unknown situation that could happen next.

It is still not known but anything can change for the better of society.

Evil is still strong but they lack their weapons. They can only use their horses in red now. It is just the thing that has to be.

An opportunity arises.

The new peasant army finds a weakness in the formation of the horses in red.

With the help of thunder, lightning, and very large hail, the new peasant army defeats the horses in red in a rage against evil.

It is all about good.

There is just the thing of the past.

The horses in red and evil are defeated and it is such a good thing.

Everything should turn back to normal but that is not the case.

It is all for the safety of humanity and that

too shall be the time of everything. Something will soon be in the works. But time is not on the side of anyone and it is just crazy. It is just how it seems to be and it is the thing of the past. And then, it appears, there is hope for all.

The ground shakes causing a quake and then a crater is opened. The horses in red fall to their deaths as they descend into the darkness of evil. It is just the last of its kind.

Then, the four horsemen appear out of thin air for the purpose of saving the day.

They ride over the crater and soon they are gone for eternity.

The four horsemen ride into oblivion racing to some distant place.

The ground and sky repairs itself.

There is now light and a sigh of relief.

It is just something that is interesting and a sign of hope.

There is no more darkness.

There is just sunlight.

Everything transform back to modern day 1939.

Meanwhile, the new peasant army is no more, and everything goes back to the way it was. Soon no one will remember anything. It might all be a dream for the purpose of nothing and that is not a lost cause of humanity.

Carina is back in South Dakota waiting at the bus stop waiting to be picked up. The bus arrives and the bus driver blinks his eyes at her as a sign for saving the day. Carina blinks back, acknowledging she knew as well.

She finds a seat next to Sean and both wink their eyes at each other. Sean proposes to Carina and the bus driver looks in his rear view mirror winking but showing the signs of wearing clergy garb with the collar and everything that resemble an Italian design exclusive to a small town not known to anyone but a select few.

Carina accepts and marries Sean just days later and they celebrate their life together.

The bus just drives in the sunset until it arrives in Washington, DC, waiting for a new day to begin so that life can just continue.

Svetlana just remains a memory of the distant past and was maybe a dream but she is just waiting for the right time.

Sean, Carina, and the bus driver, well they are just all smiling with a strange look on their faces, as a way to say they were behind everything that occurred in the distant past.

www.ingramcontent.com/pod-product-compliance
Lightning Source LLC
Chambersburg PA
CBHW060609310726
48982CB00003B/495

* 9 7 8 0 9 9 8 4 3 1 1 6 1 *